WASTED . . . MAYBE

Choices Are Ours To Make

by MK

ISBN: 978-1-4669-8104-1 (sc)
ISBN: 978-1-4669-8544-5 (hc)
ISBN: 978-1-4669-8545-2 (e)

Library of Congress Control Number: 2013904466

Trafford rev. 03/14/2013

 www.trafford.com

North America & international
toll-free: 1 888 232 4444 (USA & Canada)
phone: 250 383 6864 ♦ fax: 812 355 4082

Dear Joyce – Enjoy this
book, enjoy life, enjoy,
enjoy – thank you –
Katherine (Mr)

Nov. 2013

Acknowledgments

I THANK THE LATE Attorney Norman Garey, for believing in my talent; Shirley Barchi for getting the ball rolling for me; Attorney Robert H. Thau and before him the late Frances Jane Hynds, Ph.D. whose command of the English language strongly influenced me; more recently, Jearri Bush, Karen Clark, and Bibbi Farashian who gave me their precious time, encouragement, support, and educated observations without sitting in judgment of the work.

I thank my mentors whose words of advice shaped my professional thinking: the late Harry Bernsen who guided me with his all-encompassing vision; Sidney Sheldon who emphasized creation of memorable moments; and television's George Eckstein, E. Jack Neuman, Lew Hunter and Michael Gleason who stressed the use of necessary pointers of dramatization. I learned from all of them. I am grateful.

I hope my work does not embarrass any of those named here—including my husband whose life would be easier if I were not a writer.

Chapter 1

"**Y**OU'RE A SLUT," SAID Biff.

"A slut?" Melody cringed.

"A nympho."

"I was a virgin," said Melody, pushing the words out her throat.

"Sure you were."

"I did it for you. Only."

"All I want is an heir," said Biff.

"I can't."

"Not funny." Biff's cynicism was scathing, sharp, hurtful.

"I didn't know for sure, but now I know that I can't get pregnant."

"You weren't sure, ha! Why should I believe that?"

"I was a virgin," she repeated.

Biff started to dress with painstaking precision, pacing himself as if he had planned that each piece of his clothing dig sharply into the nude girl.

Melody got out of bed and, like a prized young animal, stared Biff down, waiting for him to surrender. For a moment, her beautiful naked body made him shiver and almost break down, but he pulled himself together.

"You should've gotten pregnant by now, but you just like the game. I would've married you. My mother wants a male heir."

Gradually, Melody's defiant stance showed weakening although she held her own and stood tall. "And love? No one else has ever touched me before you . . . for a whole year you talked to me about love and marriage. I trusted you." Holding back tears, she continued. "Biff, I let you make love to me. You said marriage will wait until you finish your education."

"Not if you'd gotten pregnant. You could've had all that money. My mother's money."

"What about love?"

Her voice trailed off as Biff finished dressing, went to the door, and without looking back, left the hotel room.

*

"Biff called me a slut." Melody got up from the *talking chair* as she named the patient's spot in the therapist office. She could have had the *talking couch*, but she chose to sit on the chair during her sessions. She walked to the window then moved close to the professional woman treating her. Tears welled up in her eyes while recalling the shameful moment of her young life that sent her for help. It had to be hush-hush. Normal people did not go to a psychotherapist.

"No. You can't say that, I told him. I pleaded with him. I love you. I was a virgin. You said you loved me," said Melody, looking into her therapist's eyes.

"I wanted to hear Biff tell me the truth. I thought he would admit that he tricked me into sex. That he just said that he loved me and it was OK to have sex because we were going to be married."

Melody continued, "We were at this hotel, not even in his apartment. I got out of bed, let him see my whole naked body. That was very hard for me to do, but he always said that I had the best body he had ever seen. He told me I had an athletic body, and he loved the tightness of my muscles. All my muscles, if you know what I mean. I told him I was all his. No one has ever touched me before him."

Melody was trying to swallow her tears as she spoke. "And you know what he said, he said he can't get his mother's fortune without giving her an heir. A male heir." Melody stood in the therapist's office reliving the gut-wrenching event.

She turned to the doctor and added, "But I can't get pregnant. I never told him that before. Some medical experiment my mother was in before I was even born. She was poor, and she got some money for participating." Melody laughed and cried at the same time.

"He called me a slut, Dr. Raina. Me? And then he turned around and left me in the hotel room. Can you believe that? Just like that."

Melody collapsed on the couch. "And what will happen to me now?"

"I understand your pain, Melody," said the psychiatrist, the first practicing female therapist in Los Angeles. "It's hard to be eighteen. We will work it out. We will find a way to make you whole." She was leaning forward, toward Melody, her body language telling Melody that she was not alone, she was getting help. The idea of a doctor reaching and touching her patient was unheard of. Dr. Raina knew not to get too close, too familiar with a patient although Melody looked like she could use a hug just about then.

"No respectable man will marry me now." Melody seemed small and felt like a broken person. "I'm used merchandise."

The therapy sessions went on, and through arduous work, Melody was getting better at facing her realities. Just the same, she withdrew and lived a solitary life yet could not forget her youthful disaster. She cried herself to sleep on many nights. She cut her waist-long dark hair to one inch. Real short. Kept her wardrobe style tailored, low-key, wanting to be invisible, unobtrusive.

Then unexpectedly, she became busy with her ailing mother who died on Melody's twenty-fifth birthday. Another downer that kept her in continuous solitude. Men and dating couldn't be further from her mind. She often thought about setting goals so that by the time she would turn thirty, she would have something to show for her life, but she never got around to it. Worked in the office every day, saw movies, read books, and kept most of her acquaintances at a distance. One of the secretaries in the office where she worked, Carla, who shared a cubicle with her, did manage to creep into her life and mind every so often.

Melody thought she was very pretty. Her shoulder-length hair surrounded a perfect Grace Kelly face, caressingly ending in a long Audrey Hepburn neck. Below that she sported unforgettable silicone breasts, a tiny waist, and pear-shaped buttocks. She was a survivor who could withstand life's blows and intimidated people by showing no weakness at any time.

One evening, Melody agreed to join Carla at the office receptionist's engagement party. It was a crowded event at a restaurant. The girl told them that their wedding will have to be real small, so they were doing the engagement real big. Melody took a drink off the tray circulated by the waiter and heard a man say, "No, not that one. This is fresh."

The man took the drink out of her hand, placed it back on the tray while getting another one for her.

"Thank you," he said to the waiter.

Turning to Melody, he said, "I'm Bill. Bill Benton. Friend of the groom to be." His eyes sparkled; his face was one huge smile. He was thin, clean-cut, wore a well-fitting designer suit, and seemed to be a take-control guy. Melody liked looking at him.

"Thank you for the fresh drink," she said.

"I saw them put it on the tray. I don't miss too many things. Especially beautiful girls."

Melody was laughing out loud. "Somehow you make this outrageous flirtation sound acceptable. How do you do it?"

"Only when I mean it."

She laughed some more. "I hope so because I think you're fun. My name is Melody Shorr."

More sparks were flying between Melody and Bill than the madly-in-love engaged couple.

Behind Bill, Melody saw Carla approaching. She had the biggest, widest smile Melody had ever seen on her. Carla excitedly pulled a large, casually dressed man toward Melody and Bill.

"This is David . . . from Texas." When she said Texas, her eyes filled with anticipation. They shook hands, and Carla quietly whispered to Melody, "I think I got a good one. Love's in the air."

She winked, waved *good-bye* with her fingers, and left the party holding David's hand.

"The night is young," said Bill. "Feel like dancing?"

"The night is young. Yes."

Bill took her to a nightclub on Sunset Strip. They had drinks and were dancing cheek to cheek. He appreciated how well she followed his lead. He was a great dancer and a gentleman. Bill liked her short-short hair, liked her humor, complimented her on her simple elegance that commanded attention. She felt reborn.

Bill took her out almost every night as if he had had no life prior to meeting her. She liked that and didn't ask questions. Neither did he. There was no discussion of premarital sex and postmarital children. Melody found out that Bill had two children from his previous marriage. So she assumed his bloodline was secured.

The marriage proposal came unexpectedly and impressively. Bill, an executive search firm's vice president, had every detail planned out. He took her to Perino's, a fine high-class restaurant. Places like this have been out of her reach after Biff dropped her from his life. The subdued murmur of the restaurant was occasionally broken by a patron's laughter or the pop of a champagne cork. Bill ordered for both of them and charmed her in every way.

"I don't want to make a sinner out of you, so we'll get married before we take any overnight trips together. What do you think?" he asked.

"I'll be happy to marry you before we take any overnight trips together," said Melody. She smiled. "That'll be nice," she added. "Where are we going?" "Well." He gently put the dessert in front of her as the waiter withdrew. Her fork clinked against something hard. A ring. A diamond ring designed just for him by his jeweler.

Watching her face, he waited a long moment. She took the ring, licked the sweet pastry off it, and handed it to him to place it on her finger. It was to the point. Everything about Bill was to the point.

"We're going on my company's annual fall bash next weekend. I want you to meet everyone. First, we will fly up to Vegas to say our I dos and get you the respect being my wife, Mrs. Benton, calls for."

"You're unreal. This is unreal," said Melody. "I must have been a very good girl to deserve you." Being in public, she could only kiss him lightly on the cheek as propriety dictated. He accepted her kudos and proceeded to tell her about the details she should know. He asked her permission to buy her clothes he thought she might like. He assumed she was a good girl, a virgin, and not once did he approach her sexually beyond some heated kisses. She was so happy. She almost felt guilty about being so happy.

The wedding ceremony was brief, and they flew back the same day. It was late at night, and Bill had a lot to do before the trip. Melody was also tired and a little apprehensive about their first night together. She didn't push, and he didn't push.

Finally, the day of the trip arrived, and everything went well. Under Bill's guidance, she got caught up in the fast-paced events of the day. First, the early-morning train trip from Los Angeles to San Diego in a chartered club car for the nearly forty-member party, employees of the Orthoner Associates. Then the endless flow of champagne cocktails and snacks, which continued on the double-decker bus that brought them to the magnificent Pink Lady, the La Valencia Hotel in La Jolla. This widely anticipated company weekend was organized and led by her new husband, Bill "Bono" Benton. She was filled with pride for him. Malcolm and Erna Orthoner, the president and Mrs. president of the company, let their vice president, Bill, handle everything except money. Bill was glad for that. He much preferred the leadership position without having to oversee bookkeeping and accounting activities.

Melody was unfamiliar with Bill's staff. Since she had met them for the first time on the train a few hours earlier, she gently refused the polite invitations by other wives to join them in swimming or shuffleboard games. When Melody had some time to herself, she walked around the grounds of the hotel admiring beautiful courtyards, hand-painted murals, mosaics, and stunning panoramic views of the Pacific before crossing the quiet cul-de-sac toward the sandy cove that stretched into the ocean. She walked up and down on the shoreline, wetting her feet as she playfully kicked the water. She headed back to find peace in the gym and rejuvenation in the sauna. There was no one around. As she went toward the showers, she involuntarily stopped in front of the mirrored wall and stared at her nakedness. Fading, but not erased, memories of the long-ago, never-to-be mentioned therapy rushed to her mind. In spite of trying to push away the past and concentrate on the now, unexpectedly but infrequently, yesterday came hastening back. Some of her therapy sessions reverberated in her mind again and again. She could still see Dr. Raina's eyes intently watching her and listening.

"I'm sensuous. It's a curse."

"Do you mean sexy?"

"No, no. That's in the mind of the beholder."

"I hear you saying that you don't think that you're pretty, only sexual."

The voice of the analyst was low, looking with unbroken gaze into her patient's eyes.

"That's right. That's exactly right."

Melody Shorr reached for a tissue, but one was not enough to dry her tears.

"Most women would give their eye tooth to look exciting to men."

"Not if they knew what it's like to be hit on by men all the time. Constantly. Everywhere."

"Would you like to be ugly?"

Melody chuckled. "No, of course not."

"Then what?"

She thought for a long beat. "Safe, I suppose. Mostly safe."

Still at the mirror, a small smile appeared on her face. Yes, this was it. The real thing. She found love and safety in Bill Benton, and she married him. The end of her nightmare. Being damaged goods was over. Bill never asked, and she never volunteered that she has lost her sacred virginity. But tonight was the night that everything would come together. She and Bill will make wonderful love. She had no high education or training to earn a good living. Why would she? Women were supposed to be homemakers. Well, she knew she would be the best.

*

Bill Benton's fashion magazine elegance, even in his casual wear, dominated the card-playing foursome. The other players at his table looked almost sloppy in comparison to him. Bill's lean good looks, accented by a perpetual gleam in his eyes, conveyed the warmth of his high spirits and, at this point, covered up his confusion. Clouding his mind was the fleeting image of the morning at the train depot when, for the last time, he ran to the end of the car on the outside platform to check on his people and something caught his eyes. He recognized Chuck Pui Hung, a handsome, chiseled-faced young Asian man, rushing up the stairs, heading directly toward the waiting figure of a soft-featured, lanky boy of no more than seventeen. After a brief welcoming embrace, Chuck took the boy's suitcase and gently, as if handling something fragile, guided him to the exit stairs. They were gone.

Bill could not move. His feet seemed to have been glued to the ground. He forgot where he was until the train whistle, marking departure, shook him back into reality. He had to run and jump up on the steps of the moving train.

Bill still felt a pang of immense jealousy as he recalled watching the two of them disappear from his view. His affair with Chuck disrupted his entire life. Bill had to end it. But two years of secret therapy, one year of living with a beautiful female to prove that he was cured, simply vanished. Troubled, he yearned to hide behind Sheila's big apron. He wanted to return to his childhood sweetheart, his wife of eight years, who went through all the changes with him, and whose fat being he abandoned for Chuck.

The cards were against him, the jokes and the cocktails flowed, and he thought that losing money at the table was better than facing his new bride, his *proof of the pudding* so to speak. Proof? His self-doubts were rising.

*

Melody walked out of the beauty salon, satisfied with her hairstyle, satisfied with everything. She wanted to look her best that evening. It was sort of a coming out for her as far as her formally meeting Bill's staff was concerned. Back in the room, she was preparing for the big banquet that night, but first, preparing for Bill, making sure that he would find her in her robe when he returned. She knew that men could not keep their hands off a woman in a wraparound robe, and she was counting on that as she ordered cocktails for them. The drinks came in minutes. Bill, however, seemed to be delayed. OK. She figured no one can predict when a card game would end.

She began to sip her sherry while reading a newspaper. When she finished the sherry, she began to sip on Bill's martini. When she finished his martini, she had difficulty standing up. By the time Bill arrived, he barely had time to shower and change before they hurried to dinner.

The banquet was a smash. Melody and Bill sat with the top echelon, Malcolm and Erna. That was the best one could do. Malcolm kept his guests on their toes by provoking witty conversation, challenging, testing, and measuring his tablemates by their responses. Melody earned Bill's approval by remaining quiet and smiling shyly. There were brief speeches, introductions of the guests of the company, such as dates, husbands, and wives, and the new bride, Melody.

Following dinner, the company descended on the nightclub en masse. Melody danced with all of Bill's friends. She was happiest, however, when Bill took her in his arms to dance to the new hit "Kiss of Fire," performed by the European singer whose version appeared to be the most popular all over the world. Melody realized they hadn't danced since she had agreed to marry Bill. Oh, she knew she would fix that. After all, part of their marvelous togetherness was the dancing and not the drinking.

Dancing was very dear to her. Back in her childhood, she was declared naturally talented. She dreamed of becoming a professional, but that wasn't in the cards. That's why, while they were dating, she especially treasured the way she fit smoothly in his arms and they moved as one, reminiscent of Ginger Rogers in Fred Astaire's.

By nearly midnight, most of the people had said *good night* in anticipation of getting up for early morning tennis, handball, or swimming. Melody asked Bill whether he was ready to leave.

"I'm having a good time. But you go ahead if you're tired."

"Well, I can't drink any more without getting absolutely drunk, and we'll have to catch the nine o'clock limousine for the airport. C'mon, Bill."

She smiled at him promisingly, wickedly. He smiled back and said, "You run along. I'll finish my drink."

Melody got up and walked out. Dizzying, she chasséd along the plush hallways. She caught a breath of the sea air. She stopped. The beach was calling. She could never resist the ocean. Oh, why not? Bill will be a while.

She was unquestionably drunk because she was convinced of being sober walking the deserted passage. The closer she got to the beach, the more excited she became. Higher and higher. As she crossed the road, she reached the sand, absentmindedly pulled off her dressy shoes, swept her long evening skirt to one side, and threw it over her shoulder.

The ocean whispered her name. She moved hypnotically toward it, seeing, hearing, and feeling nothing else. The water between her toes gave her a shiver, but she kept on walking. "Oh, my god. How fantastic nature is. To be part of something this exquisite!"

Answering the call of the waves, she compulsively moved forward.

The water was knee-high when she stepped on a rock and easily lost her already faulty balance to the oncoming billow. She fell back, feeling no pain, smiling, as she became part of the water, soft as velvet, enveloping her body. Peace, at last.

She sensed strong arms picking her up and carrying her to the sand. She felt strong fingers loosening her own, which still clutched her shoes and dress. She felt a warm jacket wrapped around her wet body and slinky dress. She started to shiver. Strong arms pulled her close to a warm chest. She smiled within. Her slowly opening eyes looked into the hard, young face of a stranger. She let him hold her. Maybe it was an eternity, maybe only a minute. His eyes were beautiful, and he was all there.

She lifted her ring finger and held it close to his face, speaking with a raspy, weak voice, "You see this expensive diamond ring? I have to go to my brand-new husband now."

He helped her up, holding his jacket around her and carrying her shoes. They headed toward the hotel. He supported her as she was hardly able to walk. She heard him talk softly, but she could not identify the language.

"Olyan szèp vagy. Ne öld meg magad. Talàld meg a boldogságod."

In a trancelike state, she thought, vaguely, that she recognized him but couldn't place him. It did not register that he was the Hungarian guest artist appearing at the hotel's nightclub.

At the entrance to the hallway, she took off his jacket and had to get on tiptoes to put it around his shoulders. He was tall and muscular. A silk scarf, matching his tieless shirt, hung casually around his neck. She spotted some embroidery in one corner of the scarf but couldn't tell whether they were fancy initials, a fleur-de-lis, or what. He was doing his best restraining himself from grabbing her. She looked so delicious. But he was raised a gentleman, who knew he was a guest in a foreign country.

"I'm a respectable woman now. Not very sane, I suppose, but definitely respectable." She rose up again to plant a kiss on his forehead and hurried into the hotel.

"Jobb lenne ha èn felkisèrnèlek," he called after her.

Somehow she thought from his tone that she knew what he said and turned back.

"It's OK. You don't have to walk me upstairs. I'll be fine alone. Nobody will see me. Don't worry."

She disappeared from view. He stood motionless. Something about her had touched him. Was she trying to kill herself? Did he save her from accidental drowning? He couldn't imagine what could be wrong with her. The way his blood rushed to his face and tripled its speed racing through his body, he thought something may be very right with her.

He thought he may never be the same again.

Chapter 2

MELODY GOT TO THEIR room unseen, damp but not cold. The stranger had had an abundance of body heat to share. Bill would understand that she had to see the ocean. He'd have to understand. He had understood everything else about her up to this point. She was confident in him.

She opened the door, grinning like a kid.

"Bill, I'm here . . ." Her voice trailed off on finding the room empty, the bed untouched. The lights, the ones she had left on before they went to dinner, were still on. *Well*, she thought, *maybe she should be angry.* She looked at her watch. It was only a half hour since she had left Bill at the club. No need to become emotional. Just hurry up and get rid of all the sand. She quickly soaked her dress in cool water in the sink, wiped her shoes, and let the hot shower run through over her feet, washing away the sand, before taking off her stockings and abandoning herself to the luxury of the hot water.

With the closet door ajar, there was enough air circulation to dry her dress by morning, and she allowed her stockings to hang in plain view in the bathroom. *That's part of marriage,* she thought. At least it is part of life with her. Her pace slowed as she put perfumed lotion on her body, got into bed, and stretched out, waiting for her man.

The rhythmic sounds of the ocean waves gently put her to sleep. She had no idea of the time when she was jarred awake by noisy hotel guests in the corridor. She was annoyed at the interruption of her sweet dreams.

"Where's Bill? What time was it?" Unable to make her numb body move to look at the watch on the nightstand, she couldn't block her mind from thinking, *Don't make a mountain out of a molehill. Jealousy is a disease. He couldn't be with a woman. First of all, he loves you, Melody, and wants only you. Second of all, everyone on this trip is married or is part of a couple. Everyone here is a friend of Bill's. But then again, why didn't he insist on my staying with him? Now, on our first night together officially? Now?*

As thoughts raced through her head, her eyes began to burn at the corners, and she couldn't breathe. Finally the dam broke, bringing on more tears than she had ever remembered. The rest of the night was spent tossing and turning through a series of restless naps. The sun was at the horizon when Bill came in, stepped out of his clothes, and crashed.

*

They were late getting on the plane, had no seat choices, and ended up with two aisle seats next to each other. Bill studied Melody. Arrogance and independence came through her every pore. Yes, she looked like a very expensive, sporty sex object, just like Malcolm described her. It bothered him that she wasn't talking. All she said in the morning was that she hoped his hangover wouldn't punish him too harshly for doing what he did to her.

She was right. *My god,* he thought to himself, *is she always going to be right? Is she only acting shy? Is she so composed that I'll feel guilty merely trying to live up to her expectations?* He could not allow himself to feel inferior. No way.

He feigned sleep under his dark glasses. He heard her complaining about something to the handsome Hawaiian steward. Bill thought she was flirting with the man, who began to pay more and more attention to her. At that point, Bill had to open his eyes to let her know that he was awake; otherwise, he might witness something he would rather not. His imagination was playing games with him in his semistupor. Melody was a good woman. She wouldn't try to do anything with another man. Men can't help themselves from reacting to her in a special way. She brings out the animal in them and demands nothing. They have good taste. After all, that's why he married her, to get her off the market and lock her up for himself. To help him forget his own past. To make a life safe and clean for himself.

Marriage? The memory of his ex-wife's phone call jolted him from his half sleep. Sheila called just hours after he and Melody tied the knot in Vegas as he was packing for the company trip next weekend.

She was polite, as always. "I thought you should know a small detail."

"What now? More money?"

"Oh, no, nothing like that. It's some mail I received today from the court. Our divorce decree. It's dated yesterday."

"What?"

"Right. That's why I called. I don't think your marriage two days ago is valid."

All the bloody marys in the world could not relax him again.

Chapter 3

MAUI. BEAUTIFUL, TRANQUIL MAUI. Bill could not free himself from sensing Sheila's presence all around. He and the mother of his children had spent a vacation on the islands before, so he was able to impress Melody with his knowledge. He knew this would be a perfect place for them to unwind from the madness of the last few weeks, to regenerate before going on to the madness of Waikiki.

Melody, quick to forgive, was eager to get to their hotel; but Bill felt like driving around in the rented convertible to see if there were any changes since the last time he was there. Finally he headed toward their home for the next three days, the Hotel Hana-Maui, or the Hana Ranch, as it was better known to guests and locals alike.

The complimentary champagne was most welcome. They touched glasses enthusiastically, glancing at each other with promises in their eyes, but it was that sip of alcohol that broke the camel's back. They both passed out exhausted.

When Bill stirred nine hours later, Melody felt it even though she was sleeping on the other end of the huge bed. She slid as close to him as their skin would allow. He gave her his big grin, and she gave him her big smile.

"Hon," he said, "I saw some instant coffee there, would you fix it?"

He pointed vaguely, perhaps toward the bathroom. She didn't move. *Gosh*, she thought, *isn't this time to finally make love? We are rested, we're in Hawaii, we're on our honeymoon. It's Monday already. We left home Saturday.* She looked at him. He was clearly waiting for his goddam coffee.

The beach was beautiful, the ocean incredible. They lounged through the morning, were served lunch and cocktails before Melody suggested they should not be outdoors in the afternoon. Their mainland skin would not take kindly to the tropical sun. After they returned to their suite with their drinks, he settled in a chair, gazing over the ocean into the unknown distance, ignoring her nude body anxiously waiting for him on the bed.

"Well, why don't we get ready for some early reservations?" he asked.

"But, Bill, are you sure you want to . . . dress, and . . . leave?"

"I know what you want, honey. But I'm not ready for that."

He didn't look at her. Stunned, she had no idea what to say next. *Ready for her? Does that take such tremendous effort?*

"Ready?" was all she could say.

"Yeah. I know you're pissed off because of the other night. I couldn't help it. I wanted to bullshit with my friends. I had things on my mind, OK?"

He kept seeing the disappearing vision of Chuck and his young boyfriend over and over again. It was agonizing, especially because he had been sure that it could never happen to him again, that he was over Chuck and over men.

"It's just that . . ." She was at a loss for words. Her fragile self-esteem was in danger. "It's just not right."

"OK, OK. Can we start fresh? Right now?" He almost said "Sheila" but caught himself in time. *Whoa! You can't just kill eight years of your life and make it go away.*

"Yes . . . ," she agreed, not moving from the bed. He headed for the bathroom to shower.

"Mel." She heard. "How long will it take you to get ready?"

"About an hour."

"Then call the desk, hon, and make reservations for the early dinner. I want you to see a Polynesian show."

"You do?"

"Yes. Very interesting cultural thing," he added.

She put on a slinky 1930s gown, one of many that Bill had bought for her. He was right. There was nothing like that in her wardrobe comprising of tailored clothes that she had favored.

The Polynesian show he wanted her to see turned out to be an amateur mess. She was happy, however, because she managed to get him to talk. Melody relaxed. As long as she had patience, she could learn to deal with Bill. She had waited for years to love and be loved again, and she loved him so much. It'd be worth it. It's that period of adjustment.

"OK, kiddo," Bill said as they were leaving the dining room. "You'll now meet your first 'Petersmasher.' And everything the name implies is true. You'll probably get hooked."

She laughed as they drove back to Lahaina, where he guided her toward the Pioneer Inn, a white New England style structure, now somewhat worn, overlooking the ocean. Bill walked her through the inside court where small benches were hidden by rich tropical foliage.

The cozy corner bar was crowded with tourists and locals alike. Merchants, professional men and their employees, everyone looking for a good time. The player piano honky-tonked nonstop as Melody learned that Petersmasher was the one-eyed, eye-patched bartender's potent specialty, another rum drink in the land of tropical rum drinks, but unlike all the others. They were too drunk when they got back to their hotel to do anything but sleep. Between the sunning, souvenir buying, and visiting of local bars, the time had slipped away. Soon they were heading back to Waikiki, in a very tipsy state. Melody realized that she had been drunk most of the past three days. So what! It's a holiday!

Wonderful Waikiki. The Royal Hawaiian Hotel's suite was a dream. She jumped into Bill's arms, hugging him immediately after the bellman had gone.

"Gosh, you sure know how to spoil a lady."

She started to unpack as Bill threw some of his dirty clothes on the floor and told her to call the valet service. He was looking at the hotel's brochure listing activities in the hotel and on the entire island.

"Listen," he said excitedly, "Peggy Lee is here on Friday night. Let me go and find out if we can get in to see her. We have four nights. Do you want to see her? Anyone else? What do you want to do?"

"Make love."

He laughed. "That's funny, Melody. I love your sense of humor. Well, I'll make arrangements. You get dressed for dinner. Oh, and don't forget the dry cleaning."

He left. She sat silently, remembering that they had brought some wine with them from Maui. She poured herself a glass before calling the operator.

Some long-ago trip caused her anxiety, and she expected the operator to speak in a foreign language. The graduating class of her Beverly Hills high school went on a ten-day ten-country jaunt on the continent, she and her mother could barely pay for it, and now the novelty of that trip surged in her mind and confused her. She suddenly couldn't think what country she was in.

"Aloha, may I help you?"

"Oh . . . uhm . . . yes!" She was delighted to hear English. "Aloha. I would like to be connected with the valet service."

"For cleaning? Tonight?"

"Yes, ma'am." She was kiddingly polite, enjoying handling such important matters.

"I think he may be gone for the day, but let me check. Put the bag out by the door, miss."

"What bag?"

"Where's the cleaning right now?"

Melody looked at the pile of clothes on the floor.

"It's on the floor. In a pile." She thought she heard the operator chuckle. Then she listened to the instructions, found the laundry bag in the closet, filled out the blank spaces, and told the operator that she would have the bag outside the door. All that accomplished, she got ready for a big night on the town. Bill, being very particular, had already approved the dress she was to wear; so she could fully attend to beautifying herself for her man.

The night promised to go smoothly. They saw a show and had a good meal, and while this Polynesian show was highly polished,

Melody wondered whether or not she could care less. She had to hype herself up to stay with it.

They danced a little; then Bill was anxious to sit at the surf-side bar and hear the bartender's pointers about where they should go. A handsome man sitting by himself steadily stared at Melody. Obviously there was nothing she could do about him but watch him be swept away by an Ivy League blonde.

She didn't like herself for noticing other men, but she was convinced that Bill's curious hands-off attitude and lack of attention was what was making her imagination so overactive.

Bill finished his conversation with a California businessman. Melody was relieved that they could be alone now. But no. Bill wanted to go dancing at a beachside club. They walked along the shore. He impatiently waited for her to put her shoes back on to enter the neighboring Reef Hotel. The Reef was brand-new and featured an underwater bar, Davey Jones's Locker. Bill and Melody had joined a group of jolly tourists in their search for the wacky place, only to find out it had closed at midnight. OK. Bill took over and, like the Pied Piper, led everyone who wanted to follow to the little club where Hilo Hattie was packing them in. The cover charge at the door of the exclusive club was too steep for the troops, so Melody and Bill were on their own. She loved the show. It felt reenergizing. They finally left at closing time. Everything was closing, but Bill was still raring to go.

Melody wouldn't object, although she was getting tired. As they looked for a cab, a tour bus, on its way back to the garage, stopped next to them. Melody graciously got on the bus. Bill was reluctant at first but then followed her. The driver, who was through working for the day, took them to his favorite breakfast joint, letting Melody and Bill join him and his colleagues for bacon and eggs.

Bill footed the tab for the entire gang. Melody talked with the driver of a double-decker old English Omnibus tour line and convinced him to let her drive the bus to the Royal Hawaiian. Several of the drivers got on the bus, watching, cheering her on as she drove the huge machine. She pulled into the narrow drive of the hotel but gave up on making the loop, abandoning the bus in the middle of the circle. The drivers looked on entertained by all this.

The doormen wondered if she were some kind of famous personality who had the right to be eccentric. After inviting all the drivers for dinner next day at a place of their choice, Bill was satisfied to get home at 4:00 a.m.

In bed, Melody reached for him and touched him. He put his enormous hard-on in her hand. "Bill?" She didn't really know what to say.

"Honey, you're my wife. This is what you have been wanting, isn't it?"

She grit her teeth as he jammed himself into her body. The pain was excruciating, worse than the first time with Biff. Tears filled her eyes, but Bill never saw that. He was already fast asleep.

Chapter 4

D INNER NEXT EVENING TOOK place at the People's Café.
Bill and Melody looked like rich Americans, which they
were. Their newfound friends, the local bus drivers,
introduced them to the genuine Hawaiian kitchen, with its
seaweeds and down-to-earth delicacies and then, of course, the poi.
Melody loved the entire scene, tried to speak Hawaiian; and even
though she could not get behind the poi, she became the darling
of the café.

Then it was time for Peggy Lee. Her black-tie audience, the
cream of the Waikiki tourists and locals, filled the spacious theater
and lounge. Bill and Melody ordered their drinks just in time for
the show to begin.

"Hey, you, cock of Broadway! Aren't you out of your
territory?"

The slurry voice, addressing Bill and interrupting the
performance, belonged to Nicae Allan Nash, the former Broadway
gypsy who married Wade Nash, superhero of Western films and a
popular member of the Hollywood community.

Nicae looked frail, had very short dark hair, her huge eyes
gleaming at Bill, as if some old memory had energized an unused,
but not yet corroded battery. She was wasted.

"Broadway missed you, kid. I missed you. And the stupid
things you stole from the girls! I'll never forget it! What a kick in
the pants. Nothing of value. Zilch!" She laughed.

"I'm afraid you're mistaken, ma'am." Bill pulled away, and Nicae came unglued. Peggy Lee stopped singing. There was silence, except for Nicae's husky voice.

"It's me. Nicae . . . *your* Nicaeeee . . ." The tall, rugged film star picked her up before anyone else could reach her and took her out of the room. All eyes followed them. Everyone knew who they were. Then Peggy Lee sang. Everything else was forgotten.

Wade put Nicae in a cab for the silent drive back to their hotel. He held her tight as they got out of the taxi. Another cab pulled up behind them; and Dale and Margo Williams, Wade's agent and his wife, jumped out, catching up with the Nashes, who were heading into the luxury hotel. Dale and Margo stood by as Wade put Nicae in bed. He looked at them, helpless.

"Why?"

Chapter 5

ON THE AIRPLANE BACK to Los Angeles, Bill carefully guarded the huge coral he had pried out of its setting all by himself. He halfway listened to Melody, who was busily getting the reception party finalized on paper. Since it was scheduled for the upcoming weekend, she knew if he approved her plans, she could easily organize and deliver a good party for Bill. It was important to her that she did everything the way he liked. She knew she could bring the laughter back into his eyes.

This was the first party she had ever given for a hundred people, and although a buffet, it required particular attention to detail. She and her mother had much smaller sit-down dinner parties. In fact, her mother insisted on Melody's learning of the niceties of the upper class, the refinement, mannerisms, and the simple elegance that spoke of money. She wanted Melody to be able to mix and blend in with the wealthy. Her mother's idea had materialized when the romance with Biff, an heir to fortunes, swept Melody off her feet and into a place of importance. Melody's mother's plans have worked out before, and Melody saw no reason to object. However, when a minor tooth infection led to illness, rapid liver deterioration, and death, Melody's pain was softened only by her love for Biff and her impending marriage to him.

Melody chased away these thoughts of yesterday and forced herself to concentrate on the task ahead, her wedding reception. Her own wedding reception. Melody knew she had the talent to organize this one. Besides, she also had maids and a bartender and was confident in her guests. Everyone there would come because of love for one or both of them. So how could anything go wrong?

Double-checking the guest list with Bill was the final item on her agenda. Didn't want to miss anyone. She also wanted to make certain that his children would attend. She did not notice that Bill was preoccupied with private thoughts of his own.

Chuck disturbed him the most, then Nicae. Why would Nicae drop back into his life like that? He was young then, just back from the service of his country and anxious to get away from men. He picked up a girl at Sardi's in Manhattan, a dancer who went crazy over his ten-inch prick. So did everyone else, all his life. It was his ticket to first-class. Somebody named it Rex. The girl roomed with Nicae, Allan, and another gypsy in Greenwich Village. He became their toy, and they kept him in fine style. Party after party was exactly what he wanted. He was twenty-two, and he could stay hard for hours. Then Nicae hit big, and her plans of moving to an apartment of her own included taking "King Cock" as her property. That was when he cut out, stealing, unbeknownst to him that they were custom, all the rhinestone and gold-colored jewelry he could find. It was amusing now, but why would Melody say nothing of the incident? He looked at Melody. He saw a similarity between her and Nicae. The short dark hair and huge bright eyes were almost identical. Maybe subconsciously that's what drew him to Melody. Except, Melody had such class and style. Poor kid. She doesn't even know she is not married. He signaled for another drink. Melody looked at the fresh drink and started laughing.

"You know, Bill, this early morning drinking gives me a guilt complex."

He nodded halfheartedly. "You're on vacation, don't worry."

"I didn't mean that. You remember my friend, Carla Silver? You met her at the same engagement party where we met. I told you about her, how she was disowned by her rich family because she got pregnant at seventeen. Then she started drinking, became an alcoholic. I met her after she had been four years on the Alcoholics Anonymous program. She's so grand about tolerating my drinking. Sometimes I think she hates me when I am happier between the two of us." Bill joined her in a chuckle. They didn't know Carla hated Melody right then.

*

Things weren't going well for Carla. Ever since meeting David Carpenter at the party and taking him home, she had envisioned her future with the great, big, jolly Texan. Although she was disappointed on finding out that he was no *Texas oil man*, David made good money in the booming Los Angeles construction industry. He went to AA meetings with Carla, and he genuinely enjoyed moving into her family, meeting and living with her two teen sons.

David and Carla sat, lingering over their after-dinner coffee, barely looking at each other. There was trouble in the air.

"Where are the boys?" David asked just to say something.

"I don't know and I don't care. They can take care of themselves." Carla's voice was angry, hurtful.

"What's eatin' you now?"

"Here, I read it." She handed David a letter from his wife in Texas and started clearing off the dishes, clattering all the way. As David read, he became more and more somber. His wife was offering him another chance to come back but also laying down her terms.

"Well, looky here." He was half amazed at the strength of the letter, clearly spelling out the changes that Sally knew had taken place in her life, the changes that she assumed had taken place in his life, the way in which they might relearn to live together again.

"That's a pretty intelligent woman, David. And she is not your ex-wife, but your wife. Why did you lie to me? Why did you lie to her about living here with a friend? I'm your woman." Carla was in tears. Thirty-eight, thirty-nine, no matter how old you are, you always get hurt. She couldn't stop crying.

"I love you. I believed you. Believed that your divorce was almost final. What a way to find out that you never even filed!"

The shoulder-length haircut enhanced her perfect-featured face; and as her blouse was unbuttoned, tied under her full breasts, showing a bare midriff above the low-riding Capri pants, she was a tempting contradiction to her sweet, child-like voice.

"You should'nta' read the letter, sweetheart." David was trying to soothe her in his awkward way. "Whatever possessed you?"

At this point, his charming Texas twang irritated her.

"I don't know, David. I just did."

She went for more coffee simply to do something, but the tears wouldn't stop.

"I was so happy. It didn't matter that we weren't married or what people said about me. It didn't matter one bit. People have always said things about me. The boys are almost old enough to leave home. Go into the service or something. All I wanted was you. And what did I get? Lies!"

Carla's little apartment became smaller and smaller as she felt life choking her for the umpteenth time.

"When are you leaving?"

"Sunday, I guess." David knew that a lot of explanations were saved by Carla's reading his letter from Sally. He felt lucky at that. It would have been a great deal more difficult if he had had to make up any other stories. Relieved from his major pressure, but still somewhat guilt-ridden, he reached out for her hand and pulled her into his lap.

"We can still go to Melody's wedding reception if you like."

Carla's artificial laughter had no meaning for him. "No way," she said, tears rolling down her face. "I hate you," she said. "I really do."

His lips closed in on hers.

The clutter of the boys' musical instruments, socks, sneakers, and school books all disappeared when she was in his arms. She forgot about the pain of tomorrow. She put revenge in the back of her mind. Revenge on men. All men.

*

On arrival at Los Angeles airport, Bill's first remark was, "Gosh, it's too late to call the kids, but first thing in the morning" What a good father.

In the crazy, crowded baggage claim area, Bill assigned Melody to a corner to wait while he located their numerous suitcases. She stood still, wanting to be helpful by letting him do things his way.

Another plane's passengers, a sizable group of noisy foreigners, poured into the area. Melody glanced toward them and then took a second look. There was a familiarity. She seemed to have heard them before.

Bill called to her. She stepped forward to take one of the suitcases from him and dragged it to the corner while Bill placed another one on the ground. He then returned to look for the rest of them. Melody was trying to identify the language of the foreigners, or figure out why it sounded familiar. She caught the eyes of a tall, muscular man. As he headed toward her, a strange excitement surged in her. She recognized the silk scarf and the wonderful face of the young Hungarian singer. Their eyes were locked. She had goose bumps all over.

"OK. Those are ours too." She heard Bill's voice speak to a Redcap.

Melody looked back at the Hungarian, gave him a small wave of her fingers, and hurried after Bill. They headed to the company car Malcolm sent to take them home.

*

The next day Bill called Melody at the law office where she insisted on continuing to work after their marriage and informed her that they were meeting his father and his lady friend of several years at the El Padrino Room of the Beverly Wilshire Hotel at eight o'clock. Melody was delighted.

Funny, because Bill knew she was as exhausted from the trip and the party preparations as he was, yet she was genuinely looking forward to meeting his father. She had put off her tiredness to some other more convenient time.

*

Melody was charmed by Louis Benton and Stephanie Mars. Stephanie, a very attractive woman in her late forties, took pride in not having accepted Louis's numerous marriage proposals. Instead, she moved in with him, kept her job because she liked it, and had a lovely man to go home to. She didn't care who frowned on that. They appeared to enjoy their arrangement. They owned property together; and Stephanie was the recipient of many expensive gifts, great luxury trips, and anything else her little heart desired. Louis was not rich, but a far-better-than-average provider for a woman who had already lived a very full life.

*

"How did you like him?" Asked Bill when they arrived home. He automatically poured two drinks, letting Melody know that he was not about to go to bed.

"Very much, of course." She meant it. "It's easy, he's only here for a visit. He seems younger than I expected."

"He could've been a goddam millionaire, you know! With his brains, years of contact with the . . . Mafia, dammit, the Mafia! I can tell you now that you're family. And the type of work that he is qualified for, that he's capable of, you wouldn't believe! He could've been a millionaire. Look at him. He's a broken-down old cocksucker!"

Melody watched the anger rise in him and was surprised. "Bill, he's here for a visit, to have a good time, to be proud of you at our wedding reception, and to go back home knowing that his son is OK. Let him be."

"I hate it. He could've been so much more. I'll show him. I'll have to. You know what he did? As soon as he left my mother, he started to make money. Real money."

"I can see where Stephanie is a far better partner for him. I know I only saw your mother for a couple of days, but there is a clear difference. Stephanie is vibrant, interested, ambitious."

"My mother was just like that. When she started to get sick, he left. But she was just like Stephanie. Always. I had to leave for the service, but he didn't. He shouldn't've left her."

"Don't you like Stephanie?"

"She's fabulous."

"You gave me the impression that you were particularly fond of her."

"I am. I really am. Believe me." He seemed to be coming out of his flare-up. He was staring into the fireplace, nursing his drink, thinking that he was rational and the rest of the world was out of whack. Tears came to his eyes.

"Melody, honey, you know, that morning on the train to San Diego?" He spoke very slowly to avoid crying. She was extremely concerned, trying to hear the words that he was not saying as well as those that he was.

"That morning on the train I was looking at all my friends from the company who knew me for a while, and I thought . . . . thought that Sheila should be there . . . like always before."

He was staring off and away from her, not moving. She couldn't move either. She curled up to become a very little person who got bad news. A very little person pressing on her churning stomach with all her might. *My god, what's happening?* She was thinking a mile a minute, maybe beginning to understand the lack of sex or rather loving in Hawaii, maybe thinking that she could understand, but no words escaped her lips.

"I know I shouldn't've said this. Especially not to you. But I had to. And . . . listen, I hated myself for thinking that, but that didn't make it go away."

Melody was speechless. He didn't seem to be aware of her pain.

"I miss the kids. I want them with me."

"Maybe we can get them in a little while. Once we have a normal household."

"I'd never take them away from their mother. She's the best. Do you realize what a responsibility that is, to raise children? Sheila is great!"

Melody sank deep into the couch.

"I'm so relieved. This is the first time in my life that I could talk to a woman. You're the first woman I trust, I can actually talk to. I'm so confused."

"I know. You're confused about your feelings for your father. You were almost belligerent to him at the dinner table."

"I didn't mean to be like that. But he gets to me."

"Bill, I love you. We could have a good life together. All you need is a little therapy."

"Therapy?" Appalled, he remembered why he had been in psychotherapy before.

"Sure. Why not? Life is fast. It's easy to get confused. I did it when I couldn't cope."

"I can't do that. It's that simple. I can't."

"Look, in some areas you are successful, in others you had no time to develop. That's normal. The only course people don't take, the course in *who am I*, affects our lives the most."

She was naively trying. He didn't answer. It appeared he might be ignoring this part of the conversation altogether.

"Let's go to bed," she suggested, thinking that perhaps such emotional relief as he had experienced would warrant a little loving.

"Yeah. I need some sleep. I'm drunk."

Chapter 6

SATURDAY NIGHT. THE NIGHT of the reception. Doorbell. Melody, dressed in a chocolate brown skin-tight gown, looked radiant as she opened the front door.

"Hello, we're the staff for the party. Would you tell your mother that we have arrived." A dapper little man stood in the doorway with three uniformed maids behind him.

"My mother?"

"Well, we meant the lady of the house, actually, Mrs. Bill Benton."

"I'm the lady of the house. Please come in." She turned, headed for the kitchen, then looked back. The four of them haven't moved.

"Well, c'mon now. There's lots to do."

They slowly came in. One of the women remembered to go back and close the door. The little guy spoke again.

"Please forgive our ignorance. But ma'am looks so young, and this is such a large house. We wholeheartedly apologize."

Melody laughed. "You're forgiven. Actually, I'm flattered, Alfred. That is your name, isn't it? We spoke on the phone. You come highly recommended by the Orthoners. Now put your things in here"—she opened a closet—"and let's get started."

Alfred headed for the bar to check whether his orders were followed. Melody took the maids, Hazel, Donna, and Mary, to the kitchen, explaining where and how she wanted everything.

"Do you agree, or do you have any better ideas? I need your expertise." The women stared at her again. No one ever asked for their opinion before. Finally the oldest one began to talk and made her suggestions, which Melody accepted.

Bill's two kids ran downstairs, looking like little five- and seven-year-old angels. They were hungry and wanted shrimp off the fancy platter arrangement. Hazel objected since that was for the guests, and until the service was set up completely, no one was allowed to touch it. However, Melody explained that if the children were hungry, they should eat. She was certain the maid knew how to camouflage a hole on the shrimp platter.

The three-piece combo that was entertaining on the company's train ride to San Diego arrived only minutes before the first guests. The party was off to a fast start. A photographer friend appeared with three cameras hanging from his neck and immediately began snapping candid pictures. Inadvertently, Melody found herself surrounded by the men, unaware of the disapproving looks from the women who belonged to the men. More and more people arrived, but she kept looking for Carla. Her appearance would have solidified their friendship. Melody needed that. She didn't really know the guests who were mostly Bill's friends and acquaintances.

Since the master bedroom and bathroom downstairs had become part of the party filled with people milling in and out, Melody went upstairs to use the telephone. She dialed and listened as the phone kept on ringing. There was no answer. "Oh, Carla, be there, please." She waited. Hung up. Dialed again. "Carla, my friend, I hope you're on your way over here." She knew she was talking to herself. She was sad.

She headed back downstairs. The young guitarist from the band materialized in the hallway, covered her mouth with his hand, and dragged her into one of the kids' bedrooms. They were alone. He held a small pill in front of her eyes.

"Here, take this, my last one, you sexy bitch. Take it and fly with me. You and me, fucker. You should be banned, you animal." His whisper and hot breath hurt her ear. "Creeping into my head, my body, you whore. I saw you on the train. I saw you on the beach. I see you everywhere."

She fought him as well as she could. When his hand left her lips, his huge mouth covered them, his tongue transplanting the pill into her mouth. He skillfully pried her gown up to her breasts and his lips were searching between her thighs when she kicked him in the groin with the high heel of her shoe and spit the pill in his face. He stepped back, eyes popping in agony, his hands over his crotch, and slowly folded up on the floor.

Melody was breathing hard. The struggle exhausted her. When she saw that his drugged body was not moving, she took a blanket off the bed and covered him like a corpse.

"Really now, really. You'd better sleep it off, Buddy."

In the bathroom, she had a great deal to fix before she could face the guests again. She quietly informed Bill of the spent body upstairs that needed removing, without mentioning the assault. He arranged for Buddy and his date to be driven home by taxi and nonchalantly posed for pictures with the body as the guys were carrying him out to the car.

Otherwise the party was an absolute success. Everyone but Carla came. There was the right amount of food, the right amount of booze. Lots of good cheer. Indeed, these friends wanted to celebrate two worthy people joining forces in love to become more worthy. Hear! Hear!

After everyone was gone, the staff cleaned up and left. Bill had another urge to talk. Melody went along with it. She wanted Bill to find his footing with her. She thought of telling him about the buddy incident but was afraid to upset him.

The phone rang. One of their guests, a former obviously very close service buddy, had been picked up for drunken driving. Bill, ever alert, jumped to his aid.

Melody passed the time for about an hour waiting for Bill to get back. Finally she checked on the children and went to bed. It was early next morning while Bill was talking to someone on the phone that she found out that after he had bailed the guy out, he and the guy's girlfriend had taken Bill to breakfast. Melody could not understand why. Before the marriage and up until the San Diego trip, he could not leave her alone. He had to be with her every possible moment. He had to hold her and touch her and share his thoughts. He had an endless need for her. And now? *Why has he none?* Why would he be out in the night with some casual friends instead of needing to cuddle close to her the way she needed him?

Chapter 7

S HE SAT IN THE office, listless. The windowless secretarial area fronted the attorney's office for whom she worked. All the windows overlooking Westwood Boulevard belonged to the offices of the bosses except for the corner conference room. Melody was down. She knew she was typing some legal document, but her mind was elsewhere as she worked by rote. With all the excitement, company, gifts, functions to attend, and maintaining some sort of a household, she and Bill had scarcely made love. When they did, it was nothing like the beauty his heated kissing had suggested during the pre-San Diego days. There was not even a heated kissing session sparking in him. She still exerted energy on looking for excuses for Bill. She refused to see that anything could be radically wrong. She even played with the idea that perhaps she had had too much youthful sex with Biff at the time that led her to believe that's how marriage would be, but in reality, this was really the normal way for married people to do things. Damn it, she loved Bill, with or without his legendary organ; but she was afraid that pretty soon she wouldn't be able to contain her sexual desires.

Carla occupied the next desk in the law office where they worked as legal secretaries for two independent attorneys who shared a long suite of offices with several more independent attorneys. Since the beginning when Melody started to work there, Carla was ready to help her since she was much more experienced.

They became best friends. Anyway, Melody thought of her as her best friend.

This was Melody's first decent full-time job, and she plunged into it to forget Biff. Melody found out the hard way how serious Biff was about heirs to his fortunes, which he would inherit from his old-money Beverly Hills mother.

The match made in heaven that was Biff and Melody turned into hell for Melody. She was nearly eighteen years old, a Beverly Hills high school senior, living on the edge of the good section of town. Broderick "Biff" Waverly, alumnus of the school, a UCLA jock, who came back for a football game, met and got engaged to the sweetest girl he ever saw, Melody. Their carnal relationship was encouraged by Bill's family, and even Melody's mother thought that in these modern times, it was probably the best way to secure Biff. Once they learned that she was sterile, he was gone. Melody was devastated and became a recluse. Eventually she saw in the newspapers that he did manage to impregnate a woman and then married her to please his mother.

Carla only knew part of the story. She never knew that Melody could not bear children. Maybe if she knew, she would not have been so openly jealous of Melody's good fortune in marrying Bill. Carla had lived with ever-growing fear of aging ever since she turned thirty-five. Now, near forty, she had lost David, had no man, only financial problems. There was no way her wealthy father would help her. Her sons had to work odd jobs at an early age. They often talked about wanting to live with their grandparents to have the good life. Carla wanted to prove that she can take care of them. Already, before her affair with David, another self-disciplined AA member, she had accepted gifts of money and clothes from some of her male friends in exchange for sexual services. An anger festered in her, and Melody's happiness only made that worse.

"I don't understand why you didn't come to my reception."

"Get over it,' said Carol.

"I can't."

"I just didn't want to, OK?" said Carol. "Isn't that enough? I don't do things I don't want to."

"I thought maybe the boys had to do with it. They could've come. It would've been OK," said Melody.

"The boys are fine." Carol gave Melody a nasty look. "The boys moved in with my mother. They didn't like those character-building part-time jobs I made them take. I couldn't stop it. I wanted to." She turned away from Melody, and only a big stifled sniffle indicated that she may have been crying.

Melody didn't know what to say. She said nothing. She had to carry her problems with Bill, alone. Carla would have been the wrong person to share them with, and running back to her shrink seemed premature. She knew the period of adjustment was supposed to be tough.

*

Sheila and the kids were going to Iowa, where her father moved and where he remarried after divorcing her mother. She and Bill agreed that the kids should see their grandfather around the holidays. Bill drove them to the airport. The travel activity of any airport, train, or bus depot had always stimulated Bill, made him restless. All the way home, he was thinking of creating some diversion.

Life with Melody was full of pressures. Keeping the upper hand with her seemed rough. Gently, with an innocent *who, me?* attitude, she kept taking control. When he saw Sheila and the kids fly off, he felt empty. He felt unsafe. Or rather, wished he had gone with them. He patted his penis, his only security.

First thing when he got home was getting his travel bag. He knew he was going somewhere. He was old-fashioned enough that he never traveled without being sure he could dress for evening. Melody's car pulled up, and the ever-cheerful woman entered the house.

"Hey, hey, hey Where are we going this time?" Melody's question was natural and lighthearted, but Bill thought for a moment before answering.

"Reno. I think Reno will be better than Vegas. C'mon. Get your toothbrush and let's go."

Trips were always exciting to Melody, short or long, any trip. However, the thought occurred to her that this might be the wrong time in their lives for another trip. Spending the weekend in a busy, glossy town would certainly not give them a chance to talk, to get closer, to make love, and clearly not to go on each other's nerves.

He quickly told her what to wear, what to take. Her lightweight flight bag was packed at the same time as Bill's.

"OK. I'm ready, you gorgeous young fellah!" She gave him an instinctive squeeze. Gosh, she loved him! He responded with a patronizing smile. Back to the airport. They took the first plane out and started drinking as soon as the stewardess was allowed to serve. Halfway into his second drink, Bill turned to her.

"Are you ready for a surprise?"

"Another one? Sure. Why not."

"Well, hon, we're not really married."

Christ, her stomach. The churning started. The cramps started. She was scared.

"As it turns out, my final divorce decree was not entered until the day after we got married. So the Vegas bit is not valid."

"Then what?"

"Then nothing. We'll do it again. City Hall or Vegas again, maybe Reno? Whatever. Relax, have a good time. Next weekend we'll have the kids, if they don't stay in Iowa. Anyway, it'll get done."

She watched him drink up and order another one.

"Why not now? This weekend?"

"Let's see. Maybe we will," said Bill.

"Why didn't you mention this before?" asked Melody.

"We were too busy," came his casual answer. "But don't worry."

She had no idea what was happening to her. She couldn't cry, couldn't scream, couldn't breathe. She signaled for another drink. She wanted to die, wanted the plane to crash. She never wanted to hurt again. Alas, the expert Western Airlines pilots brought the plane down light as a feather. Melody had to face the future.

The taxi ride to the Hotel Riverside was short. However, no matter how much Bill insisted on their reservations having been confirmed by telephone, they told him that the previous guest decided to stay on. There was no room at the inn. Bill was fuming. They brought them drinks. In less than ten minutes, the desk clerk announced that they secured a suite for Bill and Melody at the Cal-Neva Lodge in Crystal Bay, on Tahoe's north shore. Bill tried to hide his ignorance of the place by further grumbling. However, when the Riverside's manager offered them a limousine for the half-hour drive, all Bill could ask for was one more drink for the road.

Melody felt lucky as soon as she sat eyes on the beautiful structure spreading across the large acreage, sitting on top of the state line between California and Nevada. The clear, fresh smell of the lake was prominent for miles. As they entered the lobby, she felt at peace. There was elegance, warmth; and however quietly, gambling fever heated the air. Bill got high on the conspiratory feeling he caught each time he entered a gambling town, a gambling casino—knowing that not too far away, these were illegal activities. At the Cal-Neva, legal and illegal were within a few feet of one another. Bill hit the tables as soon as he showered and changed. Melody decided to walk around. She wanted to absorb the fascinating surroundings, learn a bit of history of the hotel. Bill never noticed the small brochure in their hotel room giving a capsule outline of the unique Cal-Neva story. A hotel straddling the California-Nevada State Line. The restaurant on the California side, the casino on the Nevada side. She walked around, dressed to kill, but too preoccupied to notice all the men who wanted to be killed.

She was not paying attention to which side she was on when she stopped at the entrance of the main showroom. She looked at the tasteful photo layout of artists appearing at the hotel's supper club on various dates. An upbeat picture of the McGuire Sisters, whom she loved. Louis Prima and Keely Smith, clowning. Funny, she thought, the man calling himself Prima, which means the finest, best, the first, and the woman is merely Smith. She couldn't decide whether or not to consider that a joke.

The current guest star was Louis "Satchmo" Armstrong. Melody hoped to be able to catch his show, but this was his last night at the Cal-Neva Lodge, and she and Bill arrived too late to get in. She noticed the photo of the featured novelty artist, a dashing young man. She looked again. The name rang a bell. Peter Szabó, European singer, who became internationally famous with his version of "Kiss of Fire." He recorded it in several languages, and when he performed it live, he always made sure that one verse was in the tongue of his host country.

She slowly remembered that he had appeared at the La Valencia Hotel when they were there, less than a month ago. She started to blush. She was trembling. As she became spellbound by the picture, she knew something had happened. She thought she knew that she had met the man. Her memory was vague, dreamlike. The ocean, the night, the silk scarf that's his trademark. Oh, yes, the silk scarf.

My god! Her heart was beating fast. She was looking at the fleur-de-lis in the corner of the scarf. She suddenly remembered that he was at the Los Angeles International Airport, coming toward her, until Bill cut them off. Her eyes were glued to the eighty-by-ten glossy. *So that's what he looks like?* She knew his music as well as any American would. The way he parodied some old hits or the way he had rearranged some sweet classic melodies, making them into new rock pop hits. Clever and entertaining. *So that's what he looks like.*

"Ah, we meet again?" The voice was clear, rich, and had a slight foreign stiffness to the English sounds. She turned to see Peter Szabó, silk scarf, no tie, and the vaguely familiar toothy smile. The bodyguards in the background were unimpressed with his numerous successful pickups.

"May I offer you a drink?"

She smiled and nodded yes. That was all she could do. The magnetism was overwhelming. She thought, but actually she couldn't think very well, that she was doing something wrong to Bill. Yet she could not resist this man. Incredible! She would follow him anywhere.

Anywhere, in this instance, was the Circle Bar. Familiar to him, famous to the more worldly visitors, and completely unnoticed by

Melody. She was in such a daze between the beauty of the man, the moment, and the incongruity of it all that she walked straight into a leggy waitress with a tray full of cocktails. As she fell to the ground, she managed to trip another guest, carrying a briefcase. Everyone and everything fell on her, but she didn't know it. She was out before she hit the ground.

*

She opened her eyes, looked at the warm, wonderful, and by now familiar face of the Hungarian. She glanced around and found herself in a hospital room. The man watched her steadily. He started to smile. His smile was gorgeous, enriched by the lush blond hair surrounding his marvelous, open face.

"Hi," he whispered.

"Hi," came the soft answer from Melody.

"Melody? That is your name?"

"Yes. Melody Shorr."

"Benton. The paper says Benton."

"It's Shorr."

"Your husband, they cannot find him."

"I don't have a husband. He left me for someone who was having his baby."

She smiled. Was she dreaming? She knew that she felt good, felt happy. The man's hand touched hers, and she trembled. He noticed it. It was all right to hold her hand.

A nurse came in. She looked at the two of them with an all-knowing smirk and spoke out loud and clear, disrupting the romantic mood of the room.

"Mrs. Benton, how do you feel? That was a pretty nasty bump you took on your head. Let me check your vitals."

She proceeded to check her out while Melody and the handsome Hungarian were holding hands, melting each other with their gaze.

"Mr. Szabó, you'll have to let go of her hand for a moment."

He looked up at her, puzzled.

"The hand. Please, I need to check Mrs. Benton's pulse." He let go of the hand but kept right on grinning. Melody smiled.

"Szabó? Mr. Szabó?" Melody looked at him.

"Peter. Only Peter."

"Peter, that's beautiful."

The nurse had heard it all before. The nurse also knew that whatever was going on was not supposed to be going on.

"Mrs. Benton, we'll let you know as soon as we locate your husband."

That was in vain. Melody fell asleep again. Benton or Shorr, she was out of it. The nurse left the room, deciding that Peter Szabó could not mean any harm to the patient.

*

Bill was on a winning streak. He thought he was a winner. He definitely felt like a winner when a young girl's smooth, firm body pressed repeatedly against him. He didn't need much contact to get excited, and he gave the girl two $50 chips as they left the table. She drove him to a small garden apartment complex a couple of blocks from the hotel. Before he knew it, he had a drink in his hand and a girl straddling his lap. He couldn't remember when sex had been this exciting to him, or with whom. He attacked the nameless hooker with the hunger and need that seemed insatiable. It wasn't.

The dirt, the bawdy, immoral flavor of his act made him happier than all the proper fucking that he had ever practiced. Impropriety gave him the best hard-on. It was the illegal that he needed. The nameless hooker dropped him back at his hotel and went on to other territories. Bill marched into the casino and was annoyed at hearing his name paged.

*

The hospital room looked calm with only a low light burning. As Bill entered, he thought he was in the wrong room. He stepped back to look at the number, but the nurse behind him urged him on.

"Who's that?" Bill asked, looking at the towering hulk of the Hungarian leaning close to Melody.

"That's Peter Szabó. He brought her in. Stayed with her," the nurse said matter-of-factly. "Is he some kind of relative?"

Bill couldn't believe his ears. The newest singing sensation of Europe? Sitting in his wife's room? Why? Life with Melody sure was different. He didn't know whether to be impressed or indignant.

"No . . . well, I mean . . . yes, he's some kind of a relative. Leave us alone, please." The nurse disappeared quietly. Bill suddenly turned back to her.

"Does he speak any Engl . . . ?"

But she was gone. However, the answer came from Peter himself.

"Yes. I speak English. Some very well. Some not so well. Mr. Benton? The husband?"

Bill nodded.

"Your wife, Melody, she will be fine. She had a bump. Accident. She has good vital signs."

"I know that. The nurse told me."

"May I visit tomorrow? See if Mrs. Benton is recovered?"

"Oh, sure. I'm taking her back to the hotel now. We should discuss the specifics. Could you come along?"

"No. I have to get some sleep."

Bill wanted the details before the insurance man for the hotel would show up. Bill decided that the best course of action would be to keep it quiet, out of the news.

"How about tomorrow, Mr. Szabó? Lunch?"

"I have rehearsal at eleven, then I can meet you at one thirty. Is that convenient?"

"Neat. We'll have lunch in my suite. I think we should be private."

Chapter 8

BILL HAD ORDERED A lavish lunch to be set up in the spacious suite. He popped a bottle of champagne, signifying his good will. Peter agreed to one glass, indicating his good will, but then he switched back to milk. The hotel provided plenty of milk just the way he liked it, on ice, once they knew he would be joining the Bentons for lunch.

Melody was quietly listening to the men, trying to control her excitement over Peter, trying to understand her guilt.

"With all the females at your feet, Pete"—Peter hated anyone calling him that but would not interrupt Bill—"I'd like to know why you make passes at married women?"

"Make passes?"

Bill was disconcerted by the Hungarian's good looks and relaxed demeanor. He wondered which one of them was better looking.

"Sorry. That's a little too colloquial for you. Let me make it simple."

Peter sensed that Bill, with his cocky attitude, would make a very bad foreigner in any country.

"I meant to say, why do you flirt with married women?"

"Offering a drink to a lovely lady is far from what we call flirting in my country. It is nothing more than a gracious gesture, a suggestion of admiration."

MK

"I didn't mean that. I meant the hospital. People look their worst in hospitals, but you were there. True blue. In the wee hours of the morning, you were there. Why?"

Bill didn't like the pleasant, self-satisfied grin on Peter's face. He felt that with his easygoing attitude, they could never have grounds to battle and for him to make Peter look bad.

"I intended to make certain that Miss Melody was well since I caused the accident."

"Aha, then it is the insurance that bothered you? But the hotel is covered for such accidents. Foreigners can't get with it."

"Just a minute," Melody interrupted. "Please, Bill, we went over this already. The hotel agreed to pay the doctor and the hospital. Peter probably didn't know that. Right?"

"Is that right? Is that why you stayed at the hospital?" Bill's eyes arrogantly pierced through Peter.

"I didn't think she looked her worst."

Melody blushed.

"See, I told ya! You were flirting with my wife."

"I'm not your wife, remember? In fact, you've transported me over the state line under false pretenses."

"Mel, this is no time for your humor." Bill was not expecting this.

"Never been more serious in my life. I feel very uncomfortable about this whole marriage issue."

Peter found himself pleasantly surprised. Then she was not suffering from amnesia in the hospital.

"I understand this to mean that I was flirting with an unmarried beautiful lady?"

"See, you're admitting it. You were flirting!"

"What the hell is the difference?" Melody angrily jumped up and looked at them.

"It makes much difference, Ms. Melody. In Europe we treat our women better. We don't leave them wandering around, and if they are as beautiful as you, we are privileged to have their company, as I almost was. With a name like Melody . . ."

"OK, OK. That's enough." Bill couldn't stand it anymore. The coffee and cigarettes turned bitter in his mouth.

"I shall go now. Thank you for lunch."

By the time Peter left the Bentons' hotel room, he was very much at ease. He realized that Melody was unattached, although she didn't know it yet. She didn't feel it. She was ripe for him. A curious magnetism drew him to the naïveté he saw in her contrasting enormous sensuality.

Back in his suite, he placed a phone call. The call would cost Melody her privacy but would also protect her. He wanted to be certain that his government's intelligence service surveyed her just in case his feelings were more than fleeting. She had to be cleared. She couldn't be just anyone. The government wouldn't stand for that. He checked his code key.

"Ya. PESZ 300. 3842 Studio City. 0800." He hung up. She was coded for him. She was taken care of inside the system that gave him strength, peace, and security.

*

"Life's absolutely fascinating." Melody had a dreamy look in her eyes. Glancing after Peter, she couldn't believe the emotional impact he had on her. *Could she be so disillusioned by Bill that she would notice another man?*

She needed to think, to sort.

"For sure," came Bill's answer.

Melody walked to the closet, took out her travel case, and started to pack. "I'm leaving."

"Now? I thought we'd stay another night."

"I can't. I've got to get away. Now." She continued her packing.

"You're forgetting that I'm the man of this household, and no one goes anywhere until I say so."

"That's right. I am forgetting that."

"Oh, gheez, spoilsport. I wanted to play tonight," said Bill as he adjusted his tie in the mirror.

"What time is it anyway? Oh, I shouldn't've asked you that. Anyhow, I thought that while I play, you'd see a show and then . . ."

"I don't care what time it *is*."

"You never do. It's strange that you can live without knowing the time," he said.

"I have to think. OK?"

"Are you seriously going to tell me that you fell for this storybook *Lothario*, this no-roots gypsy? You're my wife!"

"Your what?"

"What am I supposed to do? I wanted to play tonight. I've been making some business contacts here, and I don't want to go back to LA yet. I need to be away, can't you see?"

"Bill, you have been away. You are away. You play. I'm through playing. I may not know what time it is, or often what day it is, but I know I have too much on my mind. I can't stay around and make merry."

"Then you don't mind that I stay?"

"I'll see you when I see you."

"You're great, you know that, Mel. Simply great."

He went into the shower. She finished packing. She could not remember when she had been this miserable. She loved Bill. She had barely gotten used to the idea of living with him the rest of her life. But now the umbilical cord was choking her. Should she cut it? Could she? There was an emptiness in her that only a man could fill. She was raised for that. Yet she didn't feel needy. The experience was a streak of bad luck camouflaged by sugar-coated luxury living. She felt stupid for having bought it all. She felt grateful to the Hungarian for snapping her back into reality. But her love for Bill was also reality.

When she finished packing, she called to be connected with Peter Szabó. As he was not reachable, she asked the operator to give him the message that she wished to say *good-bye* to him.

She got into the hotel limousine for the airport. She could hardly believe her eyes when she saw Peter at the wheel and the regular driver next to him in the passenger seat. On seeing Melody, Peter laughed his robust, self-satisfied laughter, until he noticed her luggage being loaded on the rack.

"You are not going away?"

"But I am."

"I was thinking maybe you found out that I was the driver and maybe you wanted a what is called joy ride. See, it's America. I get to try things!"

Melody couldn't control herself from breaking into a smile. His joie de vivre was contagious.

"No. I didn't know you were interested in this kind of work. I am really going to the airport. Someone told me that tomorrow is Monday. A day of work."

"Mr. John, you drive. Please!" Peter said this with absolute urgency then jumped out of the front seat and got next to Melody. He looked at her surprised face, pulled her close to him, and slowly, passionately kissed her. Melody felt herself melting in his arms and wondering whether she really heard bells. Another couple got into the limo. They were off to the airport. Peter held on to Melody's hand. His eyes never left her.

"Three times. Thrice. No, three times it is now that you came into my life. Correct?"

Melody nodded.

"Why? For what reason, I ask!"

Melody looked at him in puzzled amazement. "Who knows?" Her answer was no answer of any kind.

"I know," he said with added drama. "Listen to verbatim translation as follows. *THREE is the supreme truth for a Hungarian!*" Peter shouted with confidence. He was positive he had stated his case eloquently. He looked back at the other passengers.

"Excuse me, but I must talk." Then he turned back to Melody. "I know the meaning, for it is destiny. You believe? Yes?"

"I don't know, Peter. I have lots of problems."

"You have none! You are my lady. No problems."

His enthusiasm was real. Charming, entertaining, and real.

At the airport, he got out of the car with her, carrying her bag, not allowing any porters to touch anything of hers! His robust, athletic body protectively moved her along the corridor to the boarding gate. John, the driver, told him to hurry up, he would wait for him, since he had a couple of shows to do that night. Peter waved him away.

"Listen, Miss Melody. I want to see you. I know you are respectable woman." He gently picked up her finger with the diamond ring, shoving it under his own nose the way she did the night on the beach. "Yet and hear me, yet," he spoke with desperate emphasis, searching for words and at the same time being concerned with the time element.

"Yet I, Peter Szabó, who am now a star, here and there, I want to see you . . ."

Melody was far too confused to know what to say.

"Peter, I'm full of serious problems. I can't bother with a new relationship."

"Ah," he lifted his index finger as if Melody had just supplied him with the right word. "It's relationship. We already got it. I kissed you, remember?"

She smiled, but was near tears. "How could I forget?"

"That's correct. It was just only now, in the automobile. You kissed me back. I know vital signs. That was vital sign."

He was on the airplane with Melody by this time. He was seating her, making her comfortable. People looked at him, smiled. Some were pointing at them. Some were trying to get his attention with autograph pads. That was impossible. His entire concentration was on getting a *yes* from Melody. The stewardess came over and politely asked him to get off the plane. Peter defiantly looked at Melody and the stewardess.

"I give you Turkish standoff. I don't leave until you say *yes*."

Melody was embarrassed at all the attention. Her head swimming. She suddenly nodded *yes* to him.

"Yes, I'll see you. And it's Mexican standoff."

The passengers applauded. Peter was so delighted he halfway bent down to kiss her, then changed his mind and reached for her hand, kissed it, and started backing out in the aisle, shouting to her.

"I finish here in ten days. I shall call you. We shall make plans, yes?"

He disappeared from the plane, jumped on a freight cart, and waved back at her as the area was clearing for takeoff. Melody sat in her seat or, rather, froze in her seat. *My god*, she thought, *what a trip this'll be. She, the cause célèbre!*

Chapter 9

WADE NASH, HIS AGENT Dale Williams, and Dale's wife Margo drove up to Wade's Malibu hillside ranch. A catering van followed them, and several cars lined the driveway in only minutes. It was a tremendous moment for Wade, a high point of his career, the gala benefit premiere of his latest film.

The party was set up rapidly by the small army of capable caterers while the select crowd, wearing evening clothes, poured in and headed for the bar making themselves at home.

The rambling one-story ranch style house stretched out in a U-shape around a pool, a guest house, a huge herb garden, and manicured patches of flowers weaved through one another as if tapestry. High ceilings and elaborate light fixtures created an added feeling of spaciousness. Lights were on everywhere. Yet when the guests entered, an eerie silence filled the unexpectedly heavy air. Someone switched on the stereo radio, and a jazz station's rich sounds took over.

"Where's Nicae?" said Margo, looking around. Through the blasting speakers, Wade's worried face led the way to the bedroom. Margo screamed, Dale froze, and Wade fell crying on his wife's dead body. The empty pill bottle, the empty scotch bottle, the glass on the floor, the marijuana joints on the bed were all the explanation they needed.

Wade picked her up in his husky arms, walked up and down with her, held her like a baby, rather like a rag doll.

Dale moved for the telephone.

"No. Give me a minute." Wade stopped him. Tears rolled down his face.

"I told her I wasn't angry if she didn't come to the premiere. I wanted her to help me enjoy being a star we both wanted for so many years."

He cried. His words came out in broken segments, as did his thoughts.

"She promised to enter a sanatorium and dry out. Before I left tonight, we called Dr. Eisner and told him to make the arrangements. Then she'd go and OD. Why? Didn't she trust me? Didn't she trust herself? Why?"

Dale dialed. When the ambulance and coroner arrived, Wade was still pacing with the limp body in his arms. They had to pry her away forcibly. The party stopped, but nobody left. They were Wade's close friends for years, all the years of small movies that had built Wade Nash, the thirty-nine-year-old child of the streets, into a sex symbol, a movie star, a box office name. He made it big.

Wade's celebration had become a wake. Everyone related stories about Nicae, and Wade stopped crying. The rising sun found the elegant show people sitting on the front porch, on the steps, some on the lawn, singing folk songs, singing quiet songs, reflecting.

Chapter 10

S TILL IN RENO, BILL was stunned by the news of Nicae's death. He had entertained the idea of picking up the old relationship with her after the stimulating scene in Hawaii. Its immoral appeal turned him on. Now she was dead.

He drove from Los Angeles International Airport to his office with no intention of working too much, but making an appearance was necessary. Two of his employees reported a couple of lucrative deals that he had to oversee.

His percentage of the take was sizable and worth the effort.

He had brought in a young business major genius by the name of Barry Sherman, a hotshot kid whose brain absorbed instructions like a sponge. Bill knew that Barry's presence would keep the office nicely balanced. He gave him a desk right in his own front area, allowed him to organize confidential papers, and encouraged him to express his ideas.

Barry admired Bill and learned from him among many other things that money was the measure of success. He wanted to take as much knowledge from Bill as possible and accepted any and all responsibilities that came his way. He didn't mind that Bill spent only short days in the office because he saw that when Bill was there, it made a difference.

Anticipating that Melody would be there, Bill drove home. In the back of his mind, he was hoping that maybe she had moved out already. He almost felt relief. Living with her was already growing more and more difficult on him. In her quiet way, she had already brought out the worst in him.

The house was empty. It made him happy to find advertisements of apartment vacancies Melody had pulled from the newspaper. At least she was getting ready to leave.

Bill had showered, shaved, and changed by the time Melody arrived.

"I see you've been apartment hunting. The romance is over, no question about it."

He certainly got right to the point. "Well, Bill, to be honest, I haven't started yet. I thought I should wait until you're back and we could talk."

"Talk? Don't expect me to talk to a woman who's off chasing around."

"You're twisting this whole thing. I'm not chasing anybody. I want a good, clean life for us. You and me. And we can make it."

Bill laughed. Good and clean. Good meant money to him. Clean was something he could never deal with since his father abused and molested him when he was only eight years old. When Bill escaped into the service as an early enlistee, Louis moved out of the family home. Louis knew he had prepared his son for other men and couldn't live with himself. He also could not stay under the roof where he had started it all.

Bill switched his thoughts about the damages of his rough childhood and returned to Melody. "Listen"—he stood erect, looking down on her seated figure—"I can't live up to you. We might as well call it quits. You're too perfect for me. It was a mistake."

"Perfect? That's the dumbest thing I've ever heard. I'm the same person you married, or whatever, a month ago."

"I know you are, but I'm not. Conversation finished." He put on his jacket.

"It's my conversation too, you know. You can't just finish it by yourself."

Bill was shocked. He didn't know Melody to be capable of such firmness. "Give up, please." He exercised forced patience.

"Without a fight? Never! You happen to be my life!"

"What's this talking back business, Mel? Where is it coming from?"

"Don't give me your big mafioso attitude. It won't scare me. I'm not—"

"I never want to hear that word *mafia* from your lips. Never!" He was raising his voice. "I told you something in confidence."

"For crying out loud, you don't even hear me!" She raised her voice. "I'm talking about *our* future!"

Bill grabbed Melody by the shoulders. His eyes pierced through her.

"Listen to me, for the last time, *we*, you and me, have *no* future. Understand? It was a mistake. *Mistake!*"

"No. No mistake. It's too soon to judge. I can make you happy." She trembled. "I'm not ready to quit."

"It's not your decision." He let her go and started for the door.

"Bill, I don't know how to be alone. I'm not good at it."

"You did fine before."

She ran after him, reaching for his arm. He pulled away and opened the door. She fought. "I'm almost feeling guilty for being in love with you. I am, you know."

"I know." A cold Bill.

"And?"

"And nothing. You'll get over it. OK? I'm going to try to be away from here when you're around. Let me know when you're moving. And don't worry. I'll pay for it. I'll give you plenty of going-away money." With that Bill was gone.

Melody held her churning stomach. Oh, how she hated that feeling. She slowly moved to the telephone, looked for a number on the classified pages and dialed.

"Hello . . . I am Melody Shorr. I'm interested in renting the loft you have advertised . . . No, I don't have to see it first . . . Fine. I'll be there in the morning. Thank you."

She submerged herself in a hot bubble bath, trying to relax. Her hands caressed her body in an attempt to massage away some of the tension. She contemplated the only physical relief she could give herself to possibly make her forget her mental pain. But no, what's the use. Masturbation was never for her. She thought of it as far too frustrating. A new fear sat in. What if she had lost all her sexual desire? What was left for her?

Wearing her elegant unused honeymoon nightgown, she curled up on the couch to watch late night TV, sipping on a glass of wine. She had given up on sleep and ran out of tears. The phone rang.

"Hello!" Through the noise of a bar came a perturbed female voice. "Where's Bill?"

"I don't know."

"Where?" The woman's voice was screaming over the crowd. "I can't hear you!" she shouted.

"Who's this?" Melody yelled back. "I'll take a message."

"This is Lara!"

Melody remembered seeing a Lara Burns in Bill's phone book. Some old girlfriend. The bastard. It was pretty rotten of Bill to be back on his old trail this quickly.

"Isn't he supposed to be with you!" she screamed, trying to trap Lara.

"No," came the answer. "Where is he? Who are you?"

"I'm just answering the phone!" The only way Melody could keep from crying was by yelling into the phone.

"Where's his wife?"

"He doesn't have a wife!" Melody hung up. She couldn't take any more. It was nearly fifteen minutes later when she managed to bring her tears under control, turn off her self-pity, and dislodge the anger she had for Bill.

The doorbell rang. "Who is it?"

"Lara."

Melody felt irritated at first then rationalized that she can't let an old friend of the man she has just dropped upset her.

"Please let me in." The voice was pleading, weak.

Melody took her time going to the bedroom, getting the matching wrap for her nightgown ensemble, checking herself in the mirror, and opening the front door. Standing hesitantly in the doorway was a tall golden blonde lanky young woman. She wore a simple cocktail dress on the casual side, and her flawless skin sported a Palm Springs tan. She didn't look more than twenty-one to twenty-two.

"Where's Bill?"

Melody noticed a sloppiness in her speech that was not apparent on the phone.

"I don't know."

"Where's his wife?"

"We went through this already. He doesn't have a wife." Melody felt completely satisfied playing the heel.

"Who the hell are ya?"

"Melody. What would you like to drink?"

Lara was too drunk to recognize that Melody was putting her on.

"You're the friggin' wife!" she shouted as the name sank in.

Melody walked to the wet bar and opened the bottle of Stolichnaya.

"Vodka?"

"Ya bet!"

"How do you want it?"

Lara was swooping around the house, coming in and out of Melody's sight, touching things, and cursing under her nose.

"Straight, rocks, mixer?"

"Rocks for chrissake!" Lara came over to her, but her anger seemed to subside under Melody's gaze. She took the drink, and half of it was gone in the first gulp.

"Melody's his wife's name. Why do ya say you ain't her?"

"Because the marriage is over. I'm no one's wife."

Lara looked at the refrigerator in the kitchen and rushed over to touch it. "That's my fridge. We picked it together!"

"You can have it."

Melody was completely detached, settled back on the couch with her glass of wine, awaiting Lara's departure. Lara was heard all about the house, announcing that this was her bed and that was her plant stand and so on. Melody had hoped that Lara would shortly finish doing inventory and the grand tour of *her* house.

Finally, Lara returned, went to the bar, and refilled her drink.

"I shouldn't drink any more but why stop now?"

She sat down across from Melody, measuring her up. "Where the fuck's he?"

"I don't know and I don't care. I'm rather glad he's not here."

"We should wait for him," Lara suggested with wicked malice in her eyes. "We should wait for him together. What do ya say?"

"Well, if he's not with you nor was he supposed to be with you and he is not with me, I have a feeling that in case he does show up here tonight, he won't give a darn about you and me being together."

Lara was still for the first time. "How c'm you're so calm? What's your shtick? Doesn't it bug you that I'm here?"

"At this point, nothing about Bill bothers me. There is nothing between us."

"I had this dream last night, you know, about Bill and his new wife." Lara spoke slowly with a touch of slurring and a lot of sensuous gestures. She got up to sit next to Melody.

"I couldn't see your face, you know, but I felt that you were a very fine woman. Classy. Not like me. I wanted to make love to ya." She moved close to Melody, whose bewilderment grew.

"I'm not gay," Lara said. "I want to kiss you. I think you're beautiful." She leaned close and kissed Melody on the lips. Melody worried about Lara's extreme need for loving and for Bill. She gently turned her head away from Lara and felt the warm tongue licking her neck, intermingled with short, sweet kisses. Melody tingled.

"Just a minute. Hold it." Melody took Lara's face in her hands and spoke right into her eyes.

"Lara, I think you are beautiful too. I'm flattered that you want to make love to me, even if it is because I'm an extension of Bill, a part of the man you love. But this is not my scene. No matter how deep in the dumps I am, I am a confirmed heterosexual. But believe me, I am really flattered."

Lara did not move away. For a moment, it seemed like an impasse. She was obviously trying to think through all the alcohol. She surprised Melody with new calmness.

"You're right. It ain't my scene either. But this dream last night, ya know, got me real fired up. It was exactly a year that we lived together and then suddenly, whoa! zap! lightning bolt!" Lara jumped up, her arms pointed to the sky as she continued, "Then suddenly, it's like everything came down, ya know? Can ya dig it?" She looked at Melody, her eyes full of admiration. Melody was far better than what she had expected.

"Yeah, ya can dig it. I can tell." She got up and pranced around like some sleek animal. She was getting more comfortable as each spurt of steam escaped her.

"This is a nice house. Me and Bill picked it."

"I know. It was supposed to be your house. But it's Bill's, OK?"

"Ya did some nice stuff to it."

"I started."

"Did he ever say anything about me? That I was his guiding light and savior from a bad life."

"No. And if he had, I doubt that I would have tolerated it."

"Little narrow-minded, ain't ya?"

"I'd call it simply refusing gossip." She saw Lara pull out a small marijuana joint, light it, and take a couple of deep tokes. Lara offered it to her.

"No, thanks, really. I don't do that stuff."

"Like I said, narrow-minded, good, classy." Lara chuckled. "Pure. And believe me, he deserved it."

"I don't know how to take that." Melody actually didn't know how to take it. She wondered why she would keep up this conversation in the first place. She didn't notice Lara slinking back until she was kissing her again.

"I wantcha'. Really." She was kissing Melody rapidly, her fingers running up and down Melody's bare arm. "I can't help it. You're beautiful. It's more than I expected."

"Lara, lay off."

Melody got up, moved toward the wet bar to do something, to get away, to try to be rational, not needy, to not get caught up in the act and be sorry later, to cover up her confusion, to get another glass of wine.

"Wouldn't it be jus' the thing if he came home and found us in bed together? Wouldn't it be something?" Lara's eyes sparkled with the viciousness of the scorned female.

"That would be something, all right. Something sick. It'd serve no purpose."

"Since when is love of any kind sick?"

"You're too fast for me, Lara. I lead a simple life, think simple thoughts."

The night was rushing by briskly. Neither of them was sleepy. They were drawn to each other. Lara broke the silence.

"I went out with this john tonight. I'm back to doin' that, ya know. An' he took me to a club in Beverly Hills where Bill and me used to go. I kept lookin' for Bill. I just knew he'd show up an' take me away from it all once again. Then the more I thought about him and livin' with him, the more I wanted to meet ya. I'm sorta' glad I did. I wanted to know what he left me for. What kind of floozy? But he shows taste. Very fine taste." She started laughing. "Look, he shuh has good taste, don't he, to first leave somebody for me and then go run away from me and pick ya."

They were both laughing.

Melody wondered why she liked this stunning whore. Melody also wondered whether she would pull away if Lara touched her a third time? She was growing weak and needy.

Lara leaned back on the couch, her hand next to Melody's, and proceeded to recall her year with Bill. Melody tried to remain noncommittal, but it was getting tough. As she listened, she recognized a pattern in Bill's method of operations. She also recognized that with all his career success, he was a loser as a human being. He never learned who he was or if he had, he hated himself. He would go through life hurting women while his wonderful facade covered his deep emotional confusion. She understood him, and it surprised her.

"I've got him to agree to go to therapy now, I think. Anyway, he said he'd try it."

"I couldn't get him to go an' fix his Jekyl an' Hyde. He said all that's for sick people, an' he ain't sick because he had done all he needed. No more shrinks for him. Anyway, I was a junky, so he never listened."

"Are you saying that he's been in therapy before?" Melody was surprised.

"Shuh. He used to call me *his celebration, his freedom from shrinks.* Guess it was a big deal for him, livin' with me or somethin'. Some kick, if ya know what I mean."

Melody felt that her decision to leave Bill was now justified. There was no way she or her love could have repaired him. She felt removed from Lara and Bill's trauma.

"I tried to explain to him that in a high-stake, high-pressure business, one needs to learn about himself. I knew that the only reason that would motivate him to better himself would be business success, money. But I was just the *little woman.*"

"Wow! I don't believe ya! . . . yes, yes, I do. I know why he'd flipped for ya, boy, do I know it. You're bigger'n both of us. He wanted to look up to a broad. He didn't like savin' one. He told me he saved himself from his past and that's 'nough savin'."

"I'm not bigger than anyone, Lara. I just never hid out from the blows life was dealing me. No dope, no booze, just face it straight on."

"I knew it in my dream, I know it now. You're a new kind of woman. Your own person." She looked at Melody as if beholding some wondrous image.

"My ma' was Pa's servant. I saw her gettin' used up, inside, ya know, not with washin' an' stuff. We had dough an' maids an' all the bullshit. They still do. But me, I earned every penny I got by usin' them. Men. Them. Tha's right. They gimme what I want 'cause they don't wanna see me sad."

"Do they see you sad?"

"I wouldn't give 'm that pleasure. They sometimes see me play sad. That's all. That's all they understand anyways."

"Don't you sometimes wonder about getting used up yourself?"

"Wonder? No!" Defiance moved into her voice. Her face flexed in arrogant hardness. "No, I don't hav'ta wonder. I know I am. But ya can't go back, if ya know what I mean."

She stood up and looked piercingly into Melody's eyes.

"I love ya . . . 'cause ya know how to shit on a man, and I can't get him out o' my mind."

She was out the door before Melody realized the impact they had had on each other. She had tears in her eyes for both of them. Lara and Melody.

Chapter 11

SUNDAY AFTERNOON. BILL'S HEART filled with joy. The drinks he had had nothing to do with it. Meeting Sheila and the kids on their return at the airport was like old times. He was so used to Sheila's fat body, round, unmade-up face, that nothing could have been more like going home. No threats, no complications, only peace and acceptance.

After driving them back to their house in Tarzana, he stayed around for a few drinks. When he left, he experienced a weird kind of nostalgia, as though he were leaving his nest going to someone else's place for the night. It made him ill at ease. He drove around aimlessly, needed another drink before he could go home to his house and face whatever awaited him. Melody's presence or the absence of it, he did not want to look it in the eye sober.

Driving in from the outskirts of the San Fernando Valley, nicknamed the bedroom of Los Angeles, he felt a new kind of confidence. He felt that his problems were smaller than he imagined and he could solve them.

He headed his Cadillac toward his own exclusive neighborhood of Studio City that was close to the Hollywood production studios and represented professional wealth. He belonged there. As he reached Encino, a rich family-style neighborhood, Bill decided to stop at Monty's, knowing full well that he was merely postponing the inevitable. He did have to get home sooner or later, but not just yet.

Monty's Steakhouse always had enough exciting patrons for diversion. The place was crowded for the early hour of Sunday evening. He couldn't get a seat at the bar. Preferred standing anyway. Chuck Pui Hung tended bar. Bill was shocked to find one of his favorite hangouts had been invaded, his privacy violated. Holding his scotch and rocks, he tried to get involved in the combo. They were good, but he was out of it. His subconscious enveloped him in a cloud of fear. Chuck's recurring presence brought on a surge of memories.

Years ago, when they parted, he told Chuck he had gone straight, he was cured of his *disease*. Chuck made him believe that this hurt him, and he warned Bill that it was not over. Now he kept trying to catch Bill's attention, but the bar was too busy, and he had to be attentive in too many directions.

Faye, the super-looking cocktail waitress, rubbed her splendid boobs against him when she brought his next drink. He didn't tingle. Was he dead? He gave her a smile along with a large tip but felt nothing. Strange. Faye was one of the best-looking women in the Valley, in spite of being over thirty-five. Everyone knew she had three children and the greatest body ever. Her tiny little waitress outfit accentuated each beautiful curve, and men outdid each other nightly to attract her interest.

I've gotta' be out of my mind, he thought to himself. He hated feeling confused. He hated feeling as if he had lost his footing. Somehow he had to get on the ball before he woke up one morning and found himself dead. Finished. He had to get his juices working. He looked around with serious intent. *No.* Faye had to work late. She couldn't be the object of his play tonight. Who else was there?

He walked toward the men's room. Always a fruitful journey, gaining him time to survey the females. He moved slowly, calculatingly, deliberately not glancing at the bartender. The bar was crowded. He never noticed the leggy brunette staring at him. As he neared her, he felt his knees bump into something. He looked down. Blocking him was a fantastic female leg coming through the slit of a long skirt. He couldn't exactly see who it belonged to but instinctively grabbed on to it, bent down, and followed the leg from the ankle to the thigh. When he straightened up, he found himself nose to nose with the owner of the leg.

"Christ, you've a great touch!" she exclaimed. Everyone around looked at them. That didn't matter. They only had eyes for each other. The one, or both, on the prowl. Looking to get away. Looking to get . . . where?

"Bonnie. I'm Bonnie, if you want a name. And believe me, it's not easy to catch your attention."

Bill felt important, grinned his best available grin. "Well, you did it, Bonnie. You got my undivided attention."

He raised his glass. They drank up. All perspectives went out the window. One more drink and a glance at Chuck to be sure he saw him leave with a woman. A quick ride to Bonnie's apartment and to the fiery excitement of new sex.

Neither of them needed to talk. Bill didn't say whether he was married or not. Bonnie didn't ask, nor did she offer any information. She did stop to tell him she loved the way he was hung. She envied his long eyelashes, letting them caress her cheek. Beyond that it was good, straight sex between two strangers. It was what they both wanted for their individual reasons. It worked. Nothing cheap and nothing fancy. A moment of peace for Bill.

Finally he had the courage to go home to his own house. He drove with the top down, feeling like the king of the mountain, speeding against the elements. It was only eleven o'clock when he entered his empty house, empty of Melody, empty of her furniture. Very empty. He undressed, pulled out the old black and white television from the closet, and settled down in the middle of the barren living room on the one and only easy chair. Next to him within reach was an ice bucket and his bottle of scotch. Several fast drinks and a lot of cigarettes later, his mind wandered off the program.

Melody, her furniture, her books, and long-playing records, her collection of memorabilia had made his house into a home. He had found new things added here and there almost every day of the short time she lived there. A living magic surrounded her, endless energy, and a vivacious attitude. Now she was gone. The house was as empty as the day he bought it.

When he had first moved in with the few pieces of his belongings that he thought were worth moving from the apartment, he felt enthusiastic about everything and looked forward to decorating. His entire staff came to the housewarming, bearing gifts useful to a bachelor. Mostly kitchen things. He left them in their boxes until Melody appeared in his life. She had found a place for everything. She knew how to use everything and has made the house *homey*.

Now there were no remnants of Melody. The huge paintings were gone, and with the drapes pulled apart, he could see forever through the endless walls of glass, through the skylight of the open-style California architecture. There was nothing to see. A definite darkness surrounded him. He pulled the drapes closed but still felt the pitch-black of the outside.

It occurred to him for the first time that perhaps he made a mistake discarding Melody so fast. She was the combination of all the things he wanted in a woman, all the things he needed from a woman, in case he needed a woman.

What else was there? Who else was there?

His alcohol-soaked mind recounted all the reliable qualities of Sheila, who would stand by him forever. Or would she? Melody did say that Sheila was incapable of taking care of herself financially. She was not about to enter any kind of a training school. She would wait on him hand and foot in order to secure her money every month. Melody was probably right. He chuckled.

And Lara. Why did he have to get away from her? She was starved for his love. She was his absolute slave. An expensive, sporty playgirl. Only he knew what class she played in. The Jewish-American princess who found a challenge in whether she could get to the bottom of the gutter in spite of her background. He found himself enthralled by this concept and by her successful descent. She was marvelously spoiled. She had always had everything she wanted from everybody. A sun goddess, losing herself in filth. She gave up the filth and her fine background for him. She had thrown away everything, on all levels of her life, for him. Her parents objected to the self-made Italian street boy. They found out through a detective that he had changed his name in the service and forced his father to do the same, using his clean-cut look and sales talents to elevate himself and to make a better future.

What had happened to Lara? The lady of high life, dope, sparkles, and nothing but endless nights. They had very little day life together. None that he could recall, anyway. For a fleeting moment, he thought of calling her.

*

Was it the phone that rang first or the doorbell? He didn't remember talking with Chuck, but suddenly there he was. Bill let him in, and Chuck found his way to the bar. He poured himself a long, stiff drink and settled down on the floor near Bill.

"I'm glad you're alone. Not just because of the check."

"What check?" Bill, in a drunken daze. He looked at the sculptured Chinese features and tried to act cool.

"Bill, old buddy, your check bounced at the restaurant. You said on the phone a half hour ago that you had the cash and I should come over after closing."

Chuck's grin was self-satisfied. He had Mr. Big Shot by the tail and enjoyed the moment. Bill was down, miserable as well as drunk. Nothing a little Asian massage wouldn't cure.

"How much cash do you have?" he asked Bill.

"A bill, bill an' a half maybe." Bill pointed toward the bedroom, casually indicating that it's in there somewhere.

"Let me get it for you. How much do you need?"

Chuck smilingly helped him up. He followed Bill into the bedroom, passing the bathroom on their way.

"Here, just so you can't say that I took the money and ran, I'll fix you up. C'mon."

He started the water running, turned on the extra-steam valves, and dropped a mimosa leaf capsule, adding a reenergizing dimension to the bath. Bill spread out comfortably on the soft lounge Melody had had built in the corner. He noticed, without great surprise, through the steam and sounds of running water, Chuck's naked body materializing and his perfectly shaped lips closing in on his. Like old times. *Happy days are here again?* Bill could not resist the flow of warmth inside his groin, his head, his entire body spinning through the visions of the sweaty glisten of the steam-heated room. His realities had vanished.

Chapter 12

THE SHRILL RING OF the telephone made him jump and almost shit in his pants. It rang through the hollowness of the house, through his aching head again and again. He opened his eyes and came close to focusing. Once in a sitting position, he could see the phone and picked it up.

"Good morning." He heard the cheerful voice of his secretary, possessor of a great deal of confidential information about him, who also controlled the flow of maids, gardeners, and pool men. In addition, she was a devoted friend. He made sure she was well paid.

"Yeah," he could barely mutter. His lips, throat were so dry. It hurt him to swallow.

She continued pleasantly.

"Bill, it's nine o'clock. In New York, it's twelve o'clock, in Chicago, it's eleven o'clock. Don't panic." But he did.

"Nothing major has gone down yet. But since I told Malcolm O you were on your way to the office, I had to make sure you won't make a liar out of me."

"You did fine. I'm on my way."

He hung up. Through the drapes, he could see the sun's rays enveloping the house, the whole damn world. Sun everywhere. Why couldn't California have a regular winter?

It took an eternity to get into vertical position. His head was swimming, and his eyes went in and out of focus. His joints seemed to have needed some WD-40. He practically crawled to the coffee pot in the kitchen; and relying on his reflexes he put in the coffee, the water, and found the damn plug.

By the time Bill "Bono" Benton was shaving, he had a smile on his face. *I'm the greatest!* he told himself. *So what if I'm late for the office? They should miss me. They should need me. I'm great!* He added up his secretary's words while grinning at his lathery image in the bathroom mirror. There must have been a call from New York, from Chicago; and of course, the beloved president, Malcolm Orthoner, needed him, as usual.

He dressed, sipped his third cup of coffee, calculating which call meant which deal, how much money he could quote, and what kind of positive statement he could make to Malcolm O to keep the old fellow satisfied that his business was in good hands. *Christ! Life's a ball! A mere game where you gotta know the players before you can lick 'm.*

The Orthoner Associates owned a two-story building in the heart of Studio City, which they rented out to other businesses. Their own suite was one of a string of several small offices. Bill's was the only formal space with a separate reception room in front. His secretary acted as receptionist for the entire organization and also did the typing of everyone's deal memos. Hers was an open entry area.

He arrived to the beehivelike office where nearly thirty bodies, including his protégé, Barry Sherman, had been busily on the phones, buying and selling other bodies, résumés, and information since before eight. The headhunters. This newly developing industry dealt in the lives of bodies. The executive placement agent also facetiously known as headhunter specialized in placing high-paid executives in even higher-paying executive jobs. Creative selling at its best. When you're a commission-only person, you start early and hit the world with your phone calls before the world can hit you. The only way to go. Your livelihood depends on how many executives with astronomical annual incomes you can relocate in new jobs with even more astronomical annual incomes.

The prerequisites were greed, smarts, persistence, and endless creativity.

Bill felt that since no one knew that Melody was out of his life, he should make some heavy points at the office, to his staff, his president, and whoever else may be watching. They can't learn anything about his personal life. He had to impress upon them that he was productive and reliable. That way whenever the news broke, it couldn't damage his position. He had no idea that Melody had already called Malcolm and his wife to say her formal good-byes, which had prompted Malcolm's summons.

There were quick hellos. People waved at him while talking on the phone. Barry had his messages and deal memos organized for him in the order of their importance. Those who needed his advice regarding deals were on another list.

He rejoiced. The type of activity that kept an executive search firm going, and all its healthy signs, was lined up on his desk.

Indeed, his first two phone calls closed two major transactions that he had going with the Eastern concerns. They wanted his recommended people, bought them. His commissions were on paper, signed, sealed, and confirmed by telegrams. The next months and months of his livelihood were secured. He now could easily get his candidates moved from town to town, city to state, and ready to report to work at their new posts on the appointed dates.

His enthusiasm reached an absolute high. He believed that no one in his field was better at making these deals, relocating families of professional people, introducing new worlds to them, warranted by their abilities but definitely unforeseen until he let them see the light. He was unequaled, felt confident and successful when he returned Malcolm's call.

"Mal, how are you?"

"I want to see you for lunch."

"Where?" came Bill's well-trained response. There is no way that you say no to the president of your company.

"The Bistro. At twelve."

"I'll be there."

*

The lunch stretched into the afternoon. During the four hours that Mal and Bill spent together, Mal assured Bill that he wouldn't hold his stupidity against him if he could keep faith with his staff. They could not agree on when to tell the staff about his messy personal fiasco. Bill thought he could fake Melody's existence for months. Malcolm reminded him that he had already wondered what happened to the bride who had suddenly come down ill the previous week when it was time for the company's executive retreat to Northern California. He and Erna had noticed her absence and Bill's lack of concern. Malcolm knew that none of the people on the staff, especially none of the executives, were so stupid, God forbid they should be as to not notice. Bill grew weary of the older man's lilting speech pattern.

"There's one more item, here. Order your salad."

Bill obediently ordered his salad although he really preferred pasta but wasn't about to press his luck.

Malcolm continued after ordering. "I don't care what you did, I don't sit in judgment. I'm a businessman, you're a businessman. That ties us together. Let the company pay for your therapy, and should you pass, I want you to take my job. Erna and I want to get away. As president, we can't. As chairman of the board, we can."

The only thing that hit Bill, fully registering, was the thing about his therapy.

"What do you mean . . . exactly?"

"Between us, you should know that your sweet, lovely, and apparently very concerned young bride called and told me not to worry about your abilities, she was sure that no damage was done to you in business, she was sure that you'll get stabilized with a few months of psychotherapy. I was very glad that she was such a kind person to you, to us."

Somehow, at this point, the slow-talking, tall, slightly pudgy man sounded so Jewish. A good man, who trained him for years, and had been nurturing him with a singular purpose in mind all along, the presidency.

"OK. You've got it. It's a deal, Mal."

Bill drank up. The momentary silence appeared enough to separate topics; and when his next drink came, eyes sparkling, Bill broached a new subject. He needed to make points, to be sure of being in Malcolm's good graces.

"Since you've been planning for our future, Mal, I want you to know that so have I." He paused, catching the curiosity in the other man's eyes. "What do you think about diversifying? A subsidiary for the company? A subsidiary in another area?"

Malcolm O expectantly waited.

"Like a restaurant, or supper club, maybe a members-only club, that kind of a thing. You know what I mean? We buy a restaurant and make it into a hot spot."

Malcolm leaned back in his chair. He looked at the ambitious young man, the son he never had. After thirty years of marriage and minimal extramarital activity, this kid was handing him a new freedom. Sort of the same freedom that he gave Bill. Good idea to have his own place. He wouldn't have to look around if he wanted to spend the evening away from Erna. He could even bring Erna sometimes and impress her with a fine kitchen. Other times he could go by himself and watch the dancing girls, so to speak. It could be a tax loss for a few years. He needed that. He was making far too much money. He looked at Bill.

The question was still hanging in midair.

"There'll be dancing, of course?"

"Of course." Bill smiled. Malcolm took the bait.

"The best food in town?"

"The best." Bill started a low chuckle that developed into a full laughter shared by both.

"Maybe a key club, like, say the Gaslight?"

"Why not?" Bill didn't care. Anything Mal wanted, he could have. All Bill dreamed about all his life was to be the fancy owner of an exclusive restaurant. Now he would do it. With someone else's money. Wow!

"And maybe we lose some money from time to time," said Malcolm, the businessman.

"Or invest the profits?"

Malcolm nodded. That's OK too, if they can't lose. Sure, invest it elsewhere and lose it elsewhere. Maybe the movies. He remained nodding and deep in thought while finishing his coffee and signing the tab.

*

It was really too late for Bill to go back to the office. After three o'clock, things slowed down. He'd catch his best business early in the day. He had a wonderful glow. Why ruin it? He needed to think. He felt like the luckiest person in the world. He made up his mind to take full advantage of this shot at bigger money, big time! He knew that having two rental houses and his own place did not mean wealth in any circles other than the streets. He was ready for a real drink. Although he was right at the Tail O' the Cock restaurant in Sherman Oaks, he drove on further west to Monty's Steakhouse.

Chuck, working behind the bar, spotted him instantly. For a fleeting second, there was fear on his face for the night before; then the con man emerged and took charge. He broke into his biggest, happiest smile, placed a Red Label and soda in front of Bill, who gulped down most of it. Chuck noticed Bill's hands trembling as he pulled his cigarettes out of his pocket. He had been drinking.

"Welcome, Billy. How're things going for you today?"

"You cleaned me out last night, didn't you?"

Chuck could not detect anger in Bill's voice. He smiled boyishly.

Bill smiled back and winked. "Well, kiddo, it's only money. There's more where that came from. And"—he took another long swallow—"if you play your cards right, you might have a grand future with me."

He finished his drink and stood up. "Come by the house after closing, hm?"

Chuck nodded. Let Bill think he is in the driver's seat for a while. Not for long, though.

Chapter 13

LARA WOKE UP WOOZY from all the dope they had consumed earlier in the evening. She rolled over to turn toward the clock on the nightstand. It was one o'clock in the morning. Her eyes wandered around the magnificently decorated penthouse apartment, and she wished and wished and wished. Why couldn't she have something really good happen to her? She felt like making a deal with the devil. How could she do that? How could she make a deal with the devil? What would interest the devil? She would give up dope and booze and possibly even cigarettes—oh, maybe not that, in trade—if she could just have something fine happen to her. On further thought, though, maybe she could keep the wine and champagne and just give up the hard stuff, hard booze, hard drugs, hard everything.

Her parents had lost faith in her and stopped trying long ago. Since her life with Bill has ended, she, very knowingly, had gone all the way back to the bottom. The place where Bill found her. No longer a challenge, getting down and dirty again was easy. She knew Bill's marriage to Melody was over because Melody said so and she, had no reason for doubting her. Bill sure did not come looking for her again. She could never measure up to Melody. What a fine lady she was. Lara was sorry, in a way, for not making love to her that night. She could have been her first female lover. It would've been appropriate. But now they would never see each

MK

other again; and she would be making love to every Tom, Dick, and Harry and whatever woman that would pay for it. Why not?

Life had lost its luster. She was twenty-six. She knew she had better make money on her body while she could because she had never been trained for anything and loathed the idea of going to school. Lots of women did it. It was the new thing of the fifties to do. Get a second start. Get an education. But not she. Not Lara Burns.

She looked at the man beside her. He was hardly breathing. He didn't look bad; but after all, he had several hours of hard loving and dope, and gave out.

"Harry," she called to him gently. "Harry?" But the man didn't stir.

"Oh, foh chrissake, if you're gonna die, you should at least gimme somethin' before you go, you asshole."

She was muttering to herself, half loud. She reached over to the night table, which was also a designer refrigerator and juice dispenser. She pressed the button and got herself some orange juice, lit a cigarette and a joint.

Snapped amyl nitrite capsules were all over the floor. How wonderful one minute and how nasty the next. The tank with the nitrous oxide stared at her, laughing, and all the other junk that was so marvelous a few hours ago looked disgusting now. She freshened up her orange juice with Moët & Chandon. It still had plenty of bubbles. A fine drink. There. It was a lot better now, with the overflow of vitamin C slightly cut.

"Harry, dammit, don't die on me. Gimme somethin', you jerk. One of your apartment houses, or your designer dress shop, somethin'!" She was whining in a half-yelling tone as she put the roach back in its container and abandoned the drink. No, nothing would help her now.

She restlessly turned and looked at Harry. He looked so peaceful. She rolled over and playfully got on top of him. Laying there, she mumbled in his ear.

"Hey, ya sweet fucker, lissen. I just got this idea, like if I could run an apartment house, maybe, I'd ya know what I'd do? I'd turn it into a hotel. Yes, a swanky hotel with a real fine little restaurant and a small, small lounge. I'd get a top o' the heap cook and some low-down, offbeat singers 'n' stuff for the small, small lounge. The upstairs'd look ever so elegant, and the customers would be friggin' chic. That's what I'd do. Harry, I tell ya, if ya wasn't asleep, I'd be afraid to say this, 'cause you'd laugh at me, but deep down in my heart I'm a really nice, nice person. I always was, Harry. I never meant to be bad. Harry . . ." She suddenly became aware of the fact that he wasn't breathing at all.

She jumped off him, shook him, checked his pulse, but had no idea if she was feeling anything or whatever she was feeling was really a heartbeat or not.

She collected her thoughts, started to resuscitate him with all her might. She didn't stop until he was breathing loud and clear. The healthiest sound she had ever heard. She was staring at him, herself out of breath.

"Harry, my god! I thought you were a goner!"

He opened his eyes and had an angelic smile for her. "Lara Burns . . . you are special."

Lara was tickled to hear him talk. She hugged him and offered him anything he wanted, water, juice, champagne, whatever.

"Come here, Lara. Sit next to me."

Neither of them were aware of the fact that she was naked. He looked at her. He looked at her like a person just back from the dead.

"I had a long sleep. Before that, I had a lovely day and evening with the most splendid young lady I ever knew."

Lara trembled. There was something eerie about the way he spoke.

"I also had a fine dream. A good dream. It was about you. I will tell you about my dream in great detail tomorrow night, actually tonight, at dinner. OK, honey?"

Lara lost interest. Tomorrow had just come in, but she had no idea how to spend it. Dinner seemed very far away. One thing she could bet on was that she would find trouble between now and then.

"Sure, Harry."

"Now, sweetheart, I'll have Mac drive you home. No other place. No stops. No escapades. I don't want you to see anyone else or even speak to anyone else between now and eight o'clock tonight. Meet me at The Place." He gave her a fatherly kiss. It was the first time that Lara realized that Harry must be near sixty. That's old. He picked up the phone, buzzed his driver.

Mac, the chauffeur, was tickled about having to get up to take Lara anywhere. He had a yen for her a long time. He was sure that she was doped, probably had a fight with Harry, and that's why he was sending her home in the middle of the night.

When she came out of the building, he was raring to go. She walked tall and surprisingly straight.

"Hello, Miss Lara. How do you feel this morning?"

"I don't feel like talkin', Mac, OK? Let's go."

She got into the limousine as if she owned it, drew up the glass, and feigned sleep. Mac kept an eye on her, waiting for some sign from the adventurous, full-of-life courtesan, to give him some space. She had been the subject of his frustrated dreams night after night ever since he had met her.

When he pulled up at her door, she got out and walked into her apartment building, rudely ignoring him. To herself, she wasn't rude. She would never dream of it. She was totally preoccupied with Harry. Should she call his doctor and have him go over there to take a look? He was definitely not breathing for a while. She was tormented with indecision. What had she imagined, and what was real? And why would he want to meet her at that stupid restaurant, The Place. *Not very hip.*

She had barely closed the door behind her when she heard knocking.

"Who is it?"

"Mac. You left something in the car."

She looked through the peephole and saw his lecherous face grinning through filth pouring out of his every pore.

"I left nothin' in the car. If I did, give it to Harry."

She loudly put the chain on the door and marched into her bedroom.

There was no way she could sleep. She decided on a hot bath. While her body was revitalizing, her mind raced a mile a second. Harry was sick. He would die. She found tears in her eyes and was surprised by her strong feelings for Harry. Gosh, he was just a rich old man paying her bills.

He was nothing to her. A fair business trade was all that tied them together. But the more she thought about it, the more she knew that he was very important to her. He was good to her in every way. He cared about her, and from all she knew, nobody cared about Harry. He had no family, no love but hers. And he was paying for it. He wouldn't even know whether that love was real or fake?

Sleep eluded her. She got out of bed, drew the drapes of her bedroom window, and watched the sun rise. It was definitely morning.

She put on Levis and sweater; jumped into her good, old, reliable MG; and drove off. She drove north, out of the Valley, against the increasing morning commuter traffic. Sometime later, she found herself at Paradise Cove, her favorite little beach north of the Malibu Pier. She took a blanket out of the trunk and spread it on the sand. As she lay there, the sun warmed up the sand, and she was finally able to doze off.

When she regained consciousness, the beach was busy with beach bums and other nonworking entities. She watched them without awareness. A cute surfer was eying her. She liked that. Then she remembered Harry's strict instructions. She began to worry. What if he called to check on her and found that she had gone out. He wouldn't believe that she was by herself.

She hurriedly drove to a telephone booth to call her answering service. Harry hadn't called. She also found out that it was nearly noon. She headed home. On the way, she decided to stop at the market then spend the rest of the day watching TV, sleeping, any way to make the time pass.

In the produce section, a man started to talk to her. She smiled, happy to know that even in casual jeans and sweater she looked good enough to be picked up. Normally, if he had appealed to her, she would have joined him easily; but this time something made her want to see Harry more than anything else. Some instinct kept telling her that he was dead, and if he was not at the restaurant, she would know that he was dead.

Shaking nervously, Lara entered the restaurant. Her eyes searched around. Harry was there. He told her about the wonderful dream he had where an angel of God told him to give Lara a gift of real value. That he let Lara know how deeply he cared about her and appreciated her caring about him.

In spite of the busy dinner crowd, Lara was in tears. She couldn't stop herself from telling Harry that she loved him and would do anything for him and never mind a gift.

Harry pulled a deed from his inside pocket and made her read it. It was his restaurant that he gave her. The Place. The very restaurant they were sitting in. Suddenly it did not look so stupid to her. He even promised to teach her the business.

Her tears dried up. She was in shock. Harry was not only not dead but also the most wonderful living man. She would never have to sell her body again. She was a businesswoman. She looked at him with loving eyes.

He dropped to the floor.

She screamed.

He was pronounced dead on the spot.

Chapter 14

L ARA ENJOYED EXCELLENT TREATMENT by several of Harry's attorneys. She came to their offices wearing a simple, soft dress that enhanced her body without being a giveaway of the wonderful curves. Her golden hair was pinned up into a loose, casually elegant pile on top of a lightly made-up face. She did her best to appear respectable. All she had to do was watch her language. She knew that she did not have to discuss her relationship with Harry with these men and one woman attorney. Four of them just to handle Harry's estate. Christ, she couldn't believe it.

There appeared to be no problems with the grant deed. After all, they had written it themselves. For a minute or two, they tried to trap her into some sort of self-incriminating admissions as to why the deed was made out the same day Harry died. But there was no way for anyone to prove Lara involved with Harry's death.

She was told that she could take possession of the restaurant, including everything on the premises, at the beginning of January. A new year. 1956.

She asked about arranging a loan to help her refurbish the place, if necessary. She found four pairs of ice-cold eyes trying to give her a warm smile along with a flat no. *OK*, she thought. *I'll show ya.* She rose, gathered the documents, slowly, deliberately, placed them in the accompanying large envelope, and marched to the door. She paused, looked back at them.

"Thanks, and fuck yourselves, fellahs and ma'am."

*

She drove by the restaurant that was to be hers, that was hers. The Place looked much better to her now than before. It was located in Sherman Oaks, on Ventura Boulevard, just east of Sepulveda Boulevard. Going west the nearest eatery was the Fireside Inn, newly opened and doing well, and then Monty's *Steakhouse* in Encino, always doing well. She tried to think if there were any other big eateries between Harry's and Coldwater Canyon. Nothing came to mind. Harry's restaurant looked pretty good but no great shakes. It was a simple, family-style eatery. Obviously not the *in* place, contrary to its name, The Place.

Too excited to go in by herself or to do anything, she drove past it several times. Knowing that on the first of next month, The Place would be officially hers, she had a lot to do to get ready in the meantime. There was no way she was going to screw this up. This might be her last chance to provide herself with a good living. There was no room for mistakes. She would even clean up her language. After all, she had started out as a product of good breeding once upon a time long ago.

Melody Benton. Or whatever her last name was. Melody flashed through her mind as if lightning. Now, there was a levelheaded person, working in a law office, probably very organized, knows about business. Lara had an urge to see her. She took a chance and called Bill's house, but there was no answer. Naturally, even if she still lived there, she would be at work. How to find her?

Caught up in the momentum, Lara became inventive. She approached a young gas station attendant and asked him to pose as a bill collector, call Benton's office to get Mrs. Benton's number. The young man was not difficult to persuade, and Lara got Melody's office number.

Melody was cool on the telephone. Lara felt she should have been more interested in seeing her but probably was too busy or couldn't talk privately. Lara found herself practically begging Melody to meet her for dinner. Lara knew she could learn from that woman. They agreed to meet at seven.

*

Inside the restaurant Lara followed the maître d' to her reserved table. She ordered a glass of white wine and a Perrier chaser, lit a cigarette and observed the activities.

It was a very large room with an occasional column separating areas. She didn't know that once it had been several different buildings, and as Harry kept buying them up, he broke through the walls to accommodate the healthy growth. The service was pleasant. As she had assumed, there were far more tables for families than for couples. Well, Harry must have felt at ease with that crowd, but she would change all that.

Melody arrived dressed in basic business clothes, wearing little jewelry. Still, the way she swept through the room in Lara's direction, she commanded space. People looked up, and Lara didn't know why. Melody was not as pretty as Lara, several years older, but somehow an unspoken sophistication and self-assurance made people pay attention. Lara smiled as Melody sat down and ordered her cocktail.

"You're looking good, Lara," she said, and Lara felt that she meant it. "I'm starving. What do you recommend?"

"I don't know. I've never eaten here. I was here once but didn't eat."

Melody looked disapproving. Lara, having used her best English, wondered what was wrong?

"Do you always suggest restaurants you don't know?"

The reprimand was uncalled for, but somehow it made Lara smile. Yeah. Melody had already taught her a thing or two, and now, a new lesson, *protect your own knowledge.*

"No. There is a special reason I wanted to try this place. I'll tell you later, OK?"

"Should we order a bottle of wine?"

She studied Melody. She felt she needed this woman, and she wanted to play her cards straight, but she couldn't tell her about this deal she made with the devil. That wouldn't go over too well with someone like Melody.

"I don't drink. I ordered this one while I was waiting. For show only. I gave up alcohol for a while." Lara was satisfied with herself. "I am trying to break a drinking history, you see."

"Well, I'm about to get myself a drinking history." Melody straightened her body, pointed the tip of her nose toward the nearest waiter.

"I never could do that," Lara said in awe, watching the waiter come over immediately carrying menu and a wine list.

"May I see the wine list, please."

The waiter handed it to her and withdrew. Melody smiled at Lara.

"There's an awful lot you can tell about a restaurant by looking at their wine selections."

"Not if you don't know wines."

"How true. How true." Melody disappeared behind the wine list, and Lara continued her surveillance of the activities.

Melody ordered a half bottle of California Cabernet for herself, Perrier and lemon for Lara; then they studied the menu.

When the maître d' appeared to take their order, Melody asked him if he had any suggestions. He happily announced a milk-fed veal, chicken, and mushroom combination dish, describing the gentle blend of lemon butter and wine sauce as if he could taste it. Melody took his advice, and Lara went with a seafood salad. She was anxious to see if their seafood was as fresh as it should be.

"You know, I'm never sure if I can take the waiter's suggestions. I always feel like they're pushin' somethin' on ya."

Melody smiled. It was nice to find out that there were things she knew better than this beautiful ex-girlfriend of Bill's.

"First of all, you should know the difference, you should know that the maître d' took our order, not the waiter. The waiter waits. The maître d' is master. True, tonight we're roughing it, but here's another clue, if you're interested. A bad restaurant will push something on a customer. A good restaurant will recommend something that you can bet they make better than any other place. A specialty. That's how good restaurants become successful and famous. The chef's creativity and the maître d's confidence in that creation can put a place on the map. I found that out with my long-term fiancée whom I did not marry in the end. We had to eat out a lot, because he wanted to be seen by his mother's friends."

Toward the end of their main course, Lara decided to discuss her problem with Melody. They were sipping espressos, pleasantly relaxed.

"Well, what do you think of this place, Melody?"

"I think the food is marvelous, the service is perfect, and whatever the name of it is, I want to come back."

Lara beamed at her. "Starting the first of next month this very fine restaurant will be 'Lara's Place'."

Melody's demitasse stopped in midair, stunned. Lara got a better reaction than she had anticipated.

"Lara's Place? Hm?"

"Yup."

"You? Lara?" She pointed at her with the cup. "It's yours?"

"Not so loud," Lara cautioned. Then she grinned. "Yes, it's mine, and I want to make it a winner.

"I thought you were in a different line of work. How, when did you get into this business."

"I didn't . . . yet. I will in two weeks when the dead owner's will officially introduces me to the staff . . . I want to make a million changes! I want to dress it up. I want it to be the most refined, absolutely the finest in town."

"Do you have that kind of money?"

"No way."

"Well, then"—Melody became the levelheaded business woman Lara imagined she might be—"the thing to do is do nothing. Let the restaurant go on without changes, other than fundamental paperwork. Start making money, your money, so that you won't need a loan. Don't do anything drastic to destroy what it has going for it now."

Lara was let down like a child. She reached for the now-warm glass of wine. She picked it up, put it down, and sipped on the soda water.

"But I wanted to close it down, redecorate an' all that, and then reopen with a big bang."

"Featuring the painted signs Under New Management, no doubt." Melody mused at the illogic. She ordered a Grand Marnier over mist and appeared to be deep in thought.

"Let's see. If I had inherited this place, what would I do?"

Lara's eyes sparkled. This was exactly what she wanted. To get Melody involved as if it was hers.

"In my opinion, but you, of course, do whatever you want, it's a mistake many new owners make with a going concern. The patrons who are eating here now come here because there is something they like about it. Don't change it. Get to know the customers, get to know the rhythm of the flow of money, get to know the kitchen and the chef. Give everybody raises, small, but an incentive. Then little by little, you change a section, change something, and on some kind of anniversary, when you're pretty secure in business, you can change the name to *Lara's Place*, you know? By the way, it has a nice ring to it. I know it's probably hard on the ego. You want the whole world to know, but the whole world doesn't care."

Melody lifted her finger, the waiter saw her point at her drink, yet unfinished, and brought her a new one. She then continued, as if there had been no interruptions, "Don't ruin a good thing because of your ego. People will take kindly to change, but not if it's pushed down their throats. And what you need, lady, is the people."

"But what if I watched all the flow an' rhythm an' stuff you're talkin' about an' I don't know what to do with it? What good's that?"

"You're right . . . OK, here's an idea. You have some time on your hands. Go to the library, get every book you can find on restaurant management, transfers, and all sorts of how-to publications and cram. That's all you can do. See what sticks in your head and use it."

"I haven't read a book in years."

"So now's your chance to catch up."

"Melody, will you be my partner? Will you help me?"

"No. I'm getting a little drunk by now, and I'll leave before I make a fool of myself, but the answer is definitely *no*. I have too many things on my mind to sort out. My neatly constructed life fell apart. I'm no more than a functioning machine on autopilot. Although I moved out last week, I'm not OK. I'm on my own again. I've never been good at that. I'm far from ready for any new interests. Especially something as complex as this. This takes a whole person. Anyway, I want to wish you luck. I'll be back here one day, and I want to see a booming business."

Lara was hurt. She wouldn't cry in front of Melody. She sat silently while Melody put her cash on the table to cover her half of the dinner. Lara pouted.

You will an' you'll be sorry then. Lara promised herself right then and there that *Lara's Place* will be everything it should be, and no one will stop her from making it. It's a different kind of prostitution. She had enough experience. It'll prove her right.

Melody left. Lara wiped a tear off her face. She could not understand what drew her to Melody. She had taken her man and had refused her in every way ever since. Still Lara wanted to be near her. She wanted her. Someone to understand her. There seemed to have been no one who had cared about her. She was more lonely than ever before. She wondered how she will be able to go cold turkey straight? Sobriety was a rough state.

At the bar, a couple of nice-looking men were drinking. Her innate urge to attract them, to make contact, surged forth. She paid the bill, rose, and headed toward the bar. As she walked through the small passage way, she saw herself in the antique wall mirror. *Lookin' good,* she thought. She noticed that she was walking almost as regally as Melody. She glanced toward the two men. One of them spotted her and made eye contact. He stayed that way. Looking at her. Lara froze in her steps. She stood still for a beat then turned.

No, this is *Lara's Place*. A very exclusive supper club.

Chapter 15

NEW YEAR'S EVE, 1956. Moving out of Bill's house in short order, Melody had rented the loft over an antique dealership one block from a residential section of Sherman Oaks. A perfect place for a fine antique shop, serving the affluent San Fernando Valley. The proprietor had designed the upstairs to be his own bachelor apartment. Spacious, no walls, small bath, and kitchenette units were hooked up to suffice. A smoked glass skylight shared a portion of the roof, making the loft pleasantly livable. Melody fell in love with it. The most unlikely place for a conservative single woman. Definitely ideal for Melody. She managed to get her furniture in, and the movers set it up the way she asked them. Her bookshelves lined the walls, and Melody used the other pieces and plants to partition different sections without breaking up the simple oneness of the space.

She counted her blessings about the good timing of the owner's marriage and his buying a house exactly when she needed a private corner in the world. No neighbors, no friends. A dog, even if downstairs, was the right companion for her. The owner didn't want the dog becoming familiar with the upstairs and play cutie doggie. His life had to be that of guarding the building. The German shepherd, aptly named Cool, lived in the store and barked at every strange noise until he heard his master's voice or now Melody's voice telling him that all was well, he had done his job by alerting the human.

Melody was happy to settle back for New Year's Eve, be alone, reflect, and try to figure out what to do next. She treated herself to an affordable bottle of California champagne and toasted the TV set. The night was young. She didn't intend to be awake by midnight.

The doorbell rang. It was Carla with a drunk guy. A very young attorney from their office building with whom she had been having lunches lately. Melody opened the door. They came right in without an invitation.

"I don't want company, Carla."

"We're friends, pretty lady. You do want friends? Everybody wants friends. On a night like this? Sure? Don't you? Mike. Mike Devlin's the name." He reached out with his left hand to shake her hand while he took a hit from the roach in his right hand.

"No, Mike, I really don't want friends, or company, or anything. Please leave."

Carla was surprised. "Not even a little bit of fun? Look at him. He's hung, and believe me he knows what to do with it."

Mike, in appreciation, stretched up to his full height and wiggled his bulging crotch against Carla.

"Carla, what are you doing? What the hell are you into," asked Melody.

Carla took the roach from Mike, inhaled deeply. There was another one who certainly could fly without alcohol. "I thought the three of us, you know, cute Mikey here and you and I could have some . . . well . . . fun. See in the New Year a new way, if you know what I mean?"

Melody didn't know whether to laugh or cry. "You're crazy. A group scene? Me?"

"Who? Me? Who? Me?" Carla parodied. "It was a mistake, maybe. But lay off this innocent bullshit number, OK? To tell you the truth, I didn't want you to be alone, so I figured two may be company, but what you need is a crowd."

Melody couldn't help laughing. "Thanks, kiddo. Nice try, but not my scene. Happy New Year."

As Melody kissed Carla on the cheek, practically pushing her out the door. She slipped a joint in her hand while dragging Mike outside with her.

Melody, who hated illegal things, instinctively hid the joint in a candy dish. Curled up in bed, watching Guy Lombardo, she considered switching channels to see if Mitzi Gaynor or Cyd Charisse might be on. She needed the uplifting feeling she got from good dancing, the dancing that was denied her by powers greater than human.

She had barely dozed off when the dog and the doorbell woke her and probably the entire neighborhood. It was Carla.

"I got rid of him. Ask me how."

"How?"

Carla came in, kicked her shoes off, threw her clothes on a chair, and marched to the bathroom.

"Well, if you really want to know, I had him drive me to my car, then I gave him head, let him think he was the man, and left him in his car. Voilà, here I am!" She was searching in her purse. "Do you have an extra toothbrush? I can't find mine."

Melody found one in the medicine cabinet and watched Carla brush her teeth, rinsing over and over again while silently grimacing at herself with disgust.

"Wow! That tastes good."

Melody had never seen Carla in the nude. It was evident that once she had great beauty. As the sagging of the voluptuous breasts slowly began, the skin and muscles took on a softness, yet Carla remained completely desirable. She pulled a towel around her body. They were talking but avoiding the subject of Melody and Bill's wedding reception. Carla particularly ignored that it had ever happened.

"Have you ever made love to a woman," asked Carla.

"No. Go to sleep, Carla." Melody took a blanket and settled down in her easy chair. She hoped the night would go fast.

"I don't want to sleep alone, Mel. Please come to bed."

Carla's voice was that of utter loneliness.

Melody shivered.

"What's happening with you? I don't understand."

"I've figured out after thirty-nine years of trying to do things right that life is a big bedroom. If you're not someone's highly esteemed wife, everyone's after that two-inch square between your legs." She yawned, stretched, and studied her body.

"You sound crude and cheap."

"No. Never cheap. Always worth my price."

"Carla, you're scaring the shit out of me. You and I've never been like that. We had a lot of fun and still had a high self-esteem."

"Yeah, and what did that get us? Zero. Zilch. Nothing. But you can keep your self-esteem. I figured out that my body is not sacred, although it must be a temple based on the number of worshippers. So I'm ready. Let the games begin!"

"And what will become of you?"

"A winner, baby. A winner."

"You're depressed. You can't mean a word you're saying."

"Depressed? Me? Not in a million years. But you, honey, are weak and unimaginative. It's time to change courses. Start fresh and build from the beginning."

"Gosh, I know I'm weak. It took me years to change courses in the first place. You know, after Biff. He was supposed to have been my Cinderella story." Melody continued to damage herself with the champagne as she recalled her previous trauma while Carla indulged in the sweet-smelling pot she had retrieved.

"When Biff and I were breaking up, he told me, *No kid, no marriage, no money.*" Oooops. She can't go into that. She quickly chased off the thoughts of *the barren female, a disgrace of God* and laughed. "The worst part was that my mother raised me as a princess. I could not do anything around the house. I realized I couldn't even clean house. I had a vague idea that there was more to it than vacuuming."

"That's a fantastic story. Thank goodness I'm stoned."

"Wait a minute. Don't you want to hear the greatest discovery I made? Ammonia! I remembered that my mother used it. It does everything. And the best part is . . ."

"Oy, there's a better part?"

"Yeah, the best part is that it's cheap."

They were laughing, kicking, and cracking up at their own misfortune. "There's more, hang on, hang on." Melody couldn't stop herself.

"I don't know why I never told you this before, but when I first got to the office, I didn't want anyone to know that I wasn't qualified for anything."

"I knew."

"I guess you would. I asked you everything."

"You asked me what a pleading was," said Carla. "That was a dead giveaway. In a law office, everything is a pleading that's not a letter. You were actually typing a pleading when you asked me that."

They were laughing. Then they went silent. A thick silence.

"Anyway, I took the separation money Biff's mother thought I should get even though I was a slut. He made me one."

She mused as if this thought had been sitting in the back of her mind. "How perverse for the mother to encourage her son to do this to a girl. A virgin. Perverse. Then she called the separation money severance. Really perverse. But if you are rich, these things are called eccentric. If poor, you get convicted," said Melody. "Is that fair? Anyway, I took the money, what else do you do but take a secretarial course before the sky falls in and the money runs out. Except it ran out anyway."

"Big deal. I had the opposite problem. Too fertile." Carla looked at a distant spot far away in the land of nowhere. "Both my boys are bastards. My dad, and I hope he's turning over in his grave, was the worst bastard of them all, cutting me off without a cent."

"I didn't know that."

"Why should anyone know? It's a rotten story. I had my firstborn in a home for unwed mothers except it was camouflaged as a *girls' school of homemaking*, otherwise the neighborhood wouldn't have allowed them to stay there. While they took care of my baby, they sent me to secretarial school. There I was knocked up by the bookkeeper who shortly after the birth changed his mind about divorcing his wife for me. So one thing led to another. I took in typing because with two small guys, you can't very well go off to work. I also took in wine, sherry, scotch, and everything short of perfume. I began to leave the boys home alone, go out, and drink myself to oblivion. I was a mess."

She started laughing through her tears, got up, and walked to the refrigerator. "Do you have any cookies, candy, any sweet stuff?

"Got the munchies?"

"Yeah, it's part of giving up drinking, or smoking . . . cigarettes, of course. Carla chuckled then shrieked with delight on finding a jar full of chocolate chip cookies. She stood in the kitchen doorway, holding the cookie jar. A sadness passed her face.

"About a year ago, I had a boyfriend, Ted. He bought me things. I don't have a stitch of new clothes since he found out I was older than his wife and left. Men have to have affairs with younger women. That's what they expect. Which means older and older men for me." She laughed out loud. Melody joined her. What else could she do?

"You were at an advantage," Carla said. "You knew how to be poor. I didn't. Two kids and no knowledge. Sad, sad."

"I think it was probably a month before I met you-know-who," said Melody, "who shall remain nameless in these halls, that I finally learned to budget to live within my income. I was really proud. Then I met money, and I liked it, again."

"Must feel great!" Carla approved of Melody's new knowledge but didn't really think she could identify with it.

"Hell, no, I want money. Now that I know how to live without it, I don't want to live without it. I deserve it."

"Wonderful. And how do you plan to get it," asked Carla.

"I dunno." The champagne was reaching her, and she slurred more than not. "I can type, and I can be a homemaker. That's all. I'm weak, and I'm getting on in years."

Carla walked around Melody.

"Take off your nightie."

Until this point, Melody had forgotten that Carla was naked except for the towel. She didn't move.

"Let me look at you."

Melody did not grasp the meaning of *looking at her* since Carla was doing exactly that.

"Your body. Let me see it," Carla insisted.

"Take it off. Now."

When Melody didn't move, Carla walked over to her and pulled the flimsy short pajama nightie off Melody. "There. You look better naked than in the most expensive nightgown." She stepped back to take in the full view. "I becha, you could make out like a bandit. Shy, classy, pretty. Guys love that."

"Bring the street into my bed."

"Ah, that's a bit of an overstatement."

"Ah," Melody imitated Carla. "That's how I feel about making commerce out of sex."

"Aha, you keep looking for *love sex*, but *work sex* pays better."

"Aha," Melody imitated her again, laughing. "You've just made that up."

Carla ignored the humor. "Please don't think all this innocence is becoming a woman your age. If you'd had children, you too would've taken money, making commerce, as you say, as soon as you were alone, without a man, without a provider. How do you suppose one supports a household of growing kids on one income?"

"I don't know. I thought my problems were real problems. But next to yours . . . I guess I almost understand your way of thinking."

Melody got into bed and pulled the cover over herself. Carla stood a moment before joining her. She slid close to Melody and put her arms around her. Melody was positive that her whole carefully structured world of propriety was crumbling down on her.

"Carla, do me a favor." The voice was weak. A vulnerable child. "Promise to keep your hands to yourself and stay on your side."

The answer took an eternity. "I promise."

Chapter 16

BILL BENTON'S HOUSE ON Fryman Avenue in Studio City had undergone a drastic change. It was not only fully furnished but also Asian style predominated. It cost Bill a pretty penny. The subtle elegance, soft comfort, and deep tones of the Far East represented Chuck's taste, who took up residence with Bill whenever the mood struck him.

The desk in the den was covered with brochures of surveys of restaurants throughout all of Los Angeles. Using Malcolm's money, Bill had hired the services of a good research firm. Based on all the information they provided, Bill started to visit different establishments on various nights. Gradually, he began to concentrate on the San Fernando Valley. He knew that the rural naïveté of a growing community had tremendous potential.

The least impressive Valley restaurant on his list was The Place, a regular eating house that had recently changed hands. Not much to look at, and all the odds were against its survival. He decided to watch it. The only good feature of it was the Ventura Boulevard location, the only street where a restaurant could set roots. Bill and Malcolm's venture was projected to becoming not only really big but also offer membership exclusivity that would appeal to the wealthy crowd.

Bill was preparing to go out on a date. Chuck lay back on the bed, watching Bill.

"Girl or boy tonight?"

"Chuck, I told you, in spite of everything we have, I'm not going to give up women. I love 'm." Bill sounded patient, happy, but Chuck knew he was drunk and hyping himself up to spend a wonderful time with some strange female. Chuck knew him, and Bill hated that.

"Anyway, buddy-boy, get lost. I want to be alone when I bring her home."

"You're the boss, boss." Chuck condescended, got his jacket, and walked out of the house. This always made Bill angry. He tried to be in charge, and Chuck let him know that he was in charge of nothing.

*

Twenty-one-year-old Mary giggled when the waiter asked for her ID. Bill was appalled since the waiter should trust that he, Bill Benton, would not be entertaining a minor.

They met Malcolm and Erna for dinner. Bill liked to do that to his girlfriends. They were impressed by the important conversation. Erna made a few friendly gestures toward all of Bill's dates, but she really didn't care to know one thing about any of them. The turnover was too rapid, and her mind refused to retain any information about any of them.

Malcolm asked about Bill's roommate, Chuck. Bill had assured Mal that Chuck would be the best man to run their club and that Bill trusted him with his life. Malcolm did not take this at its literal sense and was unaware that Bill did.

After dinner, Bill took Mary dancing and got her very drunk. Mary didn't mind. Anything Bill said was OK with her, including going back to his house. Nobody important waited for her, only her mother. That didn't count.

She was impressed with Bill's house and thought the pictures of his children were *marvey*. It was Bill's best idea to keep Melody's decorating and leave the pictures centrally located where she hung them. It showed all his dates an insight to Bill. They thought that he was a good man who loved his family. It made them relax and, as Bill learned, made them accept his advances readily.

They were necking in the living room, spread out on the low, modular pillow arrangement, when Chuck silently appeared from the background. While Bill was heatedly kissing Mary's lips, Chuck began to massage her toes. Mary stopped for a split second in an attempt to absorb what was happening. In her fuzzy mind, she decided that maybe she could do anything now that she had turned twenty-one.

Bill, Mary, and Chuck woke up together in the California king-size bed, nude, tired, and each of them somewhat surprised. How high were they? They sleepily looked around. It was not just another sunny California morning. It was different. The silence was thick. None of them had any idea what to say. Actually, Chuck was really only waiting to see what the others would come up with. Initiations always fascinated him.

"Gosh," said Mary. Chuck thought she should have done better than that. She was realizing that she was part of a small sex orgy and wondering if she ought to be unhappy, upset, or happy about the whole thing. She looked at Bill, in between her and Chuck. They're both bisexual, was her final evaluation. She could not decide whether she was scared of this realization. She had heard about it before, but she had never come in contact with it. They were such hunks.

"I wonder if you should call your mother and tell her that you're OK?" Bill spoke without looking at her. Chuck didn't think that was much of an opening line either.

"Guess I should." Mary slowly rose out of bed to reach for the telephone on the night table. She dialed.

Bill turned to Chuck. "You big shot Chink, I told ya a hundred times not to butt in on my dates. You piss me off. Can't ya lemme be! Dammit." He felt Chuck's hand touching him.

"Mother, it's me . . . I wanted you to know that I'm fine . . . yes . . . right here . . . on the couch . . . Bill felt that he drank too much . . . no, Mother, how could you even think that . . . I didn't . . ."

Bill could faintly hear the conversation because, as always, he lost ground to everything but the excitement of his body when Chuck worked his magic. By the time Mary got through explaining to her mother how she went to sleep on the couch in order not to be unsafe on the road, driving home, Chuck was completely and totally involved with Bill, oblivious to everything else. Mary looked at them. She was at a loss. She looked at Bill's passionate face. His eyes opened just then, and he reached out and pulled Mary into the action. His kisses were maddening, making her body burning hot.

Amidst the moans, groans, and sighs, Mary discovered a new kind of sex. She wanted to like it and be accepted by Bill, maybe even by Chuck, if that's the way things were.

Time came to drive Mary home. Chuck ordered a taxi, and they sent her on her way.

"I don't like sending my dates home by cab." Bill added brandy to his coffee.

"I'm the one giving you what you like. The rest is my business."

"Get off it. Who the hell do you think you are talking like that to me?"

"You don't really want to know, Billy, but I'll tell you. Your old man is back on the payroll."

"What payroll?"

"My innocent friend, as if you didn't know it. He couldn't seem to satisfy the needs of his sweet Stephanie and had to make a couple of hits. We have the goods on him, and I can blow the whistle any minute sending him to that great syndicate in the sky."

No. Bill did not know this. Suddenly he wished he had never known about his father's executioner role in the Mafia.

"And you want to blackmail me with that?"

"I am, Billy. You'll get your restaurant, I'll run it for you, except I need a spare room or two for different action. For real business."

Bill saw no choice. Chuck had already introduced him to the wonderful world of fast cash. Dealing in the hard stuff. Heroine, cocaine, acid. Trafficking was the way to Chuck's heart, and Bill thrived on life in the fast lane. He didn't think he would need

Chuck for long. He would go along with Chuck as long as he needed him. Bill believed he would prevail no matter what. What he did not know was that his dream of becoming a famous club's famous owner was but one small link in Chuck's growing empire.

Chapter 17

"**G**ODDAMMIT!" LARA EXCLAIMED AS she pranced up and down in her pink-and-pastel frills-and-lace apartment, wearing bikini underwear. "I'm gonna do it right! I'll show them. I'll show every friggin' one o' them!"

The apartment was filled with books, some open, notes hanging out of others. There were piles on the floor, on the coffee table, everywhere. The books were a direct contradiction to the baby-doll-flavored surroundings. She had glamour books written by famous restaurant personalities, *Holiday* magazine, *Ladies' Home Journal*; and she was devouring everything she thought was related to her quest. The business of owning a place became more important than flaunting it. She was going to make it work. She lived with these books and yelled at them as if they fought back.

"I can read! I can understand! I can do it! Nobody's gonna take it away from me!" The dainty desk had never before been used for anything as important as an accounting ledger.

"Hold it! Hold everything!" She stopped herself and looked in the mirror. "Priorities!" For years and years she had heard people use that word and had no idea what it really meant. "A list! A priority list! A daily priority list!"

She finally screamed with excitement. Of course, that's the thing to do. If she couldn't begin a day with an organized approach, she would never get all the work done. She would always be overwhelmed. She smiled with satisfaction. "See, girl, your momma didn't raise no idiot. An idiot." She corrected herself and knew that as long as she could train herself to keep a daily checklist, she would have it licked. It'd be tough, but so is everything else. Why not go for it?

*

She returned to the restaurant at three o'clock in the afternoon. For some people, it was still lunchtime. For her, it's been a long morning, checking in the fresh foods as they were delivered, going home to study; and today was not just going home to study. Today was the day. The day when things, the basis of her puzzle, fell into place. Discipline alone was not enough. Reading was not enough. Control could not be hers without a checklist.

She was dressed in white. A new color for her. She recently had become very fond of white and bought several things of subtle elegance to wear in the restaurant. Maybe if she dressed classy, it would be easier to act classy.

She pulled out the priority list. It was dated and categorized in sections. The first section was titled "In the Kitchen." She checked everything that was being prepared for the dinner reservations.

Another category started with "In the Dining Room." She walked around to see how it looked and how the staff looked. She had a victorious smile on her face. It seemed like even Walter, the old warhorse maître d', noticed that something had changed in the lady. She even walked with a different spring. She spent the first few weeks since taking possession of The Place just hanging around and keeping mental tabs, without making any demands, other than placing small vases with live daisies on every table. They all accepted the fact that she was a daisy freak who didn't know anything about restaurants and who probably spent her time away from the restaurant talking with her girlfriends about the problems of owning a restaurant. No one took her seriously. They ridiculed her street English while their own wasn't much better. They laughed at her ignorant questions, and they were planning to look for other jobs shortly, in the event that The Place started to lose business and they started to lose tips.

There was very little doubt in their minds that Harry's good, old family eat-out would go down the drain. They had no emotional interest in it and could not conceive that she would. To them this was not the last lifeline. To Lara it was.

The next category on her list was "In the Bar." She walked through it, as always, but she knew immediately that it was different. Prior to this day, each time she walked by the booze, she tempted herself to break down and start drinking again. Today the thought of drinking did not enter her mind.

"Larry," she spoke to the handsome bartender, "I'd like to learn the bar business. Could you help me?" He melted away to nothing around Lara.

"Anything you wanna know, just ask, boss."

Oh, the patronizing bastard. Lara was steaming inside.

"Well, I bought a copying machine, so that every night, after closing, I could take home copies of not only the accounting, but the inventory." He glanced at her from the corner of his eyes and hoped that this would pass quickly. But she came close to him; and as he looked into her big, innocent brown eyes, he felt he was talking to a ten-year-old.

"The inventory, you say?"

"Yes. You see, I was thinking that I would like to learn the rhythm of our bar business."

"The rhythm of our bar business?"

"Yes. The rhythm." She smiled out of pride. "You'll help me, won't you?"

Larry appeared to be thinking this over. A turn of events was taking place, he couldn't put his finger on it, but it had him spellbound.

"I'll try, Lara, OK?"

Lara floated on joy. She felt secure. Her checklist had provided her a new footing. She knew, deep in her heart, that she was finally embarking on the realities of being a restaurateur. She returned to the kitchen, carrying a glass of water and sipping it between swallows as she started to taste everything.

"Chef! Chef! C'm'ere!" Bobby rushed over to her. He was new since Harry's old chef left almost immediately after Lara took over. Bobby was the sixth new chef in five weeks. Young, good-looking, wiry in build, with a very good education as far as Lara could tell, and a brief but good working background.

"Bobby, we gotta talk!" He stared at her in fear. This was his first job out as full chef, and he wasn't yet in complete charge of the entire kitchen staff of five, four excluding himself.

"OK, Lara, talk."

"What da ya drink, ki . . . Bobby?"

"What do I drink? What do I *drink?*" He was at a loss. His eyebrows raised. He was the squinty-eyed New Yawk kid he used to be before going to school in France.

"I drink iyced teay, OK? I ain't drunk."

"Oh, no, baby, you got me wrong." She turned to one of the Mexican dishwashers. "Where's the ice tea?"

The Mexican also looked at her bewildered and wasn't sure whether he was amazed at her or at the fact that he understood what she said. He trained himself for years to misunderstand *gringos*. He pointed to a tall glass cooler-dispenser. Lara fixed an ice tea for Bobby, pulled him over to the table where the help ate, and pushed him to sit down.

"Let's talk."

"Shuh." Bobby slurped on his drink. He was certain this was the time for him to be canned.

"I tasted your lemon sauce. We're famous for our sauces, right?" She didn't wait for anything past a nod of an answer.

"Yours stinks. Now what's wrong? What the hell is wrong? You went to school. Did you forget your little recipe book at home? And the guacamole! The guacamole tastes like lemon sauce for white fish, all pleasantly preserved in green film. Now wait a minute. There's more. Wait." She was quieting him down before he could rebut her. "I don't wanna fight. I've learned lately that cookin's an art. That makes you an artist. Right?"

"Nobody's ever said that to me since I left school." He was overwhelmed.

"Well, Bobby, I need an artist. I *need* one. You understand? We're gonna make this place go. Capital GO. I can't have anythin' tastin' wrong. Not slightly, not a touch. Not *at all*."

She held his hands, and he felt the urgency of her life reaching him.

"Don't disappoint me, Bobby. Without you, I can't make this place happen. You understand?" Her eyes were moist, and he knew that without him, his art, she would be hurt. He did not want to hurt her. She was dumb enough to give him a full-chef job. He would show her that she made no mistake.

"I do, Lara. I really understand."

Lara stood up before she would start to cry.

"Help me, Bobby. Fix your goddam' sauces."

He knew, as he watched her walk out of the kitchen, that he would stand by her, no matter what. *That's the lady that will make him into the great chef he has always dreamed of being. He will pour in the customers so they'll never stop.* When he returned to the stove, he was sure he was a new man. A man Lara could count on.

The dinner crowd started to arrive, and Lara remained in the background. She was, for the first time of her life, observing something in a knowledgeable manner. She knew that if she would keep track of all the activity, food, drink, entertainment, she would get a complete picture of the business. Just like Melody told her. Control's where it's at. The key.

She wished Melody would come in, announce that she had changed her mind, and would work with her. She still did not understand her deep feelings for Melody, but she was grateful for the rough way in which she had laid out the future of Lara's Place.

At eight o'clock, a distinguished man in his late fifties arrived with an attractive-enough wife and daughter, who looked just like him; and the daughter's husband rounded out the foursome. They were given a choice booth, and Lara noticed Walter making a big fuss over them. He looked familiar to her but could not place him. After all, there had been a lot of men in their fifties. They had the money to buy a good evening and send her the gifts and keep her in dope when that was what she needed.

As soon as Walter became available, she asked about the man. Who he was? Why the big fuss? Walter grandly explained to her that he was, is, Mr. Martin D. Schoenfeld, esquire, the late Mr. Harry's attorney. She remembered him right away from the day of the deed and the whole hullabaloo he and the others made over her acquisition of the restaurant.

"Introduce me, please."

Walter was flabbergasted, but he had no choice.

"Come along, if you will." He guided her through the tables to the Schoenfeld party.

"Mr. Schoenfeld, excuse us for interrupting, but Ms. Burns wishes to meet you."

Schoenfeld was overly gracious, and Lara was about to throw up.

"Ms. Burns, it's a pleasure. It looks like you are attending to the affairs of this concern eminently. May I introduce Mrs. Schoenfeld and my daughter Mrs. Barr and her husband, Malachy Barr, also an attorney. Won't you join us?"

"Oh, by no means. This is a very busy night. Just the same, I appreciate your kindness. Mrs. Schoenfeld, it's a great honor to have you here. I know that you were all old friends. I try not to feel like an intruder, and I do my best to continue in Harry's fine tradition."

Mrs. Schoenfeld smiled, grinned, nodded, raised her hand to be kissed, and did everything she could think of, instead of speaking. Lara recognized that she was stoned out of her mind. Her daughter saved the moment.

"Uncle Harry was a terrific guy. I'm glad that you're thinking of him when you're keeping the business going." Under the table she kicked her husband, causing him to take his eyes off Lara.

All the bullshit smiling made Lara pretty sick.

"Well, I certainly hope you'll enjoy the evening and will return soon. The entertainment is about to start. Do let me know if it suits your tastes."

That was a mouthful. She bowed in a half-assed manner and backed out of the corner as fast as she could. This time she saw Mrs. Barr kicking Mr. Barr, whose eyes were again glued on her. Nobody kicked Mr. Schoenfeld for the same crime, however. Mrs. Schoenfeld was out of it.

Lara absolutely had to have a tonic and lime to calm her down. By the time she finished, Larry saw her laugh almost out loud. She knew she won the round, but she could not define the arena.

Kay Dennis started up at the piano bar. Her sexy, mellow voice calmed Lara. The entire restaurant seemed to settle down as they listened to the velvety tones expressing a deep, rich soul. "Wayward Wind" by Lebowsky and Newman although made famous by Gogie Grant, never sounded better than Kay's rendition. She also did justice to Duke Ellington's "Sophisticated Lady," and frequently revisited Peggy Lee's hits as well as jazz numbers popularized by Ella Fitzgerald. The lights dimmed, the spot on Kay, the illusion of an intimate nightclub in Manhattan soothed the soul, elevated the spirit. Magic of its own kind.

"Last Call!" saw everyone out of the restaurant, and Lara begun to collect the photocopies of all the daily records. No, she did not forget anyone or anything. Her checklist kept her on top of things. Somehow she knew she was no longer the dumb blonde she may have accidentally turned into for a phase.

After she said good night to one and all and left Larry to lock up, she walked out to her car. She still had the old MG but allowed a flirtation with the idea of a shiny new car. When she reached the car in back of the restaurant, she was stunned to find Martin D. Schoenfeld, esquire, in his full regalia, leaning against it.

"Hello," he said as if they knew each other. "You did mention to return soon. This was positively the soonest I could do."

"Not funny, man. And how's Mrs. Schoenfeld?"

"Oh, she's all tucked in for a long sleep. How about a nightcap, shall we say at your place?"

"Oh, shit! I should've known better!"

She grumbled and started to prance and pace, this time around her car.

"What the fuck are we doin'? What's goin' on? Sir? Esquire, sir? Are you out of your bloody skull?" Then she looked at him. Her old street timing came back and led the way.

The man knew now that this spirited young woman who has been on his mind ever since he first laid eyes on her in his office was everything he ever wanted. He knew he was in a ludicrous position, and he also knew that he was not about to walk away.

"Coffee then? I wish to talk."

"Call for an appointment."

"I'm too shy."

"It's two thirty ayem."

"Bob's Big Boy is open. I have it on good authority. They're my clients too."

He had a boyish smile. Almost shy, as if he, too, were out of his element.

"If this is a put-on, an' ya have nothin' to say that I wanna hear, an' ya wanna shoot the breeze 'bout your wife's addiction, I'll kill ya, Mr. Martin D. Esquire."

"One will be sufficient. Mr. or Esquire. You don't need both. Actually, I prefer Martin from you. And let me remark how astute it is of you to notice Mrs. Schoenfeld's drug habit."

"It takes one to know one."

They had about ten cups of coffee. He was impressed with her attitude toward the restaurant, the way she defied all probabilities and applied herself to something that tough. It was four in the morning when they finally got up to leave. She wondered why she had told him so much about her thoughts and plans for The Place.

"Harry was like you. He always wanted to know my plans, and I always disappointed him."

"Not now. Not when it counts, you didn't. And I still cannot fathom how you could simply turn your lifestyle around like this. This kind of willpower is unheard of."

"Hey, no one knew more about bein' down and nothin' 'bout bein' up there than me. Ya know what I mean? Here I was tryin' to read, to learn, to use my chance, and nothin' stuck to my mind. Blank. One night I got so stoned on real hard stuff that I knew if I

didn't kill myself, I gotta change. So how do you change? By doin'
it. Cold turkey. Not easy, but it can be done."

She saw Harry in Martin D. and then she saw Martin D. only.

"Well, go get some sleep and give me a call tomorrow."

"I don't have time to sleep. I have to be at the restaurant at six
for the deliveries."

"You do? You will?" Martin was not surprised at this point.

"Yes, Martin D. I will."

She got in her car. What made her smile? Was it that she made
some points with a man of respectable brains? Was it that he made
her feel warm and wanted like Harry did? What was it?

"I'll be too busy to call you," she yelled out the window.
"Maybe some other day." She waved and drove off.

At six in the morning, as she oversaw Bobby checking in the
fresh meats and vegetables, a dozen red roses were also delivered.
They were from "Dartin M." *Very clever, Martin D.* She laughed,
placed the flowers on the piano bar, said good-bye to Bobby, and
headed for the gym.

During her workout and sauna, she seriously thought about
the next immediate step in her life. She knew she didn't need a
sugar daddy. Harry was the best, and Harry was the last. Oh boy,
how much love and adoration she felt for that man.

Her thoughts shifted. She wondered when would it be
the right time to change the name to Lara's Place? Now? It's
been almost three months. Was it too soon? She flashed on the
enticing advertisements she had seen in her recent readings. Of
course, that's the answer . . . advertising! It's time for a slow, small
campaign and build up to the name change by some holiday, like
July 4. No, that's too close. Christmas. That'd be nice.

At home she took a nap. She went to sleep thinking of
Melody. *Why couldn't she call her and ask her over to the restaurant.
Does she think about her at all? How could Melody make such a deep
impression on her and she make none on Melody?*

Chapter 18

MELODY ARRIVED HOME, SLIGHTLY weary from the day's work. Lots of rushes, lots of pressure. Too much for too little. She had to get serious about finding a better-paying job. Maybe a bigger law firm was the answer? Somehow she would have to get up her courage to start looking, start facing strangers again. She knew she could get more money for doing the work of a litigation secretary than her small, one-man law firm could pay her. She also knew it was time to start a savings account, start thinking about investments. After all, she would be thirty-one this year, and she no longer believed in the *prince on the white charger* showing up to take her away from it all.

She took a leisurely bath, pampering her body. She wasn't hungry. She was rather numb. When she lay in bed, she was sure she would fall asleep in no time and have a good night's rest, be ready for tomorrow and do tomorrow well.

However, her thoughts, instead of easing up, became more active and inevitably led to Peter. The weekend of wonders.

He came for her in a chauffeur-driven limousine, claiming that as much as he liked driving, he really preferred to concentrate on Melody. Melody smiled but did not invite him into the house. It was Bill's house, even if he wasn't there when Peter arrived and even if she was moving out next Monday.

Peter measured up the beautiful two-story structure and knew that no woman would leave this house, would leave a marriage that offered this kind of money, if she was not honest with herself.

He was gentle and caring, not boisterous like the last time in Reno. As if he had already thought it over and Melody was more special to him than other women. Melody could not perceive that anyone would be interested in her.

"Are you very hungry?" was his first question after the shaky "hellos" while they got into the car. Melody noticed that his pronunciation became very clear and knew that he had spent a lot of his free time since they last saw each other studying English.

"No. Not too much."

"Good, because we have reservations in a quaint little place, some distance due north . . . in Carmel. It was suggested to me by . . ."

"Never mind, Peter. I'm confused enough about you and me, and being with you. I don't want to know all the famous people who recommend you restaurants, who loan you their limos, and who probably even loan you their private airplanes."

They drove directly to the Van Nuys airfield where the pilot and the Cessna 310 were ready.

"Well, they like me. I'm a nice fellow, as you say. When they come to my home, to Hungary, I shall do the same for them. I don't like that you don't want to know whose airplane this is, whether it's Eddie Fisher's, or Nat King Cole's, or George Gobel's? But you will be pleased to hear that the young man up front is not anyone's private pilot. He is ours. I rented him. I should rather say I hired him."

"That's a relief. I simply don't know how to mingle with famous people and their famous things."

"You're mingling with me very excellently. Gold star for your effort and performance."

She spent the short flight laughing with Peter and at Peter's foreignisms.

They landed on a private air strip, were met by a car that took them to a secluded residence in the hills. Their luggage unloaded,

Peter took over. He drove Melody to a restaurant on the cliff that overlooked the ocean.

"I know you don't want me to think that you will go to bed with me this weekend, so we go to public restaurant."

Melody didn't know whether or not to be appalled at such a forward remark, but it seemed too funny and harmless. A week ago, a day ago, she was still battling with Bill; and now, even though she was on a date with another man, the thought of going to bed with another man was absurd.

The restaurant had only two small dining rooms. One was filled to capacity. The next room had eight tables, but there was no one else.

"For you, Melody, we came to a public place," he said. "For me, we had to be private."

She lost track of the incongruities that had been her life for the recent past. Too much. Too funny. Too uncanny. She didn't remember what she had to eat for dinner because the champagne kept coming, the service was unobtrusive, and Peter entertaining. Now that he had a better grasp of the language, she realized a worldliness, a subtle sophistication in him, that was not at all apparent in their other brief interludes. What did a man of the world like this want with her?

"I'm over thirty," she said it out of the blue. She could have killed herself for offering this information so readily. She didn't know why she said it. Was she so insecure that she wanted to know whether Peter really would deal with her and really wanted her for herself?

"I'm thirty-nine. I shall be forty in October. We shall have a big party. You must come."

"Where?"

"I'm not sure right at present . . . now," he corrected himself. "Maybe in Budapest, maybe in Paris, or wherever I shall perform. I'm big star now, you know. I get to travel."

"Do you like being a big star?"

"It's new. It's entertaining. I am having much joy I never dreamed of. But the best part is that I have money to spend."

"You spend it all?"

"I have a very fair partnership with the Hungarian government. They take part of my international money. If I spend more, they get less to take. It is simple."

By the time they drove back to the house, she knew that he was basically not rich. He started out as an Olympic soccer player, was part of some important game between England and Hungary in 1953, where the Hungarian team, the underdog, beat the English 6:3. He had a special spark in his eyes as he related that particular event. Gradually, as he aged out of soccer, he transformed his fame into a singing career. She understood the reasons for his athletic physique and his top-of-the-heap comfortable personality. He didn't care about owning things, but more about enjoying a day at a time.

They sat on the balcony of the luxurious home, marveling at the view of the ocean and talked about things in general. It was easy. She felt at home with him.

"Why don't you go out with famous women?" *Gosh, here she goes again, showing insecurity.*

Peter smiled. He knew exactly what happened inside Melody.

"I do. No, let me clarify. I did. I see famous women at parties, we meet, have dinner, have good times. Much fun. But God sent you from the ocean to me. You could have been famous. But you are who you are. That is fine."

Melody felt silly and wonderful all at once. How easy things were when you liked yourself. Peter liked himself and liked life. That was so nice. She was certain that Peter's life had to have been much more difficult than Bill's, yet Bill was such a mess. She looked at Peter and wished he would kiss her. Peter seemed to have read her thoughts.

"I'm not good at one kiss."

"I remember one kiss that you were very good at."

"That was a special occasion. I wanted you to know you were kissed by me. I wanted you to know for certain. Now, if I touched you, just your hand or finger, I would want all of you. Everything at once."

She didn't know how to reply. *Why is this man who would travel out of her life any minute so cautious?* Peter continued, talked more to himself than to her, searched for the right words, and put them in the correct order.

"I believe, somewhere inside me, that we have here a special situation. Something real. Maybe fragile? I feel we may be something for a long time in this life. I do not want to play with sex and find out very late that it could have been love."

He got up, walked around. "When I found you first, you were walking into the ocean. Your soul was lost. Second time, at the airport, you were still lost. I watched you walk behind the man. Woman must walk side by side with her man."

He leaned down, put his face near hers. "The third time, when I saw you the third time, I knew somebody up there gave you to me to help you find yourself. Maybe to love. It was no accident."

Turning his back to her, he took a few steps away from her then turned to face her. "No one should be lost. No one."

His words ran through her mind for days after he had gone. They seemed to be words of another, more respectful era. She hung on to his gift of a seashell, small and breakable, built into the solid strength of gold, making a beautiful medallion for a chain. When Peter bought it for her that Saturday, it was the embodiment of his feelings toward love, the way you build strength around it so it can remain in permanence.

Chapter 19

S EVERAL WEEKS HAVE PASSED. Melody had not heard from Peter. She stifled her need for him and spent a lot of energy in trying to stop thinking about him. He was but a fantasy. She should forget their paths had ever crossed. She should get on with her own life. It's been screwed up twice, royally. The first marriage did not happen because her shortcomings had fouled it up. It was first love, first sex, first everything. It should have lasted.

Then Bill was a fiasco. Was that due to her shortcomings too?

Why couldn't she attract the nice, stable type of man? She knew they existed. But where? Had she, at any time, managed to overlook such persons? What will her life become? Two major relationships and still have nothing to show but her age barely over thirty.

She quit her job for another one, but the improvement was minor.

She wasn't confident in herself. She thought she should graduate herself up to a better position when she felt qualified. Dumb, dumb, but she couldn't do what she couldn't do; and one of those things was lying, lying to anyone about anything, especially to a potential employer about her qualifications.

When she walked into the large Beverly Hills law firm for the interview, she was energetic, and she handled it well. The young attorney, one of the associates of the fancy organization, hired her on the spot. But when she had to report for work after her two weeks' notice, she had the weirdest visions. She was the lone stranger in a Western movie who came to town. Everyone watched, stared, sparred, judged. Was she a fast shot? How fast? She didn't know.

She thought she bluffed a lot, but each time they called her on it, she had the answer. She actually could hold her own in her new job. She became aware of the amount of law office knowledge she had accumulated by sheer listening.

The New Year's Eve incident evolved into a more serious gap in her friendship with Carla than the marriage and divorce did. She moved on from Carla's office as well as from her life. Although Carla never mentioned it, Melody knew she had disappointed Carla that night. Did Carla mean to have a threesome? Was she testing her? Melody didn't understand many things. At any rate, it was time to do something bizarre, something she was not cut out for. She couldn't get over the feeling of being a second-rate, boring female. Bill really got the best of her. Life was easy with a man. Alone it was tough.

Carla could always do new things with ease. She kept her job mainly for show. She could move in with a man, get things, get expensive theater tickets, clothes, jewelry, trips. How did she do it? One guy she lived with, she ripped off thousands of dollars of cash he had kept in his apartment, and Melody carried her secret to this day. Loyal and righteous as she was, she always understood Carla's adventures. Maybe that comes with the years. Whatever.

Like a little mouse, Melody was concerned with good health, good thinking, paying bills, and planning investments. She felt like a first-class square. A bore. She didn't know how to change, but she knew she would have to become assertive. Her mother would think that unladylike, but times are changing.

Here it was nearly eleven o'clock Friday night. No one called her on the phone, and not one of her girlfriends invited her to join them in anything. What happened? She was not about to abandon them when she got married; why did they abandon her now when she needed people the most? She heard the girls talk about their frequent Friday nights out celebrating each other's birthdays and such.

She got dressed in her expensive casuals that Bill had bought her. Because it was a little damp outside, she added her long, dark wool cape and headed out to one of the restaurants where she knew her girlfriends hang out some Fridays.

The drive in itself was a difficult trip, but she had to make it. She had to liberate herself from her own old-fashioned traps. If her friends, any of the girls, were there, they would realize that she too needed company. She was nervous. Never ever has she done anything this bold in her life. But she was going to stick to her plan and be strong enough to at least enter the restaurant.

The Fireside Inn, a beautifully decorated seafood house, had opened little over a year ago. Melody had dinner there a few times, loved the oyster bar, and enjoyed recommending it to friends.

It was crowded. Every dining room, the bar, the lounge, and the in-between hallways buzzed with excited, tipsy, noisy people. Loud singing came from the piano bar. She couldn't tell which voice belonged to the young black singer because everyone around him joined in singing the Mitch Miller favorites. Wow! She thought. How should she handle this?

She proceeded toward the dining room, made sure that she appeared to be in a state of looking. She didn't want anyone to see that she was alone. She was more than scared of the possibilities of a stranger speaking to her. She was petrified. Why was she doing this to herself?

Through her bewilderment, she saw tailored-looking women, flashy blondes, as they eyed ugly men, plotted to start up conversations with them in order to get their bar tabs picked up. She hoped she would never have to do that.

She passed the third table where four young men dined. They spotted her at the same time. The best looking and obviously the most outgoing fellow jumped up, blocked her way, and invited her to join them. Her eyes met the young man's, and her puzzled look gradually changed to a small, curious smile.

"No, no. I'm sorry," she barely whispered to him. That was not in her. She needed a proper introduction. Still she wondered if they really meant that she should join them, or what would happen if she did. She gently slid by his side, mumbling thank-yous, and moved along. Only a couple of tables later, he caught up with her.

"It'd be a pleasure, really." His look was eager. "Won't you change your mind?"

She noted that she was not irritated by him. If anything, as she looked in his eyes once again, she felt warm and lingery. *Gosh, I must be very hard up,* she thought. Her smile expressed an insecurity that fired him on. She moved away, haphazardly looked at the faces at other tables, tried not to intrude on anyone, and wondered all along what was the appropriate way to handle this persistent man. He looked so good. Carla would probably take him.

Past the dining rooms, she was in the connecting passageway to the oyster bar. The young man closely behind. He couldn't fail in front of his buddies.

"You know this is just a put-on and you're not looking for anyone. You're here to pick up, aren't you? Except you won't go for the first shot until you've checked out the whole joint for a better catch."

An absolute insult. How anyone dared to call her bluff and give it a name. She turned and slapped him. That had never happened to him before. In his surprise, he lost his balance, hit a couple whose drinks flew out of their hands; and yes, that was the end of a tray full of drinks being delivered by a waitress to the dining room.

The glasses broke, drinks spilled all over, mostly on her wool cape. *Fine,* she thought. *She deserved it. How could she let herself sink so low? God punishes.* The young man faded into the background, and she was left with the responsibility of paying for the damages. *Good. It served her right. Once she got out of here, she would never set foot again in a public place without an escort. Never ever. She would have to assert herself some other way.*

Her knees were about to give out, and tears welled up in her eyes. She trembled when the manager introduced himself.

"Put the whole thing on my bill, Jack!" came the voice of God through the fog, or so Melody thought.

"Sure thing, Mr. Taylor." Jack, the manager, had one of the waitresses brush off the lady's cape. It was a little help. The lady turned in search of her savior and saw Ben Taylor, a handsome Jimmy Dean lookalike, standing next to her. His longish blond hair did not conform to the crew-cut style of the day as it softly waved around his face, featuring a sparkly Colgate smile. The upper portion of his sideburns were angled lightly, artistically under his eyes, away from the straight line leveled with the earlobes, giving his face catlike qualities. He gently put his arm around her shoulders and led her to his table in the safety of the attractive wrought iron railing. As she thanked him and for the first time took a good look at him, they recognized each other.

"I don't remember your name, but I'm Ben Taylor. I'm a client of the tax attorney, David Schmidtliner, where you were a receptionist a few years ago."

"Yes, of course," she exclaimed. That was before she graduated to serious litigation secretarial work. "I remember you too. And thanks again for saving my skin. I'll pay you back, Mr. Taylor, don't worry. It's just that I only started a new job and don't have the cash right now."

Ben Taylor felt as if he was talking to an eighteen-year-old blushing Alice in Wonderland. He was amused. He handed her his own drink and signaled for another one.

"I don't remember your name."

"Oh, yeah, Melody. Melody Shorr."

"That's right. I wanted to ask you out to dinner a dozen times when you were at David's office, but the jealous old grizzly objected."

"David had a strict code about fraternizing with clients."

"And you obeyed?"

"Always. Sincere, simple, boring. But he still didn't own me. Why didn't you ask me?"

"OK. I'm asking now. How about dinner tomorrow?"

"OK. Fine. Thank you. See how simple it was?" She giggled silently to herself, as always, when she felt that life was, after all, a little bit all right.

"While I'm at it, making fast plans like this," Ben continued, "my secretary just quit. Can you start working for me Monday, or do you love your new job too much? I'll double your salary."

"Yes, sure." Melody laughed and could hardly answer without mutilating her words. "Why not, Mr. Taylor. One of us must be good and drunk. Why not?" She guzzled up his drink, getting a quick shine in her eyes.

She was in an indescribable state of daze as Ben walked her to her car. She did not notice the buxom young woman who entered in haste, ran into them, and Ben pointed her to his table. She did not catch a glimpse of the petulant young man who was the cause of her misfortune, or fortune, as it were, looking after her in angry silence.

Saturday rushed by as nothing more than minutes. Ben called in the morning as he promised and got directions to her loft. She spent the rest of the day cleaning the house and herself, dressing and getting ready for her date. This time she would make a success of it. She had a sweet tingle in her bones. This man was definitely not a nobody. Very wealthy, owning homes in Los Angeles, Palm Springs, Cape Cod, and London. He had been written up in numerous social columns, and she remembered well that his initial money came from oil. She didn't worry about why he wasn't married. Why worry about good news? She recollected the information in the files a few years ago when she worked for Schmidtliner and learned to become a legal secretary that he had many businesses and, with the attorney's guidance, was on the right side of the law.

She put on the finishing touches of her makeup. Peter came to mind. She had to make herself stop that since the tears followed so fast that she knew she would ruin a perfectly fine makeup job. She remembered a Peggy Lee hit and started singing it. "I can't believe the way I feel, like riding on a ferries wheel, I've never been so happy in my life." She had to stop that happy song too because it made her cry.

A little marabou shawl hung carelessly around the neck of the mauve dress she wore that gave it an expensive look. Ben was proud as they walked into one of his favorite Malibu hideaways. Dom Pérignon and Romanoff Blue Label caviar were on the table before they even settled down. They had privacy and impeccable service. She decided to go along for the ride. Why not? As the old saying goes, what's to lose? When Ben repeated his job offer, she accepted it formally.

"Now, I don't want any misunderstandings, so I'm telling you up front that you may have to sleep with your boss from time to time, but I have it on good authority that I am not too shabby in the sack." Ben was honest. She flashed on the street in her bed thought. Maybe she could skip that and go with a boulevard, Park Avenue, Fifth Avenue. Shoot for the stars. Who knows, working for the guy could become an exciting opportunity and help her forget Peter and Bill and whoever else that had intruded on her life with love. She wanted to forget love itself. Carla's words of *making out like a bandit* rang in her ears. Could she? Would she? She looked at Ben with moist eyes and knew she was about to say *good-bye* to the nice lady she used to be. He popped something under her nose, and she inhaled the first amyl nitrate of her life. Immediate response. The blood surged to her head, she leaned close to Ben and put her hand on his penis. He blew gently into her ear, and she was surprised by an involuntary contraction in her crotch.

The waiter brought them ice-cold ceviche appetizer, and like lady and gentleman, they dug in.

They had breakfast in Palm Springs, sex in the car, marijuana for lunch, and sex in the pool, dinner in a desert hideaway for the famous; and it was three days later when she went home.

Ben suggested that she move into his house in Holmby Hills just east of Beverly Glen Boulevard, but she insisted on maintaining some of her privacy by keeping the loft. She agreed to adding a telephone answering service on her line. One never knows who may call. Except, she knew very well that no one would call.

Ben dropped her at the side entrance to the antique store and drove off. At the bottom of the steps to her place, she found a telegram.

"I'll be working in New York for two weeks. Your ticket is at the TWA office in Los Angeles. The car will meet you. You are booked into the Plaza. I'll be there on June first. Signed Peter Szabó."

She sat down on the lowest step and stared into space for a long time.

Chapter 20

*I*T STARTED. MELODY KNEW it would be a different life and plunged into it, forcing herself to make a total escape from the old one. She was determined to be everything she never was, to go against her grain, to live for the job. No more nine to five. If she had to work around the clock some days, why not. Whatever Ben needed. He didn't realize right away what a treasure he had found. Her grasp was quick. She took charge with ease. Areas of her brain that have been dormant for years suddenly got a chance to surface and function. She felt important, was fulfilled.

Ben's contacts included some of the biggest names in international industry, sports, and art. His network of business involved him on various levels of participation anywhere from partnership to advisory capacity, from research to efficiency organization, from supplier to procurer, and so on. Anything anyone needed Ben could produce if that's what he wanted.

"Taylor Unlimited Taylor" was exactly that. Unlimited and Taylor. Hollywood penthouse suite furnished with subtle dignity, spacious enough to accommodate a staff of twenty if action required that.

The front reception desk was generally unoccupied when they did not need any temporary outside help. She learned that Ben liked to use short-term temps, liked not to rehire anyone frequently, which kept them from learning too much about his business. He told her the first week she was there that he was the silent partner in a temporary office personnel agency, and she will never have any problems getting help. He was right. She came and went as needed and sensed when it was essential that she be there for him.

Ben had been on the phone all morning. As soon as she arrived, he came into her office, walked over to her, and hugged her tight. She understood that he was troubled. She let him hold her.

"What's wrong?"

"Maury Wolf, damn it" He unfolded himself from her tender hold and stared out the high-rise window at the smog smothering the City of Angels.

"This tops everything. His courier married her parole officer, and afterwards, when it's all done, her job for Maury unfinished, mind you, she sends Maury a telegram and tells him she can't work for him anymore. Two more runs, and she couldn't wait with the marriage!"

"Tough shit, hm?"

"At least." They laughed.

"Are you going to punish her?"

"Ah, nah!" He discarded the whole thing with a wave of his hand.

"She was small potato to us. A runner. She didn't really know anything. There's no sense in bringing down an investigation for murder on me for something that little. It's just asinine timing, th's'll."

It surprised Melody that by punishment he immediately meant murder. *OK,* she thought. *She obviously has passed the point of no return, no recourse. She knew too much already. So what. Who cares. What's life without love anyway? It's no more than a washbasin of lukewarm water. You put your feet in it, it may make your feet feel good, but you need a full bathtub to get the whole body in it to feel good all over.*

"I can make a run in June. If that helps," she volunteered. "I have to meet someone in New York the first of June."

"Who!"

The tone of his voice was charged, and there was a sudden alertness in his eyes.

"A friend from Europe. We have some unfinished business. He invited me, and I'd like to go if you can spare me."

He thought about it for a moment. "Why don't you make both runs? One next week, the other in June?"

She nodded agreeably.

He continued, "The first one you'll make in a turnaround. The second and final one for a while, you'll do in June and take the week off. How's that?"

"Marvelous."

"There are two footnotes. One, your bonus will be deposited in your Swiss account, and two, you treat Maury like dirt, because that's what he is."

"Deal."

Ben was puzzled. "How come you don't ask how much the bonus is?"

"OK. How much is it?"

"It's a surprise."

"How come you don't ask who the man is?"

"OK. Who *is* the man from Europe?"

"None of your business."

"Ha ha. That's cute."

"And the same to you, Charlie." They laughed. Neither of them knew why they were so comfortable with each other.

It was time to get to work. Ben suddenly turned back from the door. "So when do you want to meet with your decorator, MGF?" He took a pause for impact and then offered his explanation, "My girl Friday."

"So finally, my title, girl Friday."

"Well?" said Ben.

"That's a delicate way to put what I do."

Ben seemed to be into the moment, but she was aloof.

"Well?" he repeated.

"What decorator?" He was relieved that she did not ignore him.

"What decorator?" she repeated.

"The one who will do your office while you're gone."

"Today."

"Deal."

They were back at work. Sometime later he buzzed her on the intercom. "There's something for you in the closet I forgot to mention. It's time for us to make a little whoopee. I'll be back around five to get you. Bye."

She wondered who "little whoopee" might be as she opened the closet door and found an elegant dinner dress with matching silk sandals and wrap. Ben had great taste. He sponsored a designer, and together they dressed Melody and several of Ben's other ladies, in exciting designs, revealing the figure but seldom showing skin. The fabrics, the colors, the areas where he used transparencies were far more sensuous than if he had made simply low-cut garments. Melody could hardly wait to finish work, shower, and dress. Really dress. She tried not to think beyond looking good.

As he was winding along Sunset Boulevard on the way to the Pacific Coast Highway, Ben told her they were going to the Malibu Colony home of Jacques Martel and his ailing wife for their season-opening dinner affair. Melody knew the name since she recently had arranged for the reopening and cleaning of the house. The Martels of Bordeaux, France, came in for a few months every spring and the Christmas holiday season.

"Jacques is a close friend and business partner." Ben casually stated the facts for her. "His wife has been in and out of hospitals for over a year. Certain extra special favors are due him, Melody. He is worth it." Ben lit a joint for her. Now she knew who "little whoopee" was. She took a couple of fast hits.

"Is he fat?" she asked. Although she had never had sex with a lardy person, she knew she would hate it. She knew that the smell of each and every fatty tissue would make her stomach turn. Even being loaded out of her gourd would not reduce her abhorrence.

"Jacques was slightly pudgy when I saw him last Christmas." OK, at least Ben didn't lie. She inhaled the powerful weed and held it for a long time. She aimed to get high enough to leave the planet.

Jacques greeted them at the door right behind the English butler. Melody was pleasantly surprised to see a man just this side of six feet, silver blond hair, suntanned, and a perfect build flexed through his evening suit. It was their tradition to dress for the first dinner of the season and then conform to the casual California lifestyle.

He and Ben hugged and kissed each other on the cheeks. He graciously held her hand as she was introduced and kissed it with more than a peck.

"You're looking better than I've ever seen you, my friend," said Ben, glancing at Melody.

"Oh, you know how it goes, with Mme. Martel so gravely ill, I took up, what you call bodybuilding this past year. So much anxiety, one needs to use one's body. So you see, here I am, a gorgeous man. No? *Cherie?*" He winked at Melody.

Mme. Martel, as well as the other guests, was happy to see Ben and one another. Little bit of old home week. Melody grinned and sparkled right through the event. It looked ever so attractive through her grass-glazed vision. She didn't need cocaine, acid, or anything harder. Ben never bothered to get her on more potent hallucinogenics. He was pleased with the effects of the amyl nitrites and marijuana on her. Sometimes little hashish was mixed in her dope, and she was off on her trip faster than anyone he knew. A chemically unspoiled body.

Wheelchair-ridden Mme. Martel was pleasantly attended through dinner by a large-boned, clean-scrubbed young Swedish nurse. Maj. Madame and Monsieur looked at each other with loving eyes and toasted everyone and everything frequently. The conversation at the table was light, after all the Martels were here on a holiday. They chatted about theater, opera, arts, and sport events.

"Talking about Sutherland. Joan, you know her, I am certain. She did the lead in *The Midsummer Marriage,* a very different opera by Michael Tippett. Poor fellow. We loved her at the Covent Garden but not the piece." Mme. Martel was naturally a respected patron of the arts.

"It looks like Otis and Dorothy Chandler are building an opera or philharmonic house in Los Angeles. Come to think of it, it could hardly be an opera house, since Mrs. Chandler is not crazy about that form of art. Just the same, we shall have a respectable theater," said Jeffrey Carson, a roly-poly entertainment attorney, with dimples and smiling shifty eyes, sporting a frail, tall young girl as his date.

"No joke?" Jacques and the others found this hard to believe.

"Would I joke about something like this," joked Jeffrey. "Ben, you were out of town when Mrs. Chandler and the Los Angeles Philharmonic gave a huge kickoff fundraising party to start the building of what will one day be the music center."

"Sure," came Ben. "I couldn't go. Gave my tickets to someone. That was the El Dorado party, right? They gave away a Cadillac El Dorado as the prize?"

"I was there, and that's where I fell in love with my next-to-last husband," said Margaret Meyer, a svelte lady, wearing a great deal of svelte jewelry, holding the hand of her current husband, a silent bejeweled Texas oilman dressed in his cowboy best.

Mme. Martel was delighted. "Would you say that one day there will be a real opera house right here? *C'est magnifique.* I adore it."

"One day, maybe ten years from now," added Jeffrey. "But as all art, it's worth the wait."

"Besides a theater the only other thing the big city needs is a rapid transit system of some type. We were talking about it in London with some very interested city planner friends." Jacques was anxious to share his information.

"Let's not get morbid, *cherie,*" madame spoke. "Los Angeles, the City of Angels, would never need such horrible contraptions as noisy trains and trolleys."

"We're going to London in two weeks. Can you recommend anything special?" Margaret turned to Jacques, but madame answered.

"*Ma cherie,* you must absolutely find Peter the Hun. I read somewhere that he was going to do concerts in Barcelona,

Amsterdam, London, and then maybe here in America. Isn't that right, Jacques?"

"Peter the Hun?" Margaret was not familiar with the name.

Melody trembled and reached for the champagne.

"That's just a wild Western nickname. He's the one with 'Kiss of Fire,' you know? The world is going crazy over him." This came from a handsome, trim middle-aged man, Dick Wagner, who actually had his lovely wife smiling and nodding and guzzling champagne on his left.

"Ah, him?" Margaret exhaled. "You recommend that we catch him?"

"I recommend that you go out of your way for him. When he was in Paris, he sang Cole Porter in French, with his little accent and the way his body moves, and what a body, *cherie*, you don't want to miss him. All of France was eating out of his hands. Especially Maj, *mon petit chou*." Mme. Martel approvingly patted Maj's hand.

"He is well managed, Ben. I don't know who handles him, but I approve. You pay attention to the *exclusivité*. One concert, one city. Excellent." Jacques insisted on awakening Ben's curiosity as if he had plans regarding the Hungarian.

Melody froze the smile on her face, breaking it only to accommodate more Dom Pérignon.

"We'll talk about it, Jacques." Ben pushed business away from the dinner table, making a mental note of the subject. No reason not to try new ventures.

"It seems to me he will do a benefit in New York sometime this spring. Shouldn't we all go?" Jeffrey was more interested for his own business than anything else.

"You find out the date, and perhaps it will be possible." Jacques looked at his wife. "We shall take our brandy in the library now." She nodded. He rose, walked over to her end of the long dinner table, kissed her hard on the lips, then he led the way out of the dining room to talk business, which left the ladies on their own.

Melody noticed an elderly woman arrive. Mme. Martel said good night, and like the classy lady she was, she excused herself.

The elderly woman, who turned out to be the night nurse, wheeled her out of the dining room.

Melody removed herself from the ladies' conversation. She had brandy on the terrace, by herself, and tried not to think about Peter the Hun, the latest craze and how she fell for all his lines. She too ate out of his hands. Yuck!

Jacques and Maj met Ben and Melody at Ben's car. Maj changed into a flimsy pantsuit and was in outrageously good spirits. In the car, Melody repeated to herself several times, "Mine is not to question why, mine is just to do or die," or something like that. Why didn't Ben tell her Maj was coming too? Didn't he know? And what's to happen later? What's happening now? Oblivious to the pleasant chatter of the others, she reached for a joint and lit it with great urgency. She wanted to block out this entire evening from her memory banks.

"Wouldn't you like something somewhat more potent, *cherie?*" Jacques purred and offered his cocaine. "Oh, later'll be fine, Jacques." She tried to purr back and wondered whether this may be the time to go for the big C.

"Madame looked wonderful, Jacques. Exciting, scintillating as ever," Ben remarked.

"*Qui*. She is rather incredible. I wished, of course, that she could come along as you are such a good friend of hers also."

"You are?" Melody teased Ben.

"She loves to watch," Maj enthusiastically added. "It does wonders for her circulation."

"I'll take the coke now, Jacques." A lightbulb flashed on in her mind. Melody realized that it wasn't going to be a mere *ménage à trois*. It wasn't going to be she with Jacques and maybe she with Jacques and Ben. It was going to be she with all three of them at the same time. This was definitely the time to find out how high she could get and on what. She hyped herself with thoughts of all the money and security she would have by the time she and Ben come to an end, in the event she lives to the moment of their parting. She told herself that girls like her don't get married and live happily ever after.

"How much longer?" Maj leaned forward to ask Ben but actually breathed into Melody's ear. Melody hoped the cocaine will work and help her through the night.

Ben turned the corner off Sunset and headed up Carolwood Drive into the hills. A couple of minutes later when he pulled into his garage, Melody cheerfully led the way through the mansion to the bedroom of bedrooms.

Melody's mind had detached itself from her body. She was outside, watching the erotic show in which her body participated with such ease and grace. She saw as the hungry hands of three people reach for Melody. They have all had each other, and they wanted someone new. Melody.

Her clothes were off before she knew it, and Jacques' hairy chest rubbed against her smooth skin. Dirty, delicious words came at her in different languages. Maj's touch made her hot. Was this real? Hallucination? Was this fun? For whom? Her mind was filled with outrageous visions as she tripped out. Her body was a separate entity. Apparently there was a contest going, with Melody as the prize. She even thought the contestants' performances were graded by points, and they all hustled and pushed.

"Come'n get it!" she heard herself yell out. She was sitting on top of the massive television console, legs spread, arms stretched up in the air.

"Here. Let's put this on." Ben proceeded to slip a purple lace bra without a cup, purple high heel slippers and purple garter belt on her.

"When I see you in your high heels I want to lick your toes, your ankles, your calves, your knees . . ." his voice faded into his actions. The race went on.

Melody couldn't tell who won. She laughed a lot as one of her selves was looking in from the outside, observing the stupidity. She thought perhaps Maj won and Ben, behind Maj, experimented with how to get more points through Maj's body. Then she thought it was Jacques's gentle rubbing and kissing her everywhere that made her feel wild. She thought she should reward Jacques.

She laughed, chuckled, screamed but didn't know why. Her mind and soul looked at her body, not quite understanding how she could have changed so thoroughly. Her mind and soul wanted some sleep. They wanted some old-fashioned reality. This did not seem to be the night for that. *Whatever happened to Melody*, she thought. *Who cares*, she thought.

In spite of everything, she still went home to her loft often, however irregularly. A little voice in her told her that she could remain the person she used to be. But she knew better. The used-to-be-Melody did not exist.

After a nearly eight-hour high, she cut out from Ben's house. It was the middle of a regular business day for the rest of the world. She parked behind the antique store. A man appeared from one of the back doors. She got out of the car. The man slid back into a doorway and watched her. She glanced back at the car. The man's eyes were steadily on her. She rushed up the stairs, quickly unlocked the door, and jumped inside. There was knocking on the door.

"Who is it?"

"I'm your new neighbor. The butcher at the end of the block. Samuel Freeman. I brought you some meat."

"Thank you, but no, thank you."

"I want to come in."

"Go away."

"I'm your neighbor."

"Go away!"

"I can't. I've been watching you leave. All the time, leave. Finally I saw you arrive. Please let me in."

"No."

"Yes."

"No! Nooo!"

She screamed at the top of her lungs. She heard footsteps. "Samuel, what're you doing up there?" came the owner's voice. "I brought your tenant some steaks. I meant no harm." Footsteps.

Melody listened to the sounds of the conversation of the gentle antique shop owner and the new butcher as they faded into the distance. She sat on the bed, looked up, and saw herself in the mirror. Eyes glazed, hair loose, her breasts heaving under the cotton jumpsuit, her legs spread as if that was the only position her body knew anymore. Lewd. Cheap. Street.

She lit a joint. Must keep the buzz going. The drum roll in her head was actually someone knocking at the door. She let the antique dealer in. She trusted the short, stubby man with an eternal sparkle in his eyes. He locked the door behind himself.

"Are you well, Melody?"

"I'm tired, that's all. I didn't mean to be rude to the butcher."

He walked her to the bed. "I'll get you some tea. Little ginseng root." Fully prepared, he produced a small packet and started the water boiling. "You lie down." She did. He brought her the tea of erotic dreams.

"You must chew this, you know. Chew it as if it were solids, before you swallow." She obeyed. He unzipped the center zipper, and the jumpsuit peeled away like banana skin. He began to massage her naked body. She relaxed and couldn't remember whether it was Ben, or Jacques, or Bill, the butcher, or the antique dealer mounting her. It didn't matter. This person she saw in the back of her mind's eye was in the gutter. A tear clouded her mind's eye. How low did she go?

Chapter 21

A NOTHING-TO-DO SPARKLY SUNDAY morning found Lara relaxed on the terrace. There were no telltale traces of the baby-doll frills of the earlier phase of her life. This apartment was decorated for a young professional woman, a trendsetting rarity of the times.

She sipped on hot chocolate while reading a magazine. Now that business made her get into reading, she couldn't get enough of it. Even a trade magazine entertained and delighted her with the new worlds it opened up.

Through careful self-teaching, she managed to clean up her language entirely on her own. Reading travel magazines started her on contemplating trips. Well, not before Lara's Place is self-sufficient. The idea of a Christmas change-over of the name, sort of like a christening party, appealed to her. She began to study magazine ads, newspaper ads of other restaurants, to determine how she would handle her advertising once she started up. She found that her concentration led her in a logical manner to more and more information that she needed in order to flourish. She almost believed that she was gifted with a good brain, just never had a chance to use it. There was no one to share her discoveries.

The prancing and pacing still existed whenever she faced unknown situations inwardly or outwardly, but the rest of her old characteristics seemed to have smoothened through the demands of her new lifestyle.

The telephone rang.

"I didn't want to wake you, but then again, I did. When I saw what a beautiful day it was, I felt that the only thing I wanted to do was to fly off into the wild blue yonder with you."

"Martin, you're out of your mind. Wild blue yonder 'n stuff. You're crazy."

"That's the nicest thing anyone ever said to me. So I gotta fly, and I want to take you along. Humor me just this once."

Lara smiled. The old fellow had been persistent all right, and she had rejected him all the way. What could be wrong with a little flying?

"OK."

"Was that an affirmative?" Asked Martin D., the great corporate attorney, of little Ms. Lara.

"Affirmative."

"I'll be there before you change your mind."

Lara could not imagine why Martin would be so determined to have her in his life. She had already made it clear that he had nothing to offer her. He still popped into the restaurant, sent her flowers, theater tickets, and once even a book. It was a long book. A saga of some Latin family living in the solitude of some island. It took her forever to read, and she could not understand his insistence on that being the best book he has ever read. Oh, well, he's nuts.

He arrived in his bright yellow Pinin Farina Berlinetta Special with black trimming and black interior. It was a fantastic-looking car, and he proudly announced that it was a prototype, painted for his specifications, and just off the Brussels showroom floor. All his life he worked hard. It was important to him to own everything new before anyone else, to be the first kid on the block especially with the unusual, whether expensive toys or useful equipment.

"It's more suited for me than for you, Martin."

"That's entirely true. I'll will it to you."

She looked at him with a start.

"That was a bad joke, Lara. I wasn't thinking."

She accepted his apologies. She trusted him by now. He had no malice for her. Through their many conversations, she began to understand that his family was a mess. He had always been out there, earning a living, only to see his wife drink her life away, one daughter became a dope addict, which reduced him to having to constantly bail her out of jail. The other one married an incompetent lawyer who could not hold a job if he weren't working for his father-in-law. His son, his last hope, turned out a total idiot. His most recent proof of that was that he married a gorgeous blonde aspiring actress, who secured herself someone to pay her bills and was away from her husband half the time already, after only six weeks of wedded bliss. Martin found Lara the only bright, intelligent spot in his life.

He applied his wealth well. At the airport, he chatted about getting a small jet as soon as possible. They were in developmental stages, the air force was using them, so private ownership was not far from realization. At this point, however, since they were going for a short flight over the city, he elected his Beechcraft BE-35, which was smaller than the B-50, parked next to it in his hangar.

They soared into the sky, and she was rendered speechless by the beautiful sensation of small-craft flying. She felt like she and the sun became one. She knew right then and there that she would learn to fly. She had to have it.

Martin spotted a clearing with an old, unused landing strip next to a large barn, somewhere in the Simi Valley. Without saying anything, he gently landed.

"What do we do here?" A surprised Lara.

"We walk around. It's very pretty."

He put his arm around her shoulders casually. They strolled. The smells and the quiet of the forest were intoxicating. At the top of the hill, they stopped to admire the endlessly sprawling barren Simi Valley. Suddenly he kissed her, tongue first, the way old men kiss, and pushed her down to the ground with the same motion. Without letting his lips leave hers, he had pinned her down with all the strength of his body. Lara was twisting, pushing, attempting to kick; but the man had power beyond her belief. His free hand was hungrily ripping at her blouse, searching for her breasts, and his body was already pumping at hers as if he had succeeded with the frequently fantasized sex. Lara finally squeezed his head at both temples with her hands so hard that his lips lifted off hers.

But he was crazed. "I have a great penis, honey, you'll love it. C'mon, don't stop now. You'll love my cock. You'll never have enough of it. Let me show you. Gimme a chance."

Wild, he was breathing heavily, pumping fast; and for a moment she thought he was going to have a heart attack, but she didn't care. This was low. This was filth.

"Asshole. You friggin' asshole!" she said. "Get off! Off! Off!" she screamed and tried to slide out of his grip, which was not getting any looser.

"Hello! Anybody here? Hello!" They both heard the voice and looked up at the same time to see Wade Nash, the superstar in the flesh coming toward them, keeping his composure as if he did not see what he was seeing.

"Thank God I heard you scream! I've been looking for you! I mean that is your plane out there, I hope." He talked nonstop as he came closer and maintained a deadpan expression. He kept his eyes on Lara and ignored the man who was getting up, straightening his clothes. Martin reached out to help her up but was too late. She already took the actor's hand and rose.

"I'm Wade Nash. My plane developed some trouble, and when I saw yours here, I figured I'd better land and get help instead of trying to make it over the hills into Van Nuys. It would've been suicide."

Lara didn't care about her torn clothes or her look. She was so glad to be saved. She ignored Martin as she put her arm through Wade's and started toward the landing strip.

"We'll be glad to help you, Mr. Nash."

"Wade."

"Lara Burns. Lara."

She let Martin follow them like a puppy dog.

"If you'd give me a lift to Van Nuys, I can get the truck out here before dark."

"Fine."

"It's a two-seater." Martin angrily interjected.

WASTED . . . MAYBE

"I'll sit in Wade's lap. You fly."

"B-35?" said Wade. "Not a two-seater." Regardless, he held Lara protectively. Her trembling hand belied the sophisticated facade. The tense body seemed delicate as if she could break like glass with the slightest touch.

Back at the airport, Lara let Wade hold her hand as they walked toward his hangar. She made sure that while they were in Martin's vision, she looked cozy with Wade. Once they turned and went into Wade's hangar, she pulled away. Wade was surprised.

"Thanks a million, Mr. Nash. You saved my life."

He looked at the mussed-up face, hair flowing wild, the torn shirt, and saw a vulnerable, confused child's large eyes looking back at him gratefully. He shivered at the animal presence.

"I'll drive you home. And it's Wade."

"No, no, thanks. I'll call a cab. I don't live far."

"I'll drive you, Lara!" His voice was firm. She needed it. She didn't move.

"Give me a second to talk to my man." He started to move toward the office. "Stay put now, hear?"

She did.

Chapter 22

THINKING OF THE EXPERIENCE with Martin made Lara shudder. Thinking of the meeting with Wade gave her heat rushes. Not thinking about either was impossible. Wade certainly was a most interesting acquaintance. She wondered whether he would show up for dinner while all along she padded herself for the disappointment of his not showing.

As far as she was concerned, Martin lied. Lying is despicable. Martin was out. There was no need for further thoughts.

The night was young. The Place started off to a fast and busy evening of diners. Lara relished the joys her successful operation brought. And yes, she did this on her own.

These were *her* customers now, who came regularly, who made The Place a meeting and visiting spot, who always looked for her specials, suiting the season, the day, or sometimes even her mood. There were light cooler drinks she created, bearing names like Lara's Zap or Not Alone or Sunday with Lara. Somehow her innate good taste kept improving, her palate became more reliable.

The clientele was better dressed, stayed longer, wanted to be entertained, and milled around from dinner table to lounge. She could almost taste the charms of the *Moulin Rouge* and other clubs of the old movies, old paintings, and old songs.

Nine o'clock was marked by Kay at the piano, her voice gently filling the lounge as she lured the patrons into her special world of selected music. It was nearly at the same time that a sudden murmur seemed to roll through the restaurant. Every eye was or was trying to be on the front entry. Wade Nash appeared. In a few seconds, Kay hit the piano with the theme song from Wade's latest movie to accompany his arrival. The maître d' efficiently took over and guided him to the booth Lara had reserved, just in case.

"Ms. Burns will join you. directly. May I get you anything from the bar, Mr. Nash." His voice trembled with reverence. He was glad that he never left Lara at the time of the change-over. This lady was doing good things for The Place.

"No, thanks. I'll wait for Ms. Burns."

He sat down and graciously signed a couple of autographs before Lara appeared. As she did, he rose and excused himself from his fans. Lara blushed nervously.

"Does everybody know you here?" he asked.

"They'd better. I sign their paychecks. Meet yours truly, the proprietress."

She said it with certain pride.

"How wonderful."

"I'm glad you came."

"I told you I would, even if you didn't own the establishment. Would you like a drink?"

"Perrier will be fine, but you go ahead." She raised her head toward the waiter then realized that Wade should not be pampered any more than any other man. Wade caught her thought and signaled to order his own cocktail.

"Do you want to talk about this morning?"

"Let's see." She was half serious as she summarized the day the way she wanted it. "This morning I met a lovely man who came to dinner." They raised their glasses and toasted each other. In fact, they spent a great many moments toasting each other. They also stared at each other in silence, and from time to time, they forgot that they were being watched by curious eyes.

"I saw a wounded small animal this morning," said Wade. "I remember the torn clothes, but I don't recall seeing fear. Lara, you send some powerful vibes." His eyes penetrated through her.

"That's flattering, especially coming from you, you know. And I want to warn you that I take words at their face value."

"I give words at their face value." He laughed his famous laughter, and the look in his eyes kept Lara blushing.

"May I see you home tonight?"

"At three in the morning? I don't think that's a real good time for a date."

"One can only live by the clock if one becomes its master."

"That's sage."

"I try."

"You've succeeded."

"Then we have a date?"

"Not tonight."

"I am going to Europe next week! You want to go with me? No strings, of course."

"Don't give me the big rush, OK? I don't need it. I don't even know if I like you yet." He sat back, absorbing her. She decided against remarking about his dead wife. "So what if you're going to Europe? You'll be back. I'll see you then."

"You're right."

"What do you mean I'm right? Are you giving up?"

There came the wonderful laughter again, trailing off across the room. "Nope, just letting you think you're getting your way. Actually I really would like you to visit me on my location. Europe or Africa or both?"

Lara would not be pushed around, even by the best. But she enjoyed it.

"Africa is not my cup of tea."

"And Paris?"

"That's more like it. But I haven't agreed, OK?"

"Let me see if we can fix that?" He went for the persuasive approach.

"Well, the company will be based in Paris, you know, rehearsals, offices, and all that. Then we will travel to other locations including Berlin, hm, you like? Trieste, a little Adriatic Ocean, warm and sumptuous, you like, hm?"

She smiled at the way he described the geographical locations as if they were tasty, exotic dishes.

"Listen, you call me when you're in a civilized place, and I'll see if I can get away."

"Little humor?"

"Like they say, I am a quick wit, fun, and scared that I might turn into a pumpkin if I have to do more than twenty minutes with a stranger."

"Not if I can help it."

Although she kept her eyes on the general flow of business, and since they were not interrupted at all, she found herself more and more interested in Wade and less and less aware of the restaurant. Some people still attempted to come over for Wade's autograph, but it was in vain. Minute by minute, they got deeper into the texture of their togetherness and away from everything else. Their lives had clicked. Wade challenged her hardheaded attitudes, which she found to be a turn-on.

"OK. I've always wanted to find a busy lady, an involved lady, and I think I just found the one. You'll give me a rough time in addition, won't you?"

"You bet." She was stimulated.

"What about tonight?" He ventured once again.

"Tomorrow morning, you mean?"

"Whatever comes next is what I mean."

She was tempted. He made her feel very good. *Yes, this might be worth her sleep. This might just be the man for her.*

In the corner of her eyes, suddenly like a glorious backdrop, she saw Bill Benton enter the restaurant. Wade, without turning, knew that someone had pulled the carpet from under him. He rose, put some bills on the table, bent down to kiss her on the cheek. She stared off, nodded to Wade, and let him sink deep into a vacuum.

"Thanks, Lara. I'll call you."

"OK. OK, fine." She waved at him while he stepped back from her, still waiting for a word of encouragement.

"I'll call you from Cairo. From Paris."

Lara smiled, but she didn't hear him.

Wade, with his long strides, elegantly passed by the wiry dark-haired man in the expensive suit and the young Asian behind him. He fleetingly heard the new arrivals ask the maître d' who the owner was. This time, on his way out, he ignored his fans still crowding him. Heat of Lara versus ice of Lara. The clash was his.

Bill, with a cigarette dangling from his lips and with the gangly walk Lara always loved, moved over to her.

"Hi. Nice place you got here." And he sat down in the middle of the largest booth.

Chapter 23

P ETER HAD NEVER CONSIDERED himself lucky in the true sense of luck coming his way and taking care of things. He felt that he had worked for everything. He did not simply become a soccer hero by playing well. He earned his recognition every inch of the way. When he didn't like any of the options available to an ex-soccer star—coaching, Olympic or local, did not appeal to him; going into government work, diplomatic work all seemed unlikely—he switched over to singing through arduous studying. When he was very young, he had a toss-up between singing and athletics; and luckily, healthy living only made his natural singing voice richer. It was an easy choice to make. Hard work to get to the point where he, the soccer star, could get up and sing without making a fool of himself, but he did it.

His first published song about a girl turning twenty-one and becoming aware of boys was cute, melodic; and naturally, on account of his fame, people went out to buy the record possibly to laugh at him. He wasn't sure of being a real pop singing star until a second record became a gold. That was unusual in his small country and couldn't have been possible any sooner because until the early 1950s, few people owned record players in Hungary.

His life changed to that of an imaginary prince. He had more material things than he could dream of, and total freedom to come and go. People living in a communist country did not have those freedoms and those things. Peter was a charming goodwill ambassador. He studied languages in order to record his hits himself for other countries and wet his feet in Yugoslavia, East Germany, Romania, hoping for an invitation to Moscow.

And the ladies. Sometimes he wished he could be six men or have the energy of six men. By his basic nature, he didn't want to miss a thing; so he was always on the go, accepting as many invitations to as many places and events as he could, while maintaining his health and practice routines. No, there was no way for him to stop studying languages, give up his physical fitness, or forget that first and foremost he was a Hungarian. *Peter the Hun.* He smiled to himself.

As he drove through the city in his Mercedes Benz, one of maybe fifty private cars permitted in the country of absolute equality, he stopped at the sports club where the famous hobnobbed to have a quick beer with his soccer teammates. Yes, Grosits, Puskás, Kocsis, and the others who were winning the European Cup once again. What a glorious way to have put Hungary on the map. To have shown the world that this country was more than agriculture, more than wine, women, and music. This little country, his little country, was the birthplace of many cultural, artistic, scientific, and sports giants.

As he got older and more traveled, he began to truly appreciate the city that was his home. Budapest. The architecture of each apartment building seemed to be special regardless of its grey, unwashed surface. There was so much sculpture and regal design all over the country that he dreaded the modernization that would bring its red brick, match-box like tenement buildings. But he saw far too many of them in other European cities and knew it was inevitable.

He arrived to his late afternoon appointment at the ministry in very good spirits. He loved his city, he loved his country, he loved his life. All he wanted now was clearance for Melody Shorr.

Miklós Barát, an old acquaintance, was head of foreign affairs. He greeted Peter with overflowing pleasure. They have crossed each other's paths for years between political and sports appearances, and this appointment was merely a formality to go on the official calendar.

Although only a few years older than Peter, Miklós looked old enough to be his father. Pudgy and balding, he proudly proclaimed that he got his looks without the aid of drinking, smoking, even indulging in espresso, which seemed to be the national drink and which the Hungarians always drank with self-destructive fury.

Miklós was jovial, full of self-mocking one-liners about how he had always promised himself, in front of his friends, that one day he would go on a binge in search of what alcohol and nicotine could do to his so far naturally aging body.

They shook hands, and Peter made himself comfortable.

Miklós, unlike ever before, spoke to him in a fatherly way.

"When I got your coded telephone call from Reno months ago, I knew that you probably lost your marbles. With all the women in this country who'd be your slaves, you go and pick a foreigner. An American!" He raised his voice a notch, and the veins on his neck seemed to be popping.

Peter had anticipated something like this when Miklós asked that he come to the office in person. Yet he was sure he could explain to his friend that he was serious about this lady.

"She came from the sea."

Miklós was about to go through the ceiling.

"OK. So she came from the sea. So you save her life, which you shouldn't've done . . ."

"Don't forget that she dropped back into my life twice more in rapid succession. That's three accidents, and you know that for a Hungarian three is *not* an accident."

"You're a romantic."

"I'm a Hungarian!"

He grew vehement as he relived the purity of the experiences with Melody.

"Then she told me she threw her wedding ring into the Truckee River, and you know what that means, don't you?"

"How the hell would I know what that means?" Miklós excitedly fell for Peter's enthusiasm.

"That's the final divorce . . . from this duck . . . no, turkey, foul. Some foul, I'm sure."

Peter continued, "When I kissed her, for the first time, she kissed me back."

"Who wouldn't?"

"You think she wants to emigrate from America and immigrate to Hungary?"

Miklós did not hear the smile in Peter's voice.

"No, no. People do that the other way around. Emigrate Hungary, immigrate America," said Miklós then realized the joke.

"You're making fun of me," said Miklós, reaching for the pitcher of water. This was too crazy for him to handle dry. Then he proceeded to explain that Peter's phone call made them gather some information about her. Now that he was certain that Peter was serious about bringing a foreigner to this country as his wife, he thought they would go to phase 2, check her references, and put some personal eyes on her.

Peter requested they do the formalities fast because he intended to bring her home in the fall, after his Western concert tour; and he was sure that she would fall madly in love with the city, with the country, and even with him. Enough to want to live there.

Miklós promised he would stay with it and would keep Peter posted during his travels. Peter gave him his itinerary and signed an authorization to investigate Melody in his behalf.

Peter assured Miklós that this woman would make his life a Sunday every day. She was shy, sweet, gorgeous, full of joy, inexperienced, and easily hurt by the strong. So high on a pedestal, no one could touch her.

Chapter 24

"ENTERTAINMENT, YOU SAY? LET me call Carla." Melody headed for the telephone on Ben's desk. Ben had concluded a long meeting with two South American connections, Ulu Bernhard and Leon Kimsky, and his good friend Timothy Vickers who owned half of Palm Springs. The room begun to cloud up with the sweet-smelling smoke of marijuana. It was the end of the seriousness. Business done, it was obvious that they were ready to play; but Melody, well, she wasn't. She never was.

Tim grabbed her by the waist as she bent down to dial. "Yes, your friend Ulu here wants her over to the house for dinner."

"Instead of," Ulu corrected Tim, wiping the small row of sweat beads off his chubby forehead.

"You can handle this, sweetheart." Ben's velvety voice gave an order. He took the receiver out of her hand and set it back in its cradle. She understood the order and took Ulu's pipe out of his hand, running for a fast high on his hashish. Fast, fast, more, more. She had to catch up with them; otherwise, she would be destroyed.

"Let's ride up to the house together." Leon fidgeted with Melody's bare toes in her high heel sandals.

"I must have that one." He licked her middle toe. She stared at him.

Ben's freebased coke had him higher than a kite before Leon finished with Melody's toe. "We're riding right here, together . . . now."

Quick touches of a few buttons on Ben's master control panel and the fabulous penthouse was lushly draped, no longer offering the view of the city. The lights dimmed, Latin music rose to curdle the blood, and Ben's hoarse voice said, "OK, Leon, that toe is all you get."

Ben's timing was fine for Melody. She felt her mind detach itself from her senses, trained like Pavlov's dog. She was thinking of dollars, thinking of early retirement, thinking of dollars, thinking of early retirement. She was thinking . . . of . . . dollars . . . early . . . retirement . . . and the hands pulled her clothes off, the mouth sucked her toe, hands grabbed at her, brought oils, planted kisses, unzipped their pants, paraded around, and she thought of dollars . . . thought of early retirement.

It was dawn by the time she met reality again. She looked at the wasted men and wondered if she was any good. *Do people in groups ever perform well? What was the objective?* She never could figure out the values, the appeal that made orgy sex inviting and apparently popular. She never could visualize herself getting into it straight or sober. She had problems doing anything she did not clearly understand.

She sat in the office sauna, felt clear, crisp, healthy; and she was certain that nothing was wrong with her. She was simply a one-man woman, which was the only place where she never needed to use any hallucinogenics. But come to think of it, she never took any dope before meeting Ben, so her reasoning would not stand up. The whole thing, actually, was rather murky.

She had enough changes of clothing on the premises to dress and settle down at her own desk in her cozy office by the time Ben's guests got themselves together.

They appeared looking slightly worse for the wear. Ben asked whether she would go to breakfast with them. She declined. The sooner they were out of her sight, the sooner her conscience would stop fighting her. When they left, she rushed for the refrigerator where she devoured an orange, some buttermilk, and wheat cookies before she made the first cup of coffee.

Ben returned several hours later alone. He didn't feel like making or returning any calls. He drifted through the quiet reception room, passed by Melody's open office door, and without stopping, went into his suite. It was sparkling clean. Melody had the janitor service in there minutes after the men had left. It was impeccable, as everything around her. She was good for him. What was he doing to her? He spread out on his couch. He did not answer his phone, and probably an hour had passed before he buzzed Melody. He anticipated her cheerful answer as if she was far away from him, not in the next room. Whether she just said "hi" on the intercom, or "yeees," or "Hellooo," sweetly trailing off, she was always ready for his instructions.

"How do you feel about a Mexican dinner?"

"Terrific." He could hear her smile.

"Get your things. We're leaving."

"Now?" Her voice wasn't surprised. She wanted to remind him that it was only three o'clock in the afternoon.

"Right now."

As always, they traveled first class. On the airplane, he talked about business, and she took notes about his plans for the next few weeks. She knew by then that they were on the way to Acapulco. After all, if you want a Mexican dinner, you go to Mexico.

She had become accustomed to his whims. She kept a travel case in the office for exactly such sudden moves. Except at this point she was curious as to why was he so lonely? Why would he need a trip when everything was going so well?

He was quiet and pensive in the taxi that took them to the restaurant. They did not call his friends in Acapulco. They did not call the usual limousine. It seemed to her that he wanted to be incognito. Why? She anticipated that he might suggest a sudden turn on the road and would have the driver take them to some new property he bought or was planning to buy, or that he meant to surprise someone with Melody, like another little party? Yuck.

They pulled up at a small, isolated restaurant on the outskirts of the city. Really Mexican. Really family style, no trimmings. People. She patiently listened to his ramblings about childhood and the time when his mother brought him there, the only woman who ever meant anything to him, but she disconnected fast. She never cared for people backtracking, looking for lost glory. When he went to the bathroom, she knew he was snorting coke because he had been straight too long. He returned with a victorious smile on his face.

"I didn't."

"Why not?"

"I wanted to show you.

"Show me what, Ben?"

"That we don't need it. That's what."

"It's too late. You know it's too late. Things go better with coke. Nothing is really fun straight."

"You didn't used to think that."

"I didn't used to know it." She felt her tears surging. "I want some."

"Oh, c'mon, honey. Forget it."

"Why?"

"Because I got you into it, and I'll get you out of it." Ben had an urgency in his voice.

"I had good reasons to get into it. I don't have good reasons to get out of it. Nobody cares."

"I do. I care about you. I hated myself this morning, and it wasn't the first time. Watching you load up every time I put your body through such abuse. We'll get another girl for that sort of work. I want you for my woman. The one and only woman."

She broke out laughing, loud enough for the few locals in the restaurant to look at her. Oh, who cared about the crazy Americans. Overdressed in cocktail party clothes in the middle of small-time Mexico. They were known to be eccentric. Rich *gringos* were expected to be erratic. But as the people looked at the crazy lady, they, along with Ben, saw the change from laughter to tears.

"You don't have the right to care, my sophisticated friend. I'm free, white, and way over twenty-one, to coin a fresh cliché. If I want to do myself in, I will. That's all there's to it."

"I'm in love with you."

"Our relationship was no grounds for love. It's too high-brow or too low-brow. Either way, don't spoil it."

"Melody, I am saying that I am deeply in love with you. I realized it in the last few days. I am in love."

"I'm not in love with you. If I were in love, I would have killed you last night and all the other times when you made me do those things."

"I wish you had killed me. I wish you had fought me."

"That's not why you hired me. You made it very clear why you hired me. There were no misunderstandings. I agreed to be your expensive whore who types, takes dictation, holds your hand, or whatever else needs holding. You did not cover up the details. I'm not your responsibility."

"But why did you do it if you hate it so much?"

"Money, dummy. I've never made this much money in my life. I was pure, good, honest, caring, considerate, loving, and everything my mother wanted me to be. Now, I get a little high, I learned a few tricks, I get royally fucked, you load me up with enough cash that pretty soon I'll be independently wealthy. You taught me investments, stocks, securities. What else could I ask for? I'm OK, Ben, so don't go soft on me. Let me have a dose."

"No."

"I'll make a scene."

"You already did. Smile. Act like you like me."

He signaled for the check; and before she knew what hit her, certainly not the coke she wanted, they were back in the car, back on the airplane, switched to a private service, and set down in Palm Springs.

She was tired.

He was keyed up. He wanted to talk. It was only around one in the morning. The Palm Springs sky was clear and full of stars. She didn't notice them.

"I don't want to talk. I don't want you to tell me that I'm a doper. I know I am, and it's OK."

"What about your unfinished business in New York? What are you going to do about him?"

She shrugged her shoulders, thinking about Peter. *What about Peter? The man who walked into her life, made her feel like a woman without ever touching her, then left.*

"I hate him," she said.

She walked through the house, through the lanai directly down the swimming pool steps, and immersed herself. She began to take her shoes off, her stockings, let them drop, unzipped her dress; and when everything settled on the bottom, he watched her swim. Swim her heart out. She did lap after lap with incredible fury until she came to a halt. Looked at him. Her eyes filled with tears. The child, the weak, unprotected person in her that never had a chance to grow up and blossom, looked into his loving face.

"I want to go to sleep now."

He took her out of the pool, wrapped a lush bath sheet around her and carried her into the bedroom.

"Do you want me to sleep with you?"

"Please," came the whimper of an answer as she went off into slumber land.

He loved her. He knew he loved her. He remembered his friend in Israel who described the fruit called sabra to him. It's the fruit of a cactus. It is tough, prickly, and untouchable on the outside, sweet, soft and juicy on the inside. Melody.

He smiled. After all, through the roughness and ugliness of his life, he found a jewel. But how could he make her fall in love with him? He thought all night, watched her sleep, touched her fingertips, inhaled her aroma. He had never spent a better sleepless night in his life. When he finally dozed off, he heard her rich, loud laughter, as it gurgled through the room.

"I did it, Ben. It's your fault." She laughed, and he loved the way she enjoyed laughing.

"What's my fault this time?"

"I spent an entire twenty-four hours without dope.

"One day at a time, as they say."

"But today, now, right this minute, we're going to turn on, aren't we? Do you like being sober all the time?"

"I get a better chance to watch you this way."

"Yuck. You know, when you're this sweet, I worry. It can't last too long. You'll have a fit and make a phone call and make a million dollars."

"Would you like me to do that?"

"I don't care. It's yours."

"I'll give you half."

"What are we waiting for?"

"I want you to make me a promise."

She responded to his changed tone of voice. She always did. She didn't like herself too much for being so sensitive. Somehow nothing could turn off her sensitivities. She asked what it was but feared that she might not want to hear the answer.

"I want you to go to New York."

"No."

"I want you to."

"You can eat your money.

"As your current boss, I order you to make the second run for me, see your man, and decide."

"I'll do the errand. I have nothing to decide. That gorgeous man is never going to see me all strung out. He'll just have to settle for his beautiful memories like me."

Chapter 25

CHUCK LAID OUT THE clothes he wanted Bill to wear, exactly as Bill did for his women. Bill had a feeling Chuck was angry with him. Chuck had stopped bringing him young girls. He cut him off from that direction and had been seriously pushing him back to Lara. But Lara had changed too much. She was involved in her business, and Bill didn't think that he could enslave her once again.

Inasmuch as Bill understood that Lara's restaurant could be his, he hated to take training lessons from Chuck in attitude toward achieving their common goal. Chuck demanded that he spend all his free time with Lara or around the restaurant.

Tonight Bill arranged to skip out on Chuck. He got himself a fifteen-year-old lanky young girl whose body reminded him of a boy. He wanted to spend the night with that body, all to himself at his hotel apartment. His only secret from Chuck.

He quickly locked up the house, jumped in his car, and drove off as if trying to get away before Chuck would appear.

Priscilla waited for him. This was her big chance to impress a grown man with her womanly qualities. She had wanted a grown man ever since her mother became the lover of another woman and gradually gave up all males. Priscilla was exposed to gay life on a daily basis. She became more and more curious about men. Not boys. Definitely not boys in her own high school, who were constantly offering themselves and who would run around naked if there were no rules against that.

Priscilla wanted a man who knew what to do and who would show her the right way the first time out. Then she would never have to worry about the questions in her mind whether a man was good or bad because she could compare him to Bill. She had no doubts about Bill being a good lover. To her he looked it.

She waited patiently in the small one-bedroom studio apartment, compact, with a kitchenette behind a sliding door, and a shower behind another sliding door. The whole place seemed like an oversized doll's house. She liked it. Settled down and wondered why Bill went home after he had spent so much time convincing her to stay with him. How could she know that he had to check in with his keeper?

Earlier in the day as she walked home from school, she noticed the small Mercedes Benz coup following her. She turned the corner, and the car took off the other way. Less than a minute later, she saw him coming toward her, catching up with her on the same side of the street. He smiled as he drove by, and he looked very good to her.

They played this cat-and-mouse game for a couple of blocks. She wasn't scared of him. She was not expected at home, and her mother would probably be gone all night. She felt OK about getting into his car. Would she like dinner? She had a steak and salad just to please him; then he dropped her off at the apartment. He promised her champagne when he got back.

She lay on the couch and looked at a *Playboy* magazine wondering if she would ever look as voluptuous as the centerfold. She heard the key turn in the door, and Bill appeared. He had changed clothes, looked extremely handsome, and had a supermarket bag in which he carried the goodies he promised her. He came over, rubbed his nose against her neck, sort of all over her neck; and by the time he licked her earlobe, she felt goose bumps over every inch of her skin. She reached for him.

"Don't get carried away, hon. This was just a sample." He stepped away, popped the champagne, took other accouterments from a small hide-away refrigerator, including cheese, crackers, and a joint. She had no trouble recognizing the marijuana. She had seen it around her house although as far as she knew her mother never used any; neither did she. Well, she figured, she might as well go along with him and find out what it is that people do.

He came over to the couch with the champagne, handed her a glass, and looked deep into her eyes. She liked how she became warm inside from his look.

"Have you ever been fucked in the ass?"

She looked at him while trying to figure out what he was talking about. The ass? She had never been fucked anywhere. She thought she had had an orgasm when one of her mother's girlfriends woke her up from her sleep by licking between her legs as if she had an ice cream cone there.

The memory of that sent a shiver down Priscilla's spine. She also remembered how her mother came in, kicked the friend out, and told her to let the child develop on her own. When she is an adult, she can decide for herself which way to go.

She smiled at Bill, her eyes reflecting the warmth of her first orgasm, long, long time ago. She would decide which way to go after Bill shows her what goes on.

Bill understood her smile to mean either "Yes," or "I'd like that," or however she might want to say it, it was what her little heart desired. He carefully undressed her and made her walk around for him. She did look gorgeous with the young body of a model. When she turned her back to walk away from him, he clearly saw a boy, whom he clearly wanted. They did not hear the key turn in the lock. They were trying to chart their many sensations, trying not to forget anything that was going through them, for different but equally important reasons.

The key turned. Chuck stood in the doorway. He smiled. He had to keep an eye on Bill before he would mess up his plans. Chuck had no margin for incompetence. His would have to become the largest Oriental-Occidental connection in the world.

"Your good taste is showing, Bill. Has she walked for you yet?"

Priscilla looked at the clean, elegant, sinister-faced Asian, whose eyes turned to velvet as he beheld her. She was excited by his gaze all over again.

"How the fuck did you find me?"

"You forgot a very important appointment, Bill." Chuck ignored Bill's question. He turned his back to Bill and looked at the girl. "When he leaves, young thing, I'll show you how it's really done up your ass."

Priscilla was mesmerized. She could not take her eyes off Chuck. She did not notice as Bill got dressed and left. In a hypnotic state, all she wanted was to feel Chuck inside her, inside her where no one had ever been, inside anywhere where Chuck wanted to be.

*

It was after midnight when Bill arrived at The Place, first having stopped for drinks in an attempt to defy Chuck and to try to figure him out. Lara was ready to leave. The dinner crowd had gone, and the bar business could not be in better hands than Larry's.

She was delighted to see him. "I thought you stood me up."

"Never. If anything, I've decided to help you."

"Help me?"

"Yeah. You need me. You can't run something like this on your own. You don't know anything about restaurants."

"I've been doing it OK."

"Believe you me, you'll be better off with my help." She gave him one of her familiar rich smiles and did not notice that his eyes were glassy. He was high. He was seeing the young, anxious, bewildered face that belonged to Priscilla.

"Would you like a drink?"

"No, silly. I'm off that stuff for now. A test run. A year or two." Bill had to handle a sober Lara.

"But I have something special for you at home. C'mon," she said.

They took both cars to her apartment. Suddenly he realized that Lara's may be the only place where Chuck would leave him alone. It may be the only home he had.

The changes that took place surprised him. She told him that she had been preoccupied with learning to and running the business that she had not had time to think about a house. But after Christmas, she would definitely find a house, something that could be a real home. She reminded Bill of how much fun they had looking for the house that eventually was not hers. Bill remembered. All that happened seemingly a hundred years ago when he believed that normalcy was what he needed. Now he knew better. He had to make *quirky* the new normal.

She lit scented candles clustered around the apartment, turned the lights off, lit incense at crucial locations, and brought him a burning French connection.

She leaned close to him. "It's a new drink someone had shown us. Half Amaretto, half Courvoisier, give it a quick flambé. To make it palatable, we switch snifters because it gets so hot." As she poured the drink over into the fresh glass, the flames died.

Bill savored the mellow flavor of the smooth drink, relighted the joint, dropped a quarter of a *lude*, and felt really OK. Warm inside, burning on the outside, he looked at the dreamlike porcelain-smooth face, illuminated by the soft candle glow. He wanted her. Well, not necessarily her. In fact he was still turned on by Priscilla, which act he never had a chance to bring to a glorious finish. Damn it. One day he'll get Chuck for that. Except he knew that he was fooling himself. He won't get Chuck for anything.

"Do me a favor, Lar."

"Sure," came the enthusiastic answer. "What?"

"I want to see you naked and walk. Just walk for me, will you?"

She was surprised. That was something new. She remembered very well through her drunken daze that he always undressed her, hung on to her, and never thought of anything exotic.

"Do you have some body oil?"

"Body oil?" It was too dark for Bill to see her smiling, but she felt like her old man went out and learned some new tricks. Oh, why not? Let him strut. She will help.

She decided on the lemon oil, which she used regularly, and handed it to him. Bill smirked and seemed to be blinded as he looked up at the towering snow-white figure. Without clothes and her long blonde hair hanging loosely to her waist, she looked like a meticulously handcrafted statue. He was delighted to see that her body had not changed in the year, and he knew what he wanted to do.

He pulled her close to him, lifted her foot, and started on her toes, working upward until he had slowly oiled her entire leg, rubbed her gently, rubbed her just right. He reached for the other foot, the other leg. He rose to do her belly, her breasts, neck, earlobes. Then he turned her around and rubbed the glow on her back. When he was satisfied with his artwork, he spoke in a hoarse voice, "Walk."

She hesitated a second, then without looking at him, she walked away from him, the length of the living room. Bill looked, watched, pulsated, and saw Priscilla's boyish backside. His hand squeezed his balls. Rex was filled to the brim. As Lara reached the wall and was about to turn, she heard him say, "No. Don't turn."

He came up behind her, put his chest against her back tightly as if he was planning to get under her skin. She was caught up in his excitement. A scream of pain escaped her as Bill achieved his anal fixation. She held back her objections in order to please him. Poor, loving Lara. She never knew that he was making love to fifteen-year-old Priscilla.

Chapter 26

THE MORNING BROUGHT LARA everything she had ever wanted: Bill in her bed.

The evening brought the unexpected. Bill came in with legal papers. He said he didn't want Lara to think that he would become a partner without putting it all on paper to protect her. She didn't want to be protected from the man she loved. Bill finally convinced her that they will need a partnership agreement for tax purposes. She agreed but, beyond that, insisted on making it clear to him that whatever he wished was fine with her. He could share the income and feel free to get involved with The Place.

She didn't mention to him that she planned to rename the restaurant to Lara's Place during the holidays. She thought of saying it then caught herself. There will be a right time for that.

She was too busy that evening to look at the papers. She told Bill she would do it in the morning. He was confident that it would be done, and before leaving, he promised to be back later.

She paid attention to business all night and remained in very good spirits. She did not know the handsome Asian dining with a prosperous looking middle-aged man because she did not know Chuck and Malcolm.

There was nothing special about Chuck and Malcolm having dinner and sitting in the bar afterward. She did not know they had plans for The Place. Wade called from the East Coast. He was on his way out of the country and wondered if Lara would care to join him at any time during his stay abroad. No, Lara would not care to join him. Lara had found what she wanted all her life. But what she told Wade was different. Too busy. Can't get away. Maybe another time.

She went home after the dinner crowd had cleared out and tried to recapture the previous night with Bill. She called his house. There was no answer. That didn't really bother her. He told her he was involved in building up some other businesses. She was tired. She would surely hear from him. In the meantime, she would get some sleep and sign those papers tomorrow.

Having slept on it, instead of doing anything as important as signing legal papers late at night, she decided she would need a lawyer. She did not understand the language of the agreement. *Can this be English?* How could she find a lawyer? Martin had begged and pleaded for her forgiveness, sent roses regularly, maybe the old fellow means to mend his ways. She decided to call Martin's office.

Martin was expected in around noon. She knew that it took her a long time to understand the restaurant business, and she had no time to get a legal education too. Let's put Martin to some use.

She called a messenger service and sent the papers to Martin for his review.

Martin had the nicest surprise when he arrived in his office. Thank goodness, there was something he could do for Lara and maybe redeem himself. He thought of calling her immediately. Then he hesitated. He should read the papers first and call her about business, call with something she wanted to hear, not that he had missed her more than he had ever missed anybody in his life and that he was remorseful.

Since he never knew Lara's life prior to their meeting, he had no idea of the corporation that intended to partner in with Lara. He also had no idea why Lara would need a partner. OK. He decided to make the few phone calls that it would take to check out the interested parties. Then he would have to ask Lara in person why she was intending to do this. Her Dun and Bradstreet rating was excellent. She should not involve anyone else in her business. Especially anyone with rights.

The only way he could get to see her fast was if he did his homework and redrafted an appropriate partnership agreement.

This was a wonderful incentive for Martin, whose business flourished but whose personal life was totally empty. He didn't even want Lara's body as much as he wanted her friendship and had hoped that he could recapture her trust.

*

Martin made a sheepish entrance to Lara's small office in the restaurant. Lara was equally nervous, considering the sour note on which they had parted. However, by this time in her career, she had developed a graciousness that pretty well camouflaged her insecurities. She didn't have to do little tricks anymore in order to get attention. If anything, she had to do less to get less attention in the world, which was what she needed.

She thanked him for coming to her office since she couldn't stand the idea of going back to a place where Harry's death brought her. Very businesslike, he accepted a cup of tea and rapidly began to question who this corporation was that intended to be her partner. Who was Bill Benton? Who was Malcolm Orthoner? Who was Chuck Pui Hung?

"What do you mean, all these people? I don't know who they are?" She was surprised.

"Well, honey, hm, Lara, there is a corporation of three individuals who want to be your partner."

"I thought it was only Bill. I wanted him as a partner. He said he was a corporation for tax purposes, so I thought it was only him."

"That's misrepresentation. He willfully led you to believe he incorporated as an individual. It was an easy process to check the validity of the corporation. Have you any knowledge or information as to who these other individuals are?"

"No." Lara was perturbed. She had only seen Bill once since that night when her body was violated, yet she decided to forgive him and try to get him back by going along with all his wishes.

"No? Then what? What are the facts? You'll have to tell me if I am to perform my job for you."

"Oh, gosh." She started crying. "Gosh, Martin. What if he was lying to me again? I'll die."

Martin recognized the ex-lover-returning-to-reap-the-benefits-of-the-lady's-business syndrome. He also recognized that he would have to let her digest this her own way. He couldn't interfere with her personal affairs after what he had done.

"Listen, Lara. Here is a suggestion. Before you sign anything, with your permission, I would like to institute an investigation of these men."

"Is that expensive?"

"Yes." Martin laughed. "But it's the least I can do to redeem myself. I never wanted to hurt you."

"Thank you."

"I have a need to have you in my life, and I know it'll have to be on your terms." He watched as she sipped her tea. Never did he know a tougher little woman in his life.

"Do you need a partner for money?"

"No. This place's bound to be big. The best."

"Then why Bill, or anyone?"

"Oh, Martin, you know very well it's not Bill or anyone. It's Bill."

"I intend to stay out of your personal dealings entirely, but I have to have your promise that you trust me completely with business. This may become a sticky situation. I wish to protect you."

"I'll let you."

"How about flying. Do you still want to learn?"

"Yes, my god, I do. Just never got around to it yet."

"Well, as a token of my apology for having behaved so poorly, would you allow me to handle the matter? Instructor, as well as finances. All I require of you is to let me know your time allotment for this venture."

"Spoken like a true attorney. But I don't need your money. I can afford any instructor. Probably any ten instructors."

"It's not the cash. I want the responsibility."

"My business is not enough responsibility? I'll be so big, you won't have time for any other clients."

"I know the value of the gift of flying, and I would like to be the one to bestow that upon you."

"And you'll also be my first passenger."

Martin was genuinely overwhelmed at the idea that Lara was not afraid to go off with him alone.

"That's an affirmative on all counts."

Chapter 27

I T WAS HARD FOR Melody to remember the most recent assault on her body a few days ago because she was back on dope. In Ben's opinion, heroin was for dealing, not for using. He limited her indulgence to *quaaludes, paarest,* and the like to help her stay in the deep fog she wanted to live in. She thought the declarations of love that came from the man of the world, both under and over, were funny, bordering on the ludicrous.

The Stratocruiser made its landing approach at New York International Airport. Melody was flying in more than one sense. The complimentary champagne gently maintained her otherwise acquired high. If she wanted anything harder, she had a feeling she could cut up the thick, creative custom jewelry Ben hung around her neck when he took her to the airport.

Ben had behaved strangely ever since Mexico. He became protective, watched every step she took. Even when he was away, she felt his presence. When she made the turnaround errand for him, she thought he never left the airport. Waited for her. Why? Why would a big-time dealer, industrialist, and all-around high roller worry about her welfare? He had used up so many women before. Why would she matter?

She had tried different avenues of life only to find that it spat on her. Maybe it's not such a good place for some people. Certainly not for her. She didn't care if she died.

No matter how stoned she was, she could not escape the memories of the almost marriage to Biff too many years ago that was going to be her future. Her ever after. The inability to give birth. Biff quickly impregnating and marrying a debutante who had the ability to give birth and who had the ability to take him and his mother on. How stupid. People and bloodlines. You're nothing if you don't have children. What she hated the most was that her story was so cliché. No, she hated most the doctor who treated her mother while she carried her, the doctor who experimented on her mother, resulting in the birth of a flawed baby. Melody could forgive her mother but could not stop feeling sorry for herself. She was a weakling all her life who had to be protected throughout childhood, who ended up with a bad heart that denied her ballet, the only thing she had a natural talent for. She and the music were one since birth. Her frustration was permanent. After that disappointment, life became a series of sand castles. Now she was damaged goods. A real slut. Or worse.

It was an endless struggle to learn a skill, to take care of herself, to hold a job and be wonderful, bright, pleasant, and reliable. Then Bill. That should've been different. That should've been right. He had the children, so he didn't want any more. Except that as his kids came out of their mother's womb, Bill moved into their vacant places.

What's left? Nothing. The only good thing she could count on was that maybe she would die smiling, high, freaked out, loaded. She knew that would be painless, and she would be a good-looking corpse.

And Peter? Yeah, a lovely romantic intrusion. It could have been the Cinderella story. She fell for it all over again, but it's over. No big deal. He left. He left her to her own devices. She was fresh out of strength and the need to survive. That happens. Poor Peter. What a nice person he probably was. He should find himself some sweet Hungarian with the blonde hair and the country-high cheekbones and those ever-so-blue eyes.

All she had with her on the plane was her purse. On landing, she was met by Maury Wolf, who took her luggage stubs; and before she knew, she was in a limousine going toward wonderful Manhattan. She had never been in Manhattan before. Her optimistic part looked forward to some kind of magical new experiences that awaited her.

Oh, yes, of course, there will be Peter. But that's tomorrow. She came in early. Today it's Ben's delivery, Ben's contacts, Ben's business. Dinner at Maury's brownstone and hopefully another night of oblivion.

"Melody, you're exquisite. A gorgeous dish if I ever saw one. Better than old Ben had described you. I am sorry I couldn't meet you on your last trip."

Maury kissed her hand in the backseat of the limo, and she knew there was nothing he could do that she would like. She didn't intend to like him. It was that simple.

"Listen, we'll go to the brownstone for supper." He referred to his own house on New York's fashionable East Side the same way as everyone else did. Brownstone. "There'll be a few friends. Ben knows 'm all, if you know what I mean?" She nodded "Don't let the turbans bother you. Heavy dudes. Their evening is completely charted. The guy from the Midwest, Bo Sattler, will eat 'n' run. But there is, of course, the senator. He's yours. OK, kid?"

"Why not?"

She smiled pleasantly and realized that Ben lied to her when he said it would be strictly delivery. He wanted to protect her by keeping her in the dark. Even heavy love can't tamper with the flow of smuggling. So she got the senator tonight and Peter tomorrow night. What's the difference? The only way she would get through the night would be on *ludes* and grass, but no alcohol. Stay away from alcohol.

The smile on her face was brought on by the $10,000 bonus, which she figured would be around or just under 5 percent of the gross value of the deal she was connecting. She hoped that she could maintain her ignorance long enough to get through the week. Ben had spent endless hours teaching her how to act ignorant, cute, and much like sweet fluff. She was to say nothing even if she had the answers. She was to walk slowly and keep 'm drooling.

That was not easy at first. To kill her natural instincts, she had to turn on. She took the job, she accepted the fringes, but she could not cope with it without dope. She felt that after all was said and done, if she wanted to dry out, she would have the money to do so. What she needed was a reason.

It was nighttime in the brownstone. She dressed. She also loaded up, having mastered the key to the amounts she needed for various functional highs. When she came out of the guest suite, Maury was watching the stock market news in the den. She stood there quietly and realized that a couple of her sober choices were doing OK. The thought that she had more money and holdings in less than a year than ever before in her life made it all worthwhile. Some of her good stocks were invested in nuclear energy. She believed the nuclear age was coming. She was sure that rockets would become like buses in the sky, that man will inhabit the moon and any other planet in her lifetime unless she killed herself first. To which singular question she did not have an answer. Will she kill herself first or not? Well, either way, she would die a rich woman. When Maury took notice of her, he jumped to attention, turned the TV set off as if she had been spying.

"Oy, this must bore you to death, Melody."

"It does. Business bores me to death."

"Ahhh, you were made for fun things. I can tell by just looking at you." He spoke educated New York with a sprinkling of the melody of Yiddish.

He came over to her and stretched up to kiss her. She gently smiled him down to his natural height.

"Maury, Maury. Ben said you never touch the merchandise first."

Maury was impressed with her reliability. He didn't care which number he took in line as long as he got a number and his turn would come. He figured that's what she meant.

Melody saw the dinner party through rose-colored glasses. The other women were French whores, very young, and probably part of Maury's stable. She was hungry enough to enjoy the meal, cute enough to disrupt the conversations, and adored enough to know that she was doing her job the way Ben had instructed her. She was collecting information that Maury may withhold from Ben.

During dessert, the two mid-Easterners expressed interest in going over to the club with their dates. Bo was taking the limo to the airport. Maury offered to drop them at the club and rejoin them after a while. The young senator just sat there. He didn't want to go anywhere. He liked it where he was.

Melody excused herself with the obvious powder room exit line and took the other girls with her. According to Ben's guidelines, the men would never discuss the tedious details of who got who and who owes what and who paid what and so forth in front of ladies. The female mind was not made for thinking. Melody loved that. They came back in a few minutes. Everyone was ready to leave.

The room cleared out with "tatas" and kiss throwings. The young senator posed by the mantelpiece, held his after-dinner brandy in its large snifter, and gave Melody a smile featuring all of his three hundred teeth. Pretty as a picture. She never trusted clean-cut men. They were the ones who carried VD, and because they were too important, no one ever told them about it.

"Well, Senator, how do you feel?"

She knew it was a stupid question, but she tried to be friendly.

"Actually I don't have time for niceties. I have to be on the 3:00 a.m. flight to Washington and back in my bed before dawn."

"Because the young Mrs. Senator will be back by that time?" She shouldn't have said that.

"She is arriving at 6:00 a.m." His answer was quick, clear, leaving no room for misunderstandings. Melody knew the deal was made because the romance was gone. What she didn't know was what it was that he wanted from her that he didn't get from Mrs. Senator? Anyway, she was glad it would be a short night with him.

*

The next day marked her officially scheduled arrival at the Plaza. She woke up around eleven and needed some juice or something to drink. She was totally dehydrated. She put on her flimsy robe and headed for the kitchen. She never forgot where a kitchen was in any house. "A poor people habit," her mother used to say.

First she attacked the milk, then orange juice, then she drank whatever other juices she could find before she started the water for the coffee. She thought she heard a noise and was not at all interested in having some busybody maid enter to help her with the morning. She wanted to do it all on her own. She turned and saw Maury in the doorway. His robe was open, giving Melody a view of his fabled cock. Another injustice, she thought. If a woman's breasts hang to her navel, that's bad. If a guy's cock hangs to his knees, that's good. Of course, she clearly saw that Maury had short thighs.

"Oh, Christ. What do you want now?"

"Coffee."

"Sure. Yeah."

Maury read the rejection in spite of his sleepiness. He was not about to bring conflict into his relationship with Ben. No woman, no person is worth damaging the constant business and his growing fortunes, due to Ben's operations.

"I think you don't like me very much" was all he said.

"Right."

"There's nothin' I can do for you that Ben can't and better. I know I'm a flunky, but, Melody, so are you."

"Right."

"There's a bit of a whore in everyone. Some admit it. Some don't."

"Right." Melody turned her back.

Chapter 28

ELODY PLANNED TO CHECK into the Plaza Hotel very quietly and wait for Peter. She did not look forward to this. How could she make him, principled, wholesome him, understand that she was not at all the person he left behind. She was not his angel from heaven, or his *Lorelei* from the Rhine River. She was nothing. She was a bad girl.

As she announced herself at the front desk, she could not believe the big to-do they had been ordered to perform by Peter. She got the red-carpet treatment literally as if she were the international celebrity and not he. A violinist appeared from nowhere, walked behind her, and played a sweet Hungarian melody. The milling in the lobby stopped. All eyes were on her as she continued walking while being serenaded all the way to the waiting elevator. She felt foolish for having traveled with only one suitcase. She wished she could give her newfound entourage something to do besides watching her with ear-to-ear grins. She smiled back. It was equally difficult to maintain her composure and to decide whether to laugh or scream.

As they escorted her into the suite, she handed twenty dollars to the lead. "Share it."

"Köszönöm," said the leader, and they ceremoniously backed out of her presence.

The door closed behind them. Melody realized they probably thought that she was Hungarian since she vaguely recognized the word she had learned from Peter what seemed like a century ago, as "Thank you."

The decorations were colorful, cheerful, and she assumed native to Hungary. The champagne, fruit, and flowers were tied by red, white, and green ribbons, the Hungarian national colors. She was thrilled. She surveyed the suite of rooms, bedroom with two queen-size beds, study, marble bathroom with separate toilet and bidet.

"We are pleased," she said in a royal tone of voice and watched as everyone backed out, leaving her alone.

A note on the bureau let her know in three languages that she had a reserved table for dinner at eight thirty if she wished one and the hotel was happy to be at her disposal.

Queen for a day. She made up her mind definitely not to have dinner downstairs. She would bathe, order up some cold snacks, watch television, and wait for Peter without any booze or drugs. The bottle of champagne, however, was inviting. TV watching is more fun while sipping on the lightest of dry bubbly. She didn't want to ask the desk about Peter's arrival time because they would have thought that she should know better anyway. The lobby episode had already embarrassed her.

She contemplated calling Maury to shoot the breeze. Instead, she placed a call to Ben. Ben was nowhere to be reached. It was just she and the TV.

She had made up her mind frequently since New Year's Eve never to watch any kind of dancing. It always depressed her too much. Just the same, scanning the program guide compelled her to tune in to the New York City Ballet's special choreographed by Jerome Robbins. Her heart broke again, as always. If she could only have been able to dance, long ago and far away, everything would have turned out different. As a child prodigy, ballet experts had predicted that she would become one of the greats. A critical physical exam, a prerequisite to being permitted to join a children's *corps de ballet* at age seven, showed a weak heart that would, under the strenuous demands of that fine art, give out by the time she reached thirty. Her mother ended her dancing career. If it had been up to Melody, she wouldn't have. She was too young to understand about death and thought it would have been a nice way to go. She thought about that time and time again. "Primaballerina's heart fails at the peak of her illustrious career. The world mourns." Her memory savored this as her favorite recurring newspaper headline. She couldn't stop thinking about it. Her pain grew, her self-pitying subconsciousness took control. The champagne needed company, and she moved from grass to her custom jewelry, which were individual pillboxes full of exactly what she was looking for. Soon she floated all around the suite, danced, and floated all around, all around.

*

Gagging and throwing up replaced everything when she next focused. Behind the yuck, she saw Peter, who held her, walked her; and they were in a goddamn hospital's goddamn emergency room, and all she wanted to do was faint. She did.

"Don't faint again." She heard Peter's voice when later she opened her eyes. By this time, she was in a private VIP room. She glanced at Peter, stared at him. She liked seeing his face.

"I'm really sorry, Peter."

"We'll talk about it later."

"What, that I'm always passed out when I see you?"

"I'm actually becoming accustomed to it. Next time I'll make reservations in a hospital instead of a hotel."

"Not funny."

"Do me a large favor. Get well so we can get out of here. I hate sleeping in this white elephant."

It was then that she realized that a daybed was made. Peter had stayed there with her. What a rotten welcome. She felt like a very bad child who needed punishment.

"OK. Call the nurse, call the doctor. I can't have this whole affair take place in a hospital room."

"I got you a good room this time around, haven't I?" He was proud of himself. He was proud of seeing that his orders were followed.

Released in his care, he took her back to the Plaza. They were escorted to their suite through the back entrance. She was weak, and he insisted on doctoring her.

"I can't stand this. You're acting like a little old Jewish mother."

"Correction," he came back. "I am, number one, not little, number two, not old, number three, not Jewish, number four, not a mother. I'm taking care of you because that is what I want to do. I want to see you well, like you were before. In Carmel. That's what I want. Joie de vivre, mademoiselle."

There was no way she could talk him out of anything. He called the hospital and was told that Ben Taylor had paid the bills the next day. That puzzled him. She told him that he was her boss who took care of her hospitalization insurance. Peter accepted that, but he was not satisfied.

"Does he know you were in for too many drugs?"

"Not if the hospital didn't tell him."

Peter went back to his sitting room and studied this situation for a while. He felt ill at ease. Something was not right, but he couldn't put his finger on it.

The phone rang. It was his manager calling to double-check details regarding Peter's appearance of the upcoming weekend. Peter was booked for a sold-out concert at Carnegie Hall, one of the most prestigious venues in the world for classical as well as popular music. All the Europeans of New York, affluent or not, would show up to hear him bridge language barriers, perform their old favorites and his new hits.

Melody did not feel like bed rest. She threw on a robe and walked over to his study. The door was open, but as she heard him talk, she stopped in the doorway. She saw the graceful, lean body stretched out on the couch. He gesticulated with hands and feet in order to be convincing on the telephone. She held back her laughter because from a mixture of Hungarian and English words and some international expressions, she thought she understood the essence of his conversation. When he hung up, she spoke to him from the doorway.

"I couldn't help overhearing. And I'm not sure if I heard correctly?"

"Yes, you did hear correctly."

"I can't have that. You cannot cancel a concert because of me. How do you expect me to carry such a responsibility?"

"That is not your responsibility. I am in love. You are my lady. You are not well. I don't go to work. Anybody would do it, no?"

"No. Anybody wouldn't and shouldn't do it. Damn it! You're making me mad!"

"Mad is a dog. Angry is a person."

"Thanks. I'll call on you for my English 101 lessons when I'm up to it!"

"We have to cure you. We have to get you off those ugly drugs. The world is full of it, Melody. They bring it to me every day, sometimes gorgeous women, sometimes gorgeous men, but I do not want to hurt my body and my mind. And I do not allow you to hurt your body and your mind. We're getting married. You'll have our babies. They will be beautiful."

She stared at him as if he looked like he just got off the boat or fell off the turnip truck.

"Babies! Babies?" She turned and ran back to her room. Pain and anger choked her. She stood firmly planted against the bed. She had been looking for just punishment, and she finally got it. She was nearly paralyzed from the onrushing flow of thoughts. She'd have to end this. Now. She began packing.

Peter appeared at the door. His face changed colors by the second. He was angry, hurt, but most of all frustrated. Why wasn't she jumping for joy like every normal woman would? A few gurgley sounds came out of him as he attempted to start a sentence, but English failed him.

She would not stop. She would not look at him. In fact, if anything, she surprised herself as she threw things in her suitcase, which was not one of her habits. She had been poor long enough to treasure her wardrobe. Throwing her good clothes and stuffing them into any place was not the ideal way of caring for things. But she could not stop. Furiously she piled garment upon garment, stuck shoes in, cosmetics, and everything. Got to get out. Got to get out fast.

Finally he lost control. He marched over to her, tried to catch her eyes. When she wouldn't give an inch, he attempted to grab her by the shoulders and force her to acknowledge him. However, as he lifted his arms in sudden fury, she turned, heading right into his hand, and got slapped. She was not about to stand for that.

"Oh, yeah? Peter the Hun! Yeah?" she screamed, put her right fist in fighting order by tucking her right thumb in with her left hand. Quicker than a wink, she punched him right in his expensive face.

He was stunned. He grabbed her whole body, picked her up in order to disarm her. But she was more than he had bargained for. She pulled his hair, kicked, bit; and he had a tough time staying out of her reach.

She was fast and dangerous with her feet. It took him a little concentration to understand the pattern of her movements. He had the advantage of the athlete. Once he caught on, he managed to stay clear of her; then he grabbed her from the back, put a lock on both arms, and threw her on the bed. She turned around with catlike quickness only to be jumped by him and his lips closed on hers. He could feel her body grow limp in his arms.

Their kiss was slow and long. As its warmth ran through them, they could not separate. They opened their eyes, which brought a new surge of burning sensation. She trembled when he kissed her cheeks. He wet her ear and blew it dry with the heat of his breath. She held him tight, kissed his neck, and pushed off his shirt to plant kisses all over his chest. Under his smooth skin, well-formed muscles rippled with each movement he made. The more he touched her, the more she wanted him. There was no returning. Her fingertips pulsated with heat. They explored each other. Their pleasure increased gradually. More. More. His buttocks fit her hands, and his arms made a strong protective shield around her. She felt dainty and light as he picked her up and changed her positions or as he pulled her up to him for more passionate kisses.

She had never been loved like that before, and she had never found responding so easy before. Sheer reflex action. Her body moved with his as if he were a magnet clasping a precious metal. They could melt each other.

They did.

"I knew it'd be the best," Peter announced when they finally broke for a brief rest.

"I didn't know what the best was." She smiled.

She had to live thirty years before she found out what sex really was. "I love you." She surprised herself as the words blurted out of her.

"And I love you, Melody Shorr. I'm so very happy." Peter stopped to think. "I am also a little bit unhappy. We should have waited until after the wedding."

"Why didn't you?"

"I couldn't."

"Me neither."

"On the other hand, Melody, I am now certain that we should get married. This kind of loving is not nothing."

"No guilt? No regrets?"

"Who, me?" He laughed his robust laughter.

"None! We'll get married, we will have so much fun, we will raise such a special family, we will have it all!" He reached for her and felt her body stiffen. He kissed her. She did not respond.

"I'm tired. I'd like to sleep now." When he didn't move, she added, "Alone."

Chapter 29

ETER CHEERFULLY WAITED FOR her to join him for a late brunch, which was already served in the suite. She came out of her room dressed for travel, sat down, and drank the fresh-squeezed orange juice.

"We go to my rehearsal at one o'clock. Fine?"

"No, Peter. It's not fine. I am leaving for home."

"How can you do that to me. Last night everything was so wonderful. I thought you loved me."

"I loved you last night, Peter. I loved you last week. I don't love you this morning, so I'm leaving."

Peter had never heard any woman say that to him. He was genuinely perturbed.

"I am not understanding you."

"Men generally have that problem with me. You don't have to understand anything. It's over."

"What's over, Melody?"

"We are over. Our affair is over."

"Did I do anything wrong? Tell me."

"You didn't do anything wrong. You are trying to change too many things about me. You don't want me. You want someone entirely different."

"Not so. I wish to convince you that it is you I want. How can I convince you?"

"You can't at this point. So sit down, eat your breakfast, and go to rehearsal."

She refused to talk about details, about him wanting kids, about him wanting her perfect, like he was, about him thinking that a doper could ever be anything but a doper. She didn't want to talk. She didn't want to argue. She was in a hurry to get out, back where she belonged.

While she finished packing, she loaded up on a *lude* and a half, saved the other half for later, and figured that would suffice for the few hours of travel without anxiety. She lightly kissed Peter.

"When will I see you?" he asked.

"I don't know."

"But I just found you," said Peter, bewildered.

"I'll call you. OK? Say yes."

"Yes, yes. You do that. Later. Give me time."

She was out the door while he still mumbled to himself about giving her time. It would be a sad rehearsal, or possibly, that might be the only thing that would help him. Work.

She got the munchies for cash. She needed to see cash. A lot of it. The taxi waited for her in front of the bank while she cashed a $10,000 check then headed out to the airport.

In the terminal, she walked ahead of the Redcap carrying her suitcase to the check-in counter. She saw a group of little old people, traveling together. It was obvious that they had just returned from Miami. One woman caught her attention as she walked out of the ladies lounge and joined up with the group.

"Mommy," she uttered to herself barely audibly and stopped cold. The Redcap stopped behind her. She stared at the old lady who went about her business. Melody was in a daze. Emotions rose high in her as the dope actualized. She handed the Redcap some money.

"Thank you." She turned away. He left her with her suitcase.

She watched them board a bus and got into a taxi to follow them. She was filled with sketchy memories of her mother, who, if alive, would probably look like that, walk like that, and be like that. She wondered whether this woman had also produced a sterile child, like her mother did. She had tears in her eyes by the time the taxi stopped at the Rego Park Community Center in Queens.

All the little old people were expected by someone. Melody's old lady got into a battered station wagon. Melody had the cabby follow the wagon only a few blocks to the older section of Rego Park. The woman got out of the car, waved good-bye to whoever it was that gave her a ride, and went into the small apartment complex.

The lights came on upstairs of the garden apartment building. The cabby looked at Melody impatiently.

"Do you know where I could rent a car?"

"Now, lady?"

"Right." She pulled out some bills from her purse, more than the fare had been so far. "I'll make it worth your while," she added.

As he stood for a moment, thinking, she wrote down the old lady's address. The taxi took a sharp turn, and they headed for the nearest Avis.

The rent-a-car office was open. It was early evening, barely dusk. She rented a convertible, paid for it in cash, and drove back to the old lady's apartment.

She sat and stared at the window. Her mind drifted back to her past. Why? Why was it that the life of one person could permanently mar that of another. Especially why, if it's a parent. Nothing ever became of her, and it all started way before she was born.

In the dark of the evening, she got out of the car, went inside, checked the name on the mailbox. V. Kelley. Upstairs, she knocked.

"Mrs. Kelley? My name is Melody Shorr. May I come in?"

The old lady was in her robe. Her soft white hair framed the apprehensive face behind the hooked-up chain of the cracked open door.

"I can't let in any strangers. Sorry, miss."

She closed the door in her face. Melody froze.

"How can such a nice lady be so cold? I could be your daughter. You could be my mother," she spoke into the keyhole with a raspy, dried voice.

"But that is not the case, young lady. You will have to go home now. It's late." The lady's voice was warm, but she was not about to let this peculiar stranger in. Innately wise.

"I don't want to go home. I want to stay here," whined a young girl named Melody.

"Then I will have to call the police and have them remove you, and you know what happens to girls who get picked up by the police?"

"No. I do not know. I do not want to know." Melody's regression was rapid. She saw the vision of her mother through the door as if the door did not exist.

"I will have to tell you then. Tell you the truth. The truth is that the bad girls who don't go home, get put into large cages, and the very bad girls beat up on the other girls. So you want to go home, don't you?"

"Yes, Mommy. I do."

Sometime in the middle of the night, she stopped for the first time for gas in Maryland. The rising sun found her on the road to Newport News, Virginia. Home. Or what it used to be. Her place of birth. She drove directly to the aging apartment house downtown where she lived her first eight years of life until her mother had received a settlement sum from a class action lawsuit against the doctor who did a lot of experimentation. There was enough money to drive to California and to move to an aging apartment in Beverly Hills. Her mother worked several jobs to make sure that Melody received the same education the wealthy Beverly Hills kids got, the same advantages as all the Beverly Hills princesses were given. She achieved her goal when Melody qualified to attend Beverly Hills High, mingle with the best, meet, and get engaged to Biff Waverly. Mission accomplished. The demise of that union, the entire purpose of her life, upset Melody's mother tremendously. Melody was never sure but sensed that until the day she died, her mother blamed herself for ruining Melody's life by allowing the premarital sex and misguiding her.

The old building was boarded up, ready for demolition. Probably another shopping center. Melody sat in the car, smoked a joint, and got teary eyed. Why? Why did everything go wrong? No ballet, no baby, no future beyond marriage?

Her anger grew. Slowly she searched her memory. She put the car in gear and let a vague recollection guide her to the gynecologist's office. The office of the gynecologist who treated her mother, who ran different birth control tests on her mother which poisoned Melody's body.

She found it. That little building was also part of the condemned area. There was no one around. Through-traffic was routed onto an overpass. She was in a ghost town of the forties. Only she saw the ghosts. One in particular, Dr. Baker.

The doctor's shingle hung on one nail. The place was boarded up. The weeds reached the windows. She threw a burning match into the weeds. Then another one. She watched the hungry flames gobble up the fire hazard that was the entire block. She got back into the car and drove away without looking back.

She stopped at Red's Pier by the James River Bridge, had two ice cream sodas, filled the car up with gas, got back on the main highway heading south and west.

"Where to, little girl?" She heard a familiar voice.

"Mississippi, Alabama, Louisiana, New Orleans?"

"Yes, Mommy, I think New Orleans would be nice to visit at this time of the year . . . and Mommy, thanks for letting me have two sodas."

Chapter 30

B ILL'S OFFICE WAS NOTHING short of a busy beehive.
Somehow he attracted the hungriest people to work for
him, who have never had any money in their lives. Bill's
methods of easy, simple, yet pressurized selling techniques showed
lucrative results after no more than a three-month unprofitable trial
and training period. The first taste of large commissions was the
greatest of all aphrodisiacs. One substantial executive placement
deal would bring more revenue to the headhunter trainee than
he had ever seen before. With Bill's guidance, the deal would be
closed just right; everyone would be happy. Bill's percentage of the
transaction didn't seem to be as big as the salesperson's take-home
money. They added up.

The headhunters. A totally new breed. The 10 percenter who
discovered new grounds other than that of show business. Bill
got into it fortuitously and liked it immediately. He found a job
for some old buddy of his that was better than he had ever had
before in his life. Bill thought he should not go unrewarded for his
efforts. Both parties, his friend and the new employer, seemed to
have been so happy with one another that neither of them minded
paying Bill 10 percent of his annual income of the first year.

Bill joined a conventional employment agency after that,
but it was too touch and go, no real money for a hungry man.
He began to survey markets previously untouched by agencies. It
was through trial and error and by curiosity that he fumbled upon

a specialized branch of executive placements that turned out to be his niche in the world of pulling strings. Uneducated, poorly raised, self-made money man.

Malcolm Orthoner became aware of the talented young man early on. He had realized that he didn't want the competition that Bill Benton represented. Malcolm sought him out and offered him a position with his own placement service, the Orthoner Associates. Within just a few months, Bill, the young employee, took over running the Los Angeles office. In one year, Bill was in charge of the entire West Coast region comprising the chain of three offices, San Francisco, Los Angeles, and San Diego.

Bill's eagerness to prove himself allowed Malcolm to work less and less and play more and more golf. He promised his young protégé everything. The sky was the limit.

Malcolm saw Lara with Bill one night. The many years of intellectual and loving companionship of his wife were the best a man could have had. Seeing someone like Lara, however, meant wanting someone like Lara. Maybe even Lara? He wanted to find a place where he could legitimately get away from his daily routine. He wondered what kind of side interest would provide him with that. He had a few doubts about Bill; they were minor. These doubts were not the result of poor performance on Bill's part, only the questionable associations Malcolm had noticed. However, Malcolm wanted to believe that his support of Bill would set him on the right track and would pay off in the long run.

As far as Bill was concerned, deep thinking was not his strong suit. When he felt pain, he turned to a different diversion. He needed money, and he would get it. He would live well. Anything else would work out. Except for money, Bill believed in short-term plans.

Being seen with a woman was a good idea after Bill separated from Sheila. Malcolm believed that men who were not in a one-woman relationship were not strong enough performers on the job. Men on the hunt could not concentrate on work. Malcolm did not know about Chuck, liked Lara, did not interfere with Bill's drastic change of course by marrying Melody. However, when that came to an abrupt end, Malcolm put his foot down and got Bill back on track. Malcolm felt presidential in the way he handled personnel things. He didn't realize Bill was doing some handling of him as he gradually regained Malcolm's confidence.

In business as everywhere, one hand washes the other. By now everything was falling in place for Bill. He was on the verge of becoming president of the company. In addition, he counted on Lara making him a partner. That would help Malcolm with his need to spend time without his wife. That would also settle Chuck down, sort of giving him a table for his under-the-table activities. Bill was satisfied. Everyone was on the right track. He put them there, benefiting him immensely.

Life was his oyster. He decided he had done enough hard work for the day, would go home, change, and figure out what to do with his evening, hopefully without Chuck. He knew he was going to get high, just wasn't sure where and with whom.

Suddenly Chuck was on the phone to remind him that he had not yet produced the signed partnership papers and why is that? Chuck had to stabilize his trafficking. A floating system has become too small. He had workmen standing by to do the necessary alterations to The Place to make it functional for unobtrusive pickup, delivery, and message service. He needed Lara's permission to do a survey of existing wiring and determine where to build a secret wall safe as well as add electrical ducts. He had a lot to do.

As soon as the real possibility of becoming a partner of The Place appeared to Chuck, he had obtained blueprints and knew of the underground storage area that was too small to be a basement but large enough to accommodate his needs to conduct additional, undetectable business.

By the time Chuck hung up with Bill, Bill knew where he would be getting high that night. He knew he had to play out his game with Lara, or Chuck would never let up on him. OK. He could do it and once and for all be free of everyone who tried to tie him down to lengthy commitments.

He called Lara. She was delighted, ignorant of his lying about being back in town, and suggested a late supper at Perino's, one of her favorite restaurants.

She didn't think anything of Bill's insistence to stay at her restaurant for dinner. He could easily convince her of his interest in becoming familiar with it; after all, he would be a partner any day. Lara had assured him that as far as she was concerned, he already was her partner.

During the course of the evening, Bill learned that Martin D. Schoenfeld, the attorney, was holding up the consummation of the partnership agreement. He made a mental note of the name.

A couple of days later, Martin was burning the midnight oil. Everyone had long gone from the office suite. He was preoccupied with dictating into his newest acquisition, a Timemaster machine that recently came on the market as the busy businessman's best friend. *Your secretary doesn't have to sit in the same room with you to take dictation. Your secretary can pick up the tape from you and transcribe it during her own working hours.* What will they think of next?

Martin could not hear anyone enter the offices and come up to his open door. They did not remove their reflecting sunglasses or their dark hats. Martin could not recognize them as familiar faces, and he tried to ignore their unorthodox entry. He was relaxed, rose from behind his desk, and offered to be of any legal assistance they needed.

"We don't need your legal assistance, mister. But you will need some medical assistance if certain documents do not get signed by a certain lady."

Martin smiled. He was cordial. He showed no fear, which they didn't like. "You will have to be a great deal more specific as to the documents, gentlemen."

"Do you want your legs broken without even feeling it?" This was spoken by the largest of the three men. He was not tall either, but husky. Martin instinctively felt that the high cheekbones hiding under the glasses might belong to an Asian face.

"No. I definitely do not, with feeling or without."

"Well, you heard the man!" This was a demand.

"You don't seem to understand that in a law office there are a great many documents awaiting signature. How am I to know which one is of your concern? How can I comply?"

The men were closing in on Martin.

"Help me out here. Is the lady old, fat, skinny, rich, poor, redhead, blonde . . . ?" He noticed that when he said blonde the two men looked at the third one in the background. The big guy with the strong street dialect grabbed Martin so fast from behind that he felt the strength in the arm locking him like steel clamps. The small guy with the softer voice who had remained in the background, looked almost attractive under the disguise. He came close to Martin and put a needle against his neck. Martin felt a painful numbness setting in, in his main artery.

The third man in the background, who hadn't said a word, looked at him, with eyes piercing through the glasses.

"Some people use the ancient Asian art of acupuncture for healing, some don't." He looked on ominously; and somehow, through a sixth sense, Martin knew Lara was in danger.

They left as soundlessly as they appeared. He felt his neck where the healing acupuncture needle, inserted a mere three-fourth-inch deeper than necessary, caused him pain. He walked to the front door. It was locked. They locked it behind themselves. He returned to his office, poured a stiff scotch, and guzzled it up unlike ever before. It was only then, in the silence following his gulp, that he heard the small flapping noise of the reel-to-reel tape of his dictating equipment.

All his life, being the first on the block in everything generally paid off. He was one of the first persons who purchased the Timemaster when it became available. He looked and thought the ribbon had broken, but no, the machine was left on, and luckily the flapping of the end of the tape had not started while the hoods were there. Sweat broke out on his face.

He sat down to listen to the tape with great interest. He played the conversation back a couple of times. His major concern was to ascertain who the *certain lady* was. He knew that the voices meant nothing to him. He knew he could never identify the men. They could have been Italian, could have been Irish, could have been Latin American, could have been Asian, any or all of those, judged by the darkish sideburns and darkish skin complexions. The reflective glasses only showed him his own image staring at himself from every direction. Wow! This was rough. Could it be Lara? What made him feel that Lara might be the woman client that could cause her corporate attorney physical jeopardy.

He called his friend, long-time aid as private investigator, Theo Sanchez. Yes, he knew he woke him up; and yes, it was important enough. It looked like something criminal had crept into his life, and the investigator's excitement was overwhelming. After all, for the first time, Martin was involved in something interesting.

"Wait till the acupuncture service really starts," he joked with Martin.

"I fail to see the humor. Just get over here."

They spent the rest of the night analyzing and figuring the probabilities. They determined that Theo's team of *private eyes* would have to get in on the action fast. At six in the morning, Martin dialed Lara Burns, the proprietress of a good restaurant whose papers had been delayed.

"I'm sending you Theo Sanchez at noon today. You will hire him as a busboy. Ask no questions now, Lara. Try to trust me."

Chapter 31

THEO SANCHEZ. THE NAME brings to mind a gorgeous, tall Greek and Latin combination male with sparkling white teeth and casual charm. Wrong. Lara's physical expectations were shattered. The Theo Sanchez who showed up at The Place was short, squat, muscular, completely unsophisticated. He did have the good white teeth and glistening smooth skin of his Greek and Mexican ancestors. However, his language reflected the streets of Los Angeles. An educated ear could detect a transplanted mid-Westerner with the high flying spirit of a Latino.

"Ms. Burns? You're expecting me. Theo Sanchez." Lara liked the way he cut through unnecessary conversation.

"Martin can't participate in person, but I know his position and your position, and all I ask is that you don't slow me down. Please."

"OK. I'll do my best even if you intend to keep me in the dark. I'll introduce you around, and all I ask is that you do a good job of bussing tables. Please."

Theo was pleasantly impressed with the restaurant, its size, looks, and the way the entire staff seemed to know what each of them was doing. Bobby was preparing for the evening, and a couple of his Mexican helpers assisted. They weren't too crazy about a new guy taking part of their tips, but they liked Lara enough to go with her decisions.

Theo was all eyes and ears, anxious to learn what he had to do. Bobby asked Juan, one of his helpers, to bring a case of canned mushrooms from the cellar. Juan thought this would be a good chance to test the newcomer, and waving his seniority like a flag, he yelled out for Theo. Theo appeared immediately.

"Oye hombre. Tu eres nuevo, ve abajo al sotano, y me traes una caja de hangos enlatados." Juan passed the buck.

"Seguro, hermano." Theo called him a brother.

"Hermano? Des pues de todo, tu eres muy bueno."

"Todos vamos a estar bien juntos."

Theo was reasonably sure that he would be accepted by the labor force in due course and headed for the basement. It appeared to be nothing but a storeroom carved under the building as an afterthought. It was well ventilated and roughly tiled for easy maintenance. As soon as he spotted the mushrooms, he climbed up to get the box off the shelf. He noticed light, barely visible marks on the ceiling, which indicated electrical wiring outline. He could not take time to find out whether or not it was covering up any work already done or yet to come. He had to hurry up. He would return as soon as possible and determine whether it was some old, fading plan or fresh in the planning or even executed.

Lara arrived home to rest up for the evening. As she pulled into the driveway, she spotted Bill. He was waiting in his parked car.

"This is the nicest surprise, Bill. C'mon, get in." He got into Lara's car, who drove to her assigned parking spot. She kissed and hugged him and practically dragged him upstairs. In the apartment, she rushed around to make him comfortable. Lara didn't know that the first thing Theo did was put an *eye* on her. One his undercover team members would be watching. Her life would become an open book everywhere she went.

"Would you like a little ice tea? Would you like anything?" She looked at him for reaction to her open invitation. She babbled with joy on seeing him. "I always miss you when I don't hear from you. It'd be embarrassing if you wouldn't make me feel so good when you're here. I have to admit you're a terrific maker-upper." Chatter, chatter.

Bill didn't mind. He knew this would be a short act. Lara must have the papers ready, maybe she couldn't reach him to tell him about it. He settled down, accepted her hospitality, and didn't find it hard to return her kiss. This lady was his ticket to freedom. Who would have thought even a couple of years ago that this skinny, flakey, drinking, doping young girl, devoted to him to the end, would indeed be devoted to him to the end, even without drinking, doping, and being dependent on him or anyone else. He knew he was very lucky to have this whole thing fall into his lap.

He watched Lara come and go, making him happy. That's all she wanted. He knew it. If he could go along with her in reality, he would have it made in the shade.

"Oh, no."

"Oh, no, what?" Lara turned to him. They casually chatted until his outburst.

"I was just thinking out loud and remembered something, that's all." As in the days when she was gullible, he used phony nonchalance to awaken her interest. "Where are the papers? Do you have them ready, hon?"

"No. Actually my attorney has been away a lot, and he said he hasn't gotten to it." Lara suddenly became nervous. Lying made her even more nervous. She watched for giveaway signs, such as turning red, mispronouncing a word, dropping something, the usual things that betrayed her each time she attempted to lie. She knew that Bill could catch her easily.

"Well, it'd be a good idea if I could start working around your place, helping you out, and so on. You know what I mean?"

"You can do that now, darling. You can come in right now, tonight, learn what's going on, and make suggestions, anything at all."

"You mean that?"

"Of course I do. My place is your place. Nothing has changed."

To punctuate her assurances, she moved closer to him, ready for some serious kissing; but he suddenly became restless. "OK. Then I'll see you tonight."

Before she knew what hit her, he was gone. She didn't mind. She was secure. Bill was back in her life. Somehow she was glad that she had to earn him back and show him that she was a capable person.

Much later that evening, he appeared at The Place. He stuck his head in her open door and walked into the office. Lara smiled.

"You'll be happy to know I've been drumming up business for The Place. Some of my friends will be coming to dinner in a couple of days."

"Every little bit helps," she said. "Just let me know when and I'll make sure they will be satisfied," said Lara while turning a page in the file in front of her indicating that she is in the middle of something.

"Well, hon, I see you're busy."

"Just finished. I'm glad you're back. You were gone most of the evening." She stood up, put the file away. "Where did you go?" she asked.

Bill's face tightened. "I never accounted to you with my time before and am not about to start," he said. His defiant posture was new to her.

"Just talking," she said. "I didn't mean anything by it."

"Well then, ask no questions," said Bill, exiting the office ahead of her. "I'm here now."

He knew he could do no wrong. Everything was fine with her especially when he saw that she chose to ignore his hostile tone.

The same night when she showed curiosity toward Theo's assignment, Theo explained to her that his report would have to be made to the man who hired him; and no matter what he sees, or thinks, or thinks he sees, he could not discuss it with her. She had no idea of the efficiency of Theo's team.

She felt overpampered on one hand and left out on the other hand. Either way, she knew she was not going to go for it much longer.

During the following days, Bill had started to make regular appearances in the restaurant, but not at her apartment. One night, she arrived unusually late. She saw Bill's car pull up with a slinky young girl in the passenger seat. Bill got out, made a small whistling sound, and like a faithful servant, Theo appeared. He then drove the girl off in Bill's car.

Inside, Lara saw Bill join an older couple and an Asian man for dinner. Theo also noted the growing ring around Bill.

Lara approached the table and was introduced to Malcolm and Erna Orthoner and Chuck Pui Hung, Bill's long-time friends. She excused herself after a few minutes of pleasantries. Malcolm and Erna looked vaguely familiar, fleetingly passing through some foggy, doped-up part of her mind. They too gave her a second look but did not dignify the moment with questions. Lara's real concern, however, was the girl and what Bill and Theo were doing in cahoots in her establishment without her knowledge. She was burning with anger.

When evening's end came, Bill suggested that he follow her home and have a glass of wine at her apartment. She was still puzzled about the young girl, but just the same, she would never say no to Bill. She served him his favorite wine but did not ask why not his usual. She then disappeared in the bedroom only to return in a beautiful negligee. It was purchased especially to entice Bill. She needed him. She had to win him.

He stayed over but was too beat for any loving. That was fine with her. But she did want to know why he had never yet invited her over to the house that she helped pick.

"Oh, that's the past." An attempt at being sage, maintaining the upper hand she had given him. He got up very early next morning, wanting to get to work. Too many deals were pending in too many parts of the country. He had to get going, so he said, unconvincingly.

Lara looked at him, tears welled in her eyes. "I don't want to doubt you, Bill. Please don't let me."

This made him want to leave even quicker.

"I don't need a heart-to-heart talk, sweetheart, OK?"

"What do you need?"

"What I really need"—forced laughter—"is a cup of coffee. You remember how I take it?"

"I remember a lot more than you think, Bill, my dear, true love."

The sarcasm in her voice was new. He stopped dressing.

"Are you coming to some point besides forgetting my coffee?"

She was contemplative. If she spoke, she might be giving up a piece of her heart and soul. She spoke, "Something's very wrong, Bill. I feel it. I feel it from many different directions. You're not having fun. You're not in love with me."

"What're you talking about?"

"Sobriety is a beautiful state. The best. I can see things now. I'd do anything for your love. Anything. I even made a little white lie for your love. To please you."

"You please me, hon, and I love you. Stop worrying."

His embrace never penetrated through their clothes. "I'll help you out in business as soon as it's official and let you be the lady of the home. I'll relieve you of the burdens. How's that? Isn't that love?"

"I used to think that was love. Being a dress-up doll and a fucking machine. That was love. But, Bill"—she drew close to him, rubbed against his back, blew gently into his shirt collar—"has anything happened just now, Bill?

No. Nothing. Right? It's morning, you're straight, and you can't feel me. Can't respond."

She picked up his jacket, handed it to him, and opened the front door. "Please have your black coffee with one and a half lumps of sugar someplace else."

He was out the door. He turned back. "What about The Place?" Only the walls heard him.

Lara was inside, trembling, crying quietly. She had cut out a chunk of herself. She had lost her baby.

She called Martin on a wild impulse. He was at his office. He had been there all night. Theo called and brought Priscilla to Martin's office before taking her to Bill's hotel apartment. They got enough information from Priscilla to put several of the pieces together. No proof but an understanding of what dear Bill was into.

Martin met Lara at the airport. She had had enough lessons, and he could let her do the flying. Up in the clear sky, they absorbed the freedom of the atmosphere in their own ways. He left his tie and jacket at his office, letting Lara see that he represented no time pressures for her.

During the flight, he outlined the situation to her. Bill was being manipulated into this partnership deal, and he had enough evidence on him right now to lock him up but not enough to keep him under lock. What does she want to do? She would have to think about it. Could she go along with Bill's scheme and let him and his cohorts frame themselves? The police would have to be informed shortly.

They landed in Santa Barbara-Goleta airport. Walked slowly toward a roadside motel. She became quiet. Too quiet. They stopped in front of the office. Martin waited. Her decision had been made. She kissed him and felt fire coming to life in him. She wanted to make love to Martin. She loved him. He was her friend.

"Martin, you are my friend. It is because of you, in a way, that my values have changed. My self-worth stops me from meaningless sex."

"Meaningless? Should I be insulted?" Martin smiled because he understood her. "You don't have to show me gratefulness with sex. We are friends."

"Forever friends," said Lara.

They continued their walk past the motel. "Martin, you take care of Bill. I'm not strong enough."

He put his arm around her shoulders, assuring her of his protection.

Chapter 32

TIME WAS FLYING. MARTIN did not keep her information up to date "to protect her." All she needed to know was that Bill's actions could jeopardize her. Martin's meticulous sheltering of Lara went unnoticed by her.

Life was unfair. You'd think you get your just rewards in this life, not in some *ever after*. Here she was, having licked the worst problems. Here she was, having turned straight, and the man she loved was a crook. No, there was no way she had it in her to have him arrested or to press charges or anything that ugly. All she could do was go along for the ride. Let Bill weave enough rope to hang himself on his own if he was guilty. She already knew that Bill did not tell her about his copartners because he was afraid of them. He must be. People always try to ignore what they fear the most. But she understood from experience that it doesn't go away. You have to face it head-on.

All right. She was glad that she grew up to be a tough cookie, but what do you do when your love has really gone wrong?

Martin was her only friend. She was on the phone with him often. Martin had been a gentleman. He had told her that making love with her was the best day of his life although he was sorry he got her by default. That was not what he wanted. Nevertheless, he could not resist pouring on his honorable gibberish. Lara didn't mind. When people love each other, they can make love together without becoming lovers. She loved Martin even if they never

made love together again. He told her he would stay in her life, try
to do all he could to make her happy, even if she could not fall in
love with him.

Martin was fair. Martin, and she almost felt guilty about it,
was more fair than Harry. But she could not really compare them
because Harry never knew her as a straight person, only as a doper
and whore. She was convinced that Harry too would have been a
gentleman had she been different. After all, who but Harry gave
her a reason to survive.

She got emotional support from Martin, which was all she
really needed in the strange world of legitimate business. She
wished she could be in love, in real love where it was returned.
That would have to take its time.

Early mornings became her and Martin's regular telephone
time. This morning, Martin came up with a fresh idea.

"Why don't you go away for a week, meet up with that
handsome fellow who saved you from me, and have fun. He is still
in the picture, isn't he?"

"Wade? I'm not sure," said Lara.

"After a break, things will look a lot better around home."

"I can't take any time now. Summer is over. I am getting into
the Lara's Place campaign. That'll take up a lot of my time. I don't
think I should go anywhere."

"Excuses, excuses. You hired a competent agency to design the
campaign, didn't you?"

"They're your clients. Did I? OK. Even if I did go away for a
few days, who would run the restaurant?"

"Think of someone you know or hire someone you don't know."

"Martin, I love the way you're looking out for me, but I can't
just pick up and go to the guy. I haven't heard from him beyond a
postcard.'

"Lar, did he give you an open invitation, or did he give you an
open invitation?"

The doorbell rang.

"Wait a sec, there's someone at the door. Don't hang up. I'll get
rid of them."

She put the phone down, giving Martin a chance to check his papers on his desk, and begin the day's work.

Lara opened the door to a Western Union delivery man.

"A telegram?"

"Ms. Lara Burns."

"That's me."

"It's for you. Please sign here."

She hurried for her purse to get a tip for the man and anxiously closed the door behind him. Back on the telephone, she practically screamed into it.

"Martin, Martin! Are you there?"

"I'm here. Watch my eardrum."

"It's a telegram."

"From whom?"

"I don't know."

"Lara, dear, open it."

"Oh."

The old-fashioned fear of a telegram representing bad news overwhelmed her and made her hands shake as she opened the envelope.

"Well, who is it from?"

She looked, reading slowly, checking the signature, the city, and gave out another scream. "Martin, it's Wade! Look, I mean, listen, 'Company will be back to civilization by October 10. Please let Kathy Simms in the producer's office at Twentieth Century Fox studios know if you can be at Hotel George V, Paris, on that date. I miss you. I could not get you out of my mind. Wade,'" she read out loud. "You know something, I could use a little vacation. Let me work on it. See ya."

She hung up, pranced about the apartment as if she had gotten a new lease on life. Well, she had.

She spent the rest of the day thinking about Melody. Wouldn't it be wonderful if she could simply call her and find out that she would love to babysit the restaurant. Wouldn't that be something? She searched her brain to try to remember the name of the law firm where Melody had worked, where she had reached her a long time ago.

She had to find her old phone book. Did she throw it away? She had been meaning to throw it away.

As soon as she could make time, she headed downstairs to the storage area of the apartment building. She would find the phone number and call Melody. Melody will be so impressed; and she, Lara, could trust her to the end. After all, she knew how to do it even before Lara ever knew how to do it. The restaurant business was special, and Melody had a knack for it.

Sure enough, in an old manila envelope, she found her hooker's log and phone book. What a terrible thing to save. As if she would want anybody to know where she came from after she had made it. Her friends, parents, and schoolmates gave up on her long ago. Why save this stuff?

She hurried upstairs, tore out the page with the phone number she needed, and threw the rest of it in the fireplace. A quick match took care of nearly ten years of filth. The early life of Lara Burns.

She dialed the law office. When she asked about Melody, she was turned over to another voice. Sweet and clearly composed, the matriarch of the firm, Carla Silver took the call. She was a little cagey at first, making sure that she knew who she was talking to. After all, working in a law office teaches you some basic caution about strangers. When Lara told her she was Bill's girlfriend prior to his marriage to Melody, Carla screamed, "I don't believe it!"

Lara smiled. It was her turn to sound ever so collected.

"Well, it's really me, Lara Burns, and I'm sure you've heard nothing nice about me."

"That's n . . . well . . ."

"That's true, right?" Lara smiled. It all seemed so long ago.

"Right. What do you need her for?"

"I have a business proposition for her."

"She has a job."

"This would be only part time, temporary. Something she could probably do on the side."

In spite of Carla's curiosity, Lara could not be probed further. Finally Carla promised to deliver the message to Melody.

It took a full twenty-four hours, but the next evening, Ben Taylor appeared at The Place, flaunting all his boyish charm, hair flowing, wearing an unusual dark-tone tapestry jacket. He told Lara that Carla had made the connection. He did not mention that he was impressed by Carla especially since he had come close to meeting her on several occasions. He was surprised, never having heard of Lara, who wished to keep the details of her and Melody's past private.

Lara was gracious, offered Ben dinner and drinks on the house, even after she found out that Melody was unavailable.

"She is traveling for me." Ben was brief. He remembered a postcard from a hotel in Biloxi, Mississippi, addressed to him in Melody's clean printing, but not a word on it. It was postmarked about two weeks after the $10,000 check was cashed by Melody in New York. He had since hired a private investigation service to try to locate her. No luck, so far. No need to discuss it with anyone.

Ben complimented Lara on the restaurant, the entertainment, and promised Lara that he will be back. In fact, he made reservations for a business dinner there the next evening. All that was all right with Lara, although her purpose had not been satisfied. She would wait a few days, and if Ben does not put her in touch with Melody, she would hire an outsider to oversee The Place while she was gone.

On her way back to the kitchen, she overheard Walter greet Malcolm Orthoner, whom she had recently met through Bill. The maître d's good memory, good manners, good brain impressed her. Maybe he could keep the restaurant in shape for an extra bonus if Melody did not work out. Lara was happy with the speed with which her mind worked.

You're not getting older, you're getting better, girl, she thought to herself and grinned.

Malcolm sat down by himself at the piano bar. Lara wondered why? What is he doing there alone? She saw Ben rise and go over to Malcolm. Theo busily bussed the nearby tables. It seemed from Lara's point of view that Ben was introducing himself. She called Walter over.

"Do they know each other?"

The maître d', always knowing who the boss was, readily offered her information.

"No. Your guest, Mr. Taylor, overheard me calling Mr. Orthoner by his name, and then it seemed that he, Mr. Taylor, may know him, or his name rang a bell, or one of those things. He asked me if this Mr. Orthoner was the same of the employment agency."

Lara looked at the two men in the lounge. They were getting acquainted.

Chapter 33

BILL ARRIVED HOME, TOOK a quick shower, fixed himself a drink, and settled by the pool with some paperwork. He hadn't used the pool in so long; the heater was turned off. Two large Hawaiian torchlights gave him all the warmth and light he needed. It had been a long time since he enjoyed his home by himself. Chuck was out of the country, and Bill couldn't be happier. True, he had a small guilt complex about being so happy alone, but it wasn't something he couldn't live with. Business at the Orthoner Associates was excellent. Business with Lara had definitely reached its dead end. He had no idea how to break the bad news to Chuck.

The bloody mary warmed him up. Tranquility surrounded him. He slowed down and gave into a little nap.

Sudden terror awoke him as he felt an ice-cold needle prick his foot. Between the first and second toes, a needle an inch and a half deep. A half inch beyond healing relief. Excruciating, sheer pain. No, it was not a dream. Chuck's Asian mafia, three hoods, dark reflecting glasses, hats, gloves, turtleneck sweaters, were there. Bill's nonexistent high blood pressure took over. The blood rushed to his face and made him tremble. As he got hold of himself, his face turned white; and he felt, or thought he felt, blood escape from his body through the tiny dry hole pricked in his foot.

"Relax, Mr. Benton." The voice was slurry and scratchy. "We ain't gonna hurt ya now. We want ya should respect this message from the boss. He'll be back on Friday. He wants a place of operations. A good place. He says it's your job. A neat place, daddio."

They disappeared as soundlessly as they appeared. Bill broke out in cold sweat and passed out. He was out for several hours. As he regained consciousness, he became more frightened than before. He threw on some clothes, jumped in his car, and sped screeching out of the drive way. A parked car in front of the next home also started up.

As if driven by some demon, he drove directly to Sheila's house in Tarzana. He couldn't comprehend how Chuck had learned about his losing The Place. Did Malcolm know too? His drug-abused mind had too many gaps.

It was late. Sheila was startled from her sleep by the doorbell. The house was quiet and dark except for an occasional night-light. Sheila, who had put on even more weight than he remembered, came to the door, dragging sleepily.

She quickly let him in. The children were asleep. He didn't ask about them.

"Sheila, I have a proposition for you." He walked to the liquor cabinet, which was empty except for a bottle of Haig & Haig. He took it out with great delight and stopped for a beat to appreciate it.

"You saved my bottle, hm?"

He didn't wait for an answer. He didn't want an answer. He poured himself a stiff shot and turned back to the obese figure.

"I want a temporary place for some business associates to work out of. I will use your garage. You'll get twice the money for the time that they're around. That's the best I can do. What do you say?"

He looked at her expectantly, fully aware of what she would say, since his was an order to go unquestioned and be obeyed.

She stared at him. She was a worn-out welcome mat that everybody stepped on.

"I saved the scotch because I love you and you love it. Nobody else drinks around here. And even though that woman you married poisoned you, still you are welcome here. I will do what you want me to do because I still love you. I know that has no meaning for you. But mainly I will do it because you are my only source of income."

"Because you've got my kids, that's'll." He flashed a near-sinister smirk at her. This was his only place of totalitarian power. He liked that.

"The one question I have is whether it'll jeopardize your children's lives?"

"Don't be crazy, woman. I'm going to have a false front built on the garage and reopen the entry from the alley. It'll never be noticed."

He was relieved. He sat down on the couch, looked at Sheila, and kicked off his shoes.

"It's settled. Bring me a blanket and go to bed."

His mind was buzzing about the next day, about meeting with an architect and ordering alterations to the garage in Tarzana. Fast. He was growing frantic. Sleep eluded him.

Chapter 34

"ONE GOOD TURN DESERVES another," Ben said when he opened the door of his impressive Tudor home to Carla. He wore a colorful, short caftan over tailored blue jeans. "I'm glad you gave me a chance to thank you in person for delivering Melody's message to me."

"Oh, it was nothing." She entered.

"It was proof of reliability. It shouldn't be underrated."

The most exciting thing about Ben Taylor was that Melody never spoke about him. Their ways have parted since the holidays. They spoke rarely, and each time it was more and more brief. Being here made it apparent to Carla that Melody tried to keep Ben to herself. It was due to her advice that Melody got wise and got hold of a man of means, and she would not share any details about him. All Melody ever said was that her new job was unique, pretty tough, well-paying, and never boring. Carla understood why.

As she looked at Ben's all-American, open face, she had an urge to pinch it.

As he looked at her ample bosoms, tiny waist, beautiful, pear-shaped, full buttocks, and the large grey eyes demurely gazing out of a small, barely detectable maze of crow's feet, Ben wanted to do more than pinch, a lot more.

She entered elegantly, glanced around appreciatively. Her mind was made up to be fascinating, to act knowledgeably, and to take the guy from Melody. She let Ben walk her through his lavish living room to the terrace, which overlooked a woody meadow of the Holmby Hills. Even the air was better here than anywhere else in town. The houseman set up the bar service and quietly disappeared.

"I thought we'd have cocktails here, hors d'oeuvres maybe, then go out to dinner someplace." Ben rolled the service tray laden with delicacies in front of her. "What's your pleasure, Carla?"

"Oh, I don't drink, thank you."

"That's commendable. You don't mind if I do? . . . a lot?"

"Oh, no, no, of course not," came the quick answer in her sweetest voice. She liked tipsy men. The main advantage she had gained as a member of the rehabilitated Alcoholics Anonymous club was a strength over those who drank and became weak. She could get anything she wanted from a man in that state. She usually did. She sat back, crossed her legs, let her skirt ride above her knees. She leaned back in the wicker love seat so utterly straight that her breasts were displayed to their best possible vantage point.

She was satisfied with the effect she had on Ben, the look in his eyes, and the distraction in his drink pouring. His eyes never left her. Carla, copying Melody, looked away shyly.

Ben flashed on the firm, trim, athletic, girlish body that Melody had and that he loved so much because Melody had it, but here was something different. A full-grown, very feminine, zaftig body with the whitest skin he had ever seen as if Carla had bathed in nothing but milk and took on its characteristics. He was excited. As a rule, he had stayed clear of older women because they think too much and grow needy, but this time he could use a nice change of pace.

"So how do you like your job at the law office?"

She remembered the simplicity with which Melody got her job with Ben.

"It's OK for now, but I'm always looking."

"For what?"

"For the right job. You know, good money, diversified, as little routine as possible, where my experience is appreciated.

"That's a swell answer." Ben wanted her to show interest in his line of employment before making any suggestions.

"You know that Melody has been with me a few months, ever since her . . ."

"Her annulment. Yes. I've talked with her a few times, but generally she is hard to reach."

"She handles a lot of errands for me, with me, and sometimes with my associates. She is very valuable to me. She is bright and absolutely the most cooperative assistant I've had in the past ten years."

Carla nearly choked on her words. "I know, she's simply wonderful."

She walked to the bar, made sure that her walk was worth watching, and poured herself another glass of Perrier. This was going to be rougher than she had expected.

"The job she is holding also entails a great deal of confidentiality.

"I can hold my mouth as well as"—she was about to say Melody, but realized that she could not attack her in any sense if she was to accomplish her goal—"anybody." She finished the sentence.

"I'm sure." Ben smiled. He liked how the lady struggled, but the vibes he picked up indicated that she was not a true friend of Melody's. In her naïveté, Melody probably didn't even know it. Sad how people step on one another.

"There's also some private entertainment involved from time to time."

"I can serve drinks just because I don't drink. I can be interesting."

"Can you be enticing? Can you be irresistible? Can you bring pleasure to a man without tears of sorrow in your eyes?"

"I can do anything she can do." This came out far too fast. Ben caught it clearly now. He was fascinated by the intense savagery this woman displayed, the hunger, quite in contrast with Melody's laid-back nature.

"What if I want you to take my shirt off?"

"Now?"

"Yes, now."

As she glanced toward the door for any onlookers, she realized that servants generally don't hang around their masters. "What shirt?"

"A make-believe shirt, darling." His gaze was heated, She walked over to him, took his hands, and pulled him up against her. She lightly kissed his lips, untied the sash, exposing his chest. Then she slowly unbuttoned his make-believe shirt, putting her body close to his. When there were only two invisible buttons left, she kissed his chest, licked both nipples on the suntanned body. Their minds caught up in fantasy, the buttons were no longer imaginary for either of them. Carla finished the unbuttoning, and he was bare.

Carla's anxious attempt to overwhelm amused Ben. He didn't find it difficult to accept her attention. He would try to put Melody out of his mind for the time being and deal with his self-serving realities.

A couple of hours later, Ben knew that Carla would do anything to outshine Melody. He liked her dedication but not her motivation. This kind of person could sell out easily. In his cutting-edge business where he was walking the wild side, the smallest degree of disloyalty, dishonesty, can bring down the curtains; and yes, even Ben Taylor could be sold out. He made his decision. He will have to limit Carla's access to information. She is bright but unlikely that she could bring him down at any time.

"Carla, luv, you're a dangerous woman," said Ben, lifting his glass in toast to her.

Carla, with eyes shyly cast down and away, said "I hope you mean that in a good way, Ben."

"You're indeed something." The way he said "something," Carla knew she had made headway for herself. "Let's make a temporary arrangement wherein you would cover selected entertainment demands, if you know what I mean, the entire show, body and soul. Then we will go from there."

"Great!" she interrupted with sudden enthusiasm.

"I'd like you to keep your regular job and help me out when I need you. Don't think in terms of clerical help, darling. Most of that is farmed out. How does that sound to you?"

He walked around, putting his caftan back on as he continued, "You'll be on a retainer of sorts. Getting additional salary almost identical with your current wages, merely for being available. Is that a sweet deal?"

Carla was nodding and calculating numbers.

"Very little labor . . . and considerable fringes."

Ben stopped talking, looked at her expectantly.

She accepted all his suggestions. She was certain something good had just happened for her and maybe for once she put her body in the right place at the right time. Her enthusiasm reignited when Ben took the little pipe off the service table and lit it. She didn't notice that he didn't take any grass. She reapproached Ben to bring him more pleasure, to express her appreciation, not knowing that she should have left after the offer was made and accepted.

At nearly dawn, she practically crawled to her car. Unaware of being followed all the way home by the surveillance vehicle positioned at Ben's house. High on weed, she wondered whether she had made a good deal? Whether she could have done better? Whether she would have all the good things Melody had? Never having any idea that Melody also had Ben.

Chapter 35

A WHITE FOX-TRIMMED NECKLINE accented the soft, white, crushed leather coat that was delivered to Melody in her room. She was packed, ready to leave. The coat came on a hanger. She screamed, "Peter! Peter!" He appeared in the doorway, dressed all in beige, he was Prince Charming personified. His gleaming face brightened up the already sunny sanatorium room. They hugged and held on. Her first hug following the arduous treatment. She was dry. She was his lady. He held her, and she was under and inside his skin. Inseparable. The kiss lasted a century. He wrapped the coat around her protectively.

There was an early fall chill in the air as they walked out of the private clinic on the Hudson River, got into the waiting limo to take them back to New York City. There was so much to say. Neither of them knew where to start.

"You never told me how you found me, Peter?" This question had been burning in her mind for weeks.

"It's too delicate for your ears."

She laughed. "You don't mean the part I lived."

"No. I mean the work of the Hungarian intelligence abroad. That is far too delicate to be discussed."

"Did you want to find me?"

"Funny, that was the only question they asked me too before they went looking."

"And what did you say?"

"What do you think I said, silly woman? I didn't want you to leave me in the first place. Naturally I wanted to find you."

"How come Ben never found me?"

"Guess I had a better team doing the looking."

His national pride brought a smile to her face.

"You went through a lot of trouble for me. Do you have any doubts now? Any second thoughts?"

"You mean the fact that you are sterile?"

"You knew that? When?"

"Oh, Melody, I've read every bit of your medical history. I know you inside and out. I love you as you are. Do you know how terrible I felt when I learned that I triggered your entire regression? On the other hand, I also triggered your complete recovery. So maybe we can enjoy some real living from now on."

Her mind raced along, wondering if there was an easier way to pose the next question than coming directly out with it. "I have a request . . . I want to take a few days now, to clean up my past."

"What's a few days?"

"Aha, you've been around, hm?" She attempted to lighten the issue. She knew that he was aware of the Americana expressions of *later*, meaning any time at all, and sometimes meaning no time at all. It was only fair that he would like to be specific about her expression of "a few days."

"I can't tell you precisely how many."

"I wish you could." He became distant. He was nobody's fool.

She thought about it. She felt that leaving him now and not traveling back to Hungary with him could destroy the whole relationship. But she had learned not to be dishonest with herself. She remained silent. She could not ease the pain for either of them.

"OK," he finally said. "I'll go one more step, the last step, Melody Shorr, to make this love affair a reality."

She was touched. She began to cry. Through the dam of tears, she saw the big man at a complete loss. She looked away and collected her thoughts. Putting her index finger gently across his lips to stop him from protesting, she said, "I want to be worthy of you, Peter. My physical shortcoming has been haunting me, but I should not have reached the degradation I did. This is my step one to redeem myself. *R E D E E M*," she spelled it out, "if you wish to look up the word."

A fleeting smile broke Peter's bewildered look. "I've always trusted my instincts," he said. "I've wrestled with the series of surprise elements that are part of your package."

"You mean baggage?" she said.

"No, package. All these surprises add up, surround, and weave our relationship since the beginning and show me that you and I are meant to be together." He held her close.

"I'll prove it to you every day, Peter."

"There is nothing to redeem," he added. Without a specific date, Peter agreed to Melody's picking up on the last leg of his European concert tour in West Germany.

The night, back at the Plaza, passed quickly. They held hands and talked. She wanted to know about her inadvertent sojourn in New Orleans. How she walked into the old hotel where she and her mother lived, without knowing that it had since turned into a brothel and where she became the resident laughingstock. Where the Madame charged extra for anyone trying to have sex with *their little girl.*

Peter would never embarrass her. He understood now what led to Melody's hardcore state. He also understood that without her will to live and love, she would never have recovered. The morning found them having coffee at Idlewild Airport, Melody going west and Peter going east. The twains shall meet . . . so they hoped.

When Melody arrived at LAX, she had a message directing her to a private prop-jet to Palm Springs.

Ben's Palm Springs home was dressed up for nothing less than a fairytale wedding celebration although it was merely her welcome home party. The dreamlike setting was filled with beautiful people. The Place, one of Ben's new hang-outs since Melody had left, catered the food and waiters.

She was surprised, pleased, and deliriously happy with all the excitement her return had caused. Ben would not only never let her down, but also he would, if he could, keep her up all the time. She drooled in the sweetness of American decadence. She, for the first time, on account of Peter, had another point of view. Nevertheless, she found it fascinating and tantalizing. Too beautiful for words.

She spread out on the chaise lounge; the flight lag, the dancing, and the noise behind her, she recalled the last night she and Ben spent there. She knew they were both straight, but how straight?

Now, she looked at it backward, not in retrospect, backward, from the current point of view of a recovering addict. Ben proved to her how good he could be when he intended it. She even wished she could love him.

Looking at the star-filled early-October night sky over balmy, wonderful Palm Springs, less than a year after her most heartbreaking fiasco, she was amazed at herself for the confidence she had in choosing her next life. A foreigner, a foreign place. But he was sent from the sea.

She was oblivious to Carla languidly moving close to her and sitting by the edge of the pool.

"I hear that you'll marry the man. How come everybody wants to marry you?"

"I don't know how come. And what the hell are you doing here? Not drinking, I hope?"

"Never."

"Well, what do you do?"

"Everything but alcohol." Her answer was choked by a slight, self-defacing chuckle. Melody had the feeling this was not the same lady she used to know.

"Is this the *work sex* you talked about, or could it be *love sex?*"

"You were a good student, I can see. A fast study," said Carla.

"But really, what's going on with you?" Melody probed.

"I'm trying to get from Ben's B-team to his A-team."

"Doing what?"

"Fucking around Melody, as if you didn't know. Mostly fucking."

"And getting a lot of dough."

"Just like little old Melody."

The silence was thick. Their thoughts were deep.

"How stoned are you?" Melody worried for her.

"Not enough."

"I wish I hadn't heard you say that."

"Why? Ben said that you tried to reach me many times for some of his parties. That means you must've wanted to hear it."

"Carla, you sweet dummy, that was before. Before I knew that no matter how old you are, there is someone out there who wants to make you whole."

Carla's laughter resembled shrieking. "Who, me?"

"Don't you understand? I felt the same way, you have to remember that. I thought I've had it. Over thirty, no family, no one to care, there was nothing but dope. But time can be made a friend."

"You're lucky and accept it." Carla's voice became harsh. "You're always lucky. Somehow you lure them to you, and they want you for keeps. What the hell do you do is what I'd like to know!"

"Mostly I have no idea what the hell I'm doing." Melody heard herself say this, but it was at the same time that she first realized that that was exactly what happened to her. Somebody up there must really like her.

She sipped the ice tea; and without thinking she stretched her legs, did a couple of straight leg lifts, just testing the old stomach muscles.

"Not bad," she announced.

"What?" came Carla's voice from a distant stupor.

"My stomach muscles."

"Oh, fuck you."

"No, thanks." Melody's voice was kidding, light, trying to change the conversation, and missed Carla's mood entirely. "I'm through with that. I have one man to do all that with for the rest of my life."

"Like you had Bill? Haha."

"Hope not."

Melody couldn't get angry. "What I want you to do is take a look at yourself in the morning and find out if this is what you really want. Ben's A-team. I never stopped to look. That was my mistake."

"You're too damn wise for your old age. I'm not buying. You wait and see. I've got Ben and all the trimmings that go with him."

"Hey, Carla, that's all right." She looked at her beautiful friend, curled over her knees in the fetal position, hanging her hands into the pool.

"I don't have any claims or hold on Ben. I just want you to know that getting back to the straight life is not bad at all. There are people everywhere who will help you. I want you to believe it."

"Bullshit." She rose to rejoin the party at the same moment as Ben appeared. On seeing Ben, Carla straightened herself up and pushed her bosoms out high, trying to gain back her fresh smile of the early evening. Melody did not see Ben at the sliding doorway, searching for his guest of honor.

"Ben, are you pleased with the party I organized for tonight?" Carla scurried up to him. "Do you like the food from The Place? Was that a good idea?"

"I like it if the guest of honor likes it." He walked over to Melody and lowered himself to one knee. He took her hand and looked deep into her sparkling, happy, clear eyes.

"I love it, Ben, Carla. Both of you are wonderful. I love it."

Carla stood in the doorway for a moment, waiting for a sign from Ben. But he was totally enveloped in his love for Melody. He searched her eyes for a slight message, a slight promise directed to him.

"I'm sober, Mel. I've had nothing."

"Ben, I should hate you for all the shit you've put me through, but I love you for loving me anyway." She leaned close to him, kissed him gently, and let him walk her over to his bedroom.

Carla looked at them and suddenly felt that maybe she didn't do something right.

In Ben's bedroom Melody kissed him and felt his blood rushing through both of them.

"Our sex was always wonderful, Ben. We were wonderful. But no . . ."

Chapter 36

THE STREETS OF FRANKFURT, West Germany, were gray with metallic overtones reflecting through the drizzly day. The sun gave up trying to get through long ago. Gloom sat in openly and freely.

Peter's new Mercedes Benz, which he had purchased and planned to drive home to Budapest with Melody, was delivered to his hotel, the Frankfurter Hof, the same morning he had arrived. His manager, other Continental friends, and entourage waited for him for their breakfast reunion. They had come back to Europe ahead of him, leaving him to take care of the *Melody matter*.

Yes, it was called the Melody matter. No doubt, there had to have been something serious about it. More than passing fancy. More than international romance. None of them knew exactly what. None of them understood the kind of love that propelled Peter.

They kept an eye on the entrance to the fabulously elegant dining room. Finally they gave up waiting and began to order their brunches. A uniformed hotel page came over to let them know that he saw Peter Szabó get into his new car and drive off by himself.

That was exactly what he did. In the misty, sad tasting day, he was more or less aimlessly driving around the city that he normally loved.

Europastrasse No. 4 & 5, the Autobahn cross of Europe, connecting six countries, did not dazzle him as he headed out to the airport. Like many other sections of the city, it too was under construction, fully operational, and on its way to becoming a major airport and architectural design showplace of Europe. He pulled off the main road and stopped at a spot where he could watch incoming planes. Melody was sorely missing. He watched the planes without really watching. Melancholic, he drove on.

The river. He always felt better near large bodies of water. Same as Melody. Good things happen near water. He remembered that on his first visit to Frankfurt, a tour bus he had taken turned off the Autobahn and went to a famous waterway. Through the fall-colored open fields, the narrow road took him to a boy scout summer camp by the river Mein. His tour had had lunch there. It was open. It was summer. Unlike now.

He got out of the car and walked down to the river. It was running fast, its icy clearness suggesting a bottomless danger. But no. This was only October. The river contradicted, saying it was winter.

Peter stared at the water. *Why? For heaven's sake, why is he so down?* In his mind's eyes, he saw himself pick up pebbles and bounce them systematically at the surface of the rushing water, but his mind's mind said, *Just a minute! Stop everything! Why am I unhappy? What am I missing? The concert tour is going well. There is a definite film offer if I ever have the guts to speak on camera. The end of the tour is around the corner. I will be forty years old in two weeks, and I am in love with a wildly exciting, delicate woman, who will be back to being her normal self as soon as she is out of the filth I let her get into. No, I didn't let her get into. She did it all on her own. Self-destruction, lack of self-appreciation, everything dependent on not being loved. She will be back to me, and I will make sure that she stays.*

"Hey, OK. Everything is OK." He jumped up into the air, kicked some pebbles away, and headed back to his car. He inhaled the crystal clear air and for the first time stared at his amazing new machine. Wow! He went through the four-speed transmission of the 300Sc Mercedes Benz coup convertible roadster in seconds and screamed "Geronimo" with each gear shift until he was driving along the open highway.

The regal, empirical stature of the hotel already had a new beton and glass building neighboring it, the product of postwar architecture, a startling contrast that even the high spouting fountain of Kaiserplatz could not offset.

He took the telegram from the desk man along with his key, started to read it on the way to the elevator. He finished reading it, looked at his watch, turned around, and played back the whole scene in reverse. The elevator man who rose to take him upstairs sat back; the desk man who gave him his key took it and hung it back in its place; the doorman who stood by the door to let him in let him out. He backed his car out of its preferred spot in front of the building and was off again.

Holzhausenstrasse housed the Hungarian Trade Bureau where Miklós Barát waited for him.

"Right on time, Peter. I'm glad I reached you before you went into rehearsals for tonight's concert."

"Good to see you, Miklós." He did not like the urgency of the telegram that summoned him over there. "What's going on?"

"I'll get to the point. The Hungarian government is not going to allow Melody Shorr to live in Hungary. She is an addict, incorrigible doper."

"She's cured."

"There's no such thing."

"Are we back in the Middle Ages? You know better than to say there's no such thing."

"Well, regardless, this was the final decision, and I wanted to bring it in person."

"So you came all the way to Frankfurt? How touching."

Miklós laughed a dry laughter. "Our friendship was the main reason for my coming here. I knew you would be upset. But it couldn't be helped."

"My birthday is in two weeks. We're having a party. I want to show her my home."

"You think that's a good idea?"

"You bet." Peter's face lit up just from the thought of showing Budapest to Melody. "You can get me a visitor's visa, right?" He paused for a moment, after suggesting a solution for his immediate problem. "I'll bring her in no matter what."

Miklós was fearful of Peter smuggling Melody into the country. He had never known Peter to possess such defiance. "Yes. That I can arrange, but are you aware of the potential emotional repercussions?"

"That's my problem. Will I see you at the concert tonight?"

"Unfortunately I'm really on my way to a conference in East Berlin."

*

Peter sat back in his dressing room after a trying day, a good run-through, and an exhilarating concert performance. He was physically exhausted and happy to be finished with the encores, finished with the day. Boy, he needed rest.

His manager, Jankó Sass, knocked and, without waiting for an answer, came in. Peter had accepted this old man of worldly knowledge. Now somewhat crumpled and bent but once a cultural attaché of prewar Hungary for years, he himself was a culture saved from the past. Jankó had his fingers on the pulse of international taste and knew the places worth booking. They made a lot of money with his good decisions, and neither of them minded sharing such amounts with the Hungarian government. They were fond of their country and had drank some of the best French champagne cheering their homeland many times together.

Jankó sat down. Peter waited for him to speak. He didn't. Peter ignored him and went about his business of changing clothes. He had no idea that the old man found out about the problems regarding Melody's permanent entry into Hungary. Jankó sat there quietly. He merely wanted to be around to take any fleck should there be some, to help Peter get some of the steam off if that's what he needed.

Jankó smoked heavily, helped himself to a brandy snifter, and poured a shot of Courvoisier, so as not to let Peter drink alone.

MK

Knocking was heard again. Peter didn't look up. When Jankó was around, he could leave everything to him. Peter could and did disconnect. But lo and behold, Wade Nash burst through the door with the energy and dynamics of a dozen mountain lions.

"It took me forever to get back here and away from my admiring crowd. Great show, old buddy! They don't call you Peter the Hun for nothing! You got it man, whatever it takes, you got it. They were eating out of your hands."

They hugged. Peter poured Wade some brandy. Wade continued excitedly. "The good news is, that (a) I can make it to your birthday party and (b) that Lara is coming over next week. I never thought I'd hear from that dame again!"

"I am not sure that I follow you." Peter was unfamiliar with the Lara situation, which Wade realized.

"Right! You don't know about her. We've gotta fix that. Wait till I tell you how I met her. How's dinner? Are you free? Are you doing a show tomorrow?"

Peter nodded in the negative while asking Wade about his work schedule. "Do you have a call tomorrow?"

"Nope, Hun. A 2 p.m. standby. Rainy day schedule."

"Then dinner it is. Jankó?"

"No, thanks, fellows. See you at brunch."

The old man instinctively felt that Wade Nash was a far better solution for Peter for the evening than he. Just the same, he would have stayed awake and listened to Peter, if that's what he would have needed.

"Stay out of trouble, boys. Don't do anything I didn't do twice."

Chapter 37

DON CURTIS, CURLY HAIRED, slightly pudgy twenty-three-year-old advertising apprentice, was Lara's personal choice to design the ad campaign for the restaurant. Martin hired the firm. Lara hired the person. Lara went for the inexperience and good education he stood for, the same as she did with Bobby. Bobby hadn't disappointed her. Don won't. Although Don gave the appearance of winging it and being more into motorcycles than advertising, Lara saw through it. Belying his own cool, Don tried to dress for this meeting with Lara and Martin. His jacket and tie were wrong in every sense, funny to the insensitive. At any rate, Lara was more interested in the layouts, in the series of publicity articles he was securing, in the clippings of small write-ups he had already managed to get published, and his plans and methods of gaining some free space in the trade magazines of the restaurant industry.

The redecorating plans were under control and incorporated in a workable timetable. Whatever she needed to have done by December 26 would be done. The rest of the budget would be spent on direct advertising and, like Lara teased, on "putting Don through law school, or medical school because he was never going to make it in advertising."

Satisfied with the presentation, Lara was assured that Don would be able to run the restaurant together with Walter while she was gone. The itineraries were exchanged. Martin D. called for a taxi, and Lara was on her way to faraway lands. The Place was on its own for the first time except for her trusted aides and undercover private eye.

Ben Taylor's imposing party consisting of Melody Shorr, Carla Silver, and Malcolm appeared for a late supper. Malcolm thought Melody had good reasons for not getting into a conversation with him about old times. He made no attempt either. To Don Curtis, seeing the group meant nothing. To Walter, it meant a free flow of money and tips. To Theo, seeing them together was an important confirmation of his theories. He wished Lara were there. He rang Martin to let him know of the curious gathering.

They occupied the largest booth, allowing for gracious comfort. Melody sat next to Ben, and Carla was closest to Malcolm. Malcolm handled the ordering as if he owned The Place and kept referring to it as the "club."

Melody looked around, studied the room that gave her a *déjà vu* feeling. She didn't search too deeply having come to accept that after the amounts of dope she had consumed, there would be a lot of gaps in her memory.

Ben and Malcolm quickly became involved in business matters. Ben had opened a lot of new doors for Malcolm, and there was mutual admiration between the two men of legitimate up-front business facades, looking for exciting risks.

"I've got to cut out a middleman, Ben." Malcolm gulped up his drink as if it were a chaser for his thoughts.

"Buy 'm out," came the simple solution.

"Not that easy. The office is no problem. But he can't handle really big business. Small potatoes never change."

"So he's out."

"He brought me into Hung's operation, remember?" Ben had no idea of the details preceding his involvement. He listened intently to information about Bill as Malcolm continued, "He never came up with a restaurant, which is how it started, but geez, things changed. He's extra baggage. Buying him out is not the answer. You don't know how mad he is. He'd talk."

Melody knew, without a doubt, that Malcolm wanted somebody or somebodies killed. Had she remembered who Malcolm was and who his objective was, she might have wanted to do the killing herself. When Ben tapped her on her knee, she was expected to listen to and. remember every word that was being said. Just like old times. Gosh, she thought she was through with all that. Ben needed a backup brain; and hers, sober, was the best.

Melody felt entrapment. She grew tense. Ben was trying to tie her back into his business. Ben was relying on her appreciation of clever wheeling and dealing, which, he knew, always thrilled her and hooked her attention.

In spite of Ben's tapping on her knee, signaling to be an additional pair of eyes and ears for him, she decided to turn to Carla and make her final lunge for freedom.

"So, Carla. Do you really want to get on the A-team?"

"That's right. I want that more than just fun and games for money, if you know what I mean." She fidgeted with her tonic and lime.

"No. I don't."

"I'd like to work the inner circle. Get really involved. Have him tell me to give up my other job and really be valuable to him."

Ben and Malcolm talked right over them, oblivious to the girl talk.

"What do you think this is? Aren't you working for him right now?"

Carla did not understand what Melody was driving at.

"I don't think so. I'm here for dinner."

"That's working, Carla. Believe me, that's working. Dining with Ben is working. Look who you're sitting next to."

Carla looked. Melody ignored Ben glancing at her. She knew he was wondering why she was defying him. Why she was having a conversation aside from his?

"Oh," Carla exclaimed. "You mean?" She nodded rapidly as if the realization of her position in this particular walk of life had just hit her. Under Melody's watchful eyes, she squeezed close to Malcolm. Malcolm could not help noticing the hot thigh against his. He stopped talking, realizing for the first time that he was not with his beloved Erna.

"Listen, Ben, business can wait, right?"

"What about the terms?"

"You name 'm." As expected, it didn't take much to derail Malcolm's reasoning. "Do what you have to do, I'll sign any terms."

Ben smirked, leaned back, and looked at Melody. He knew that she had just turned Carla officially over to him and his causes. "Are you sure this is what you want, Melody? I want you to be absolutely positive."

"I am," came the quick answer. "Please," she pleaded, her eyes searching Ben's, searching for some assurance that she could leave in peace, unharmed. "Please, I do want out."

"She's not as smart as you."

"She is very clever, believe me. Besides, she has a purpose. I never did."

He felt many different feelings for Melody. *Does he love her enough to let her go? That could have been his woman, if . . .*

"*If* is for children," he blurted out of his thoughts.

"What?"

"Oh, nothing. Actually I was thinking that it would have been wonderful if you had decided to stay and marry me."

Melody had no answer. She looked away. Carla rubbed her cheek against Malcolm's. "I'll be back in a jiffy, luv." She headed toward the ladies' room. A few seconds later, Melody knew she should give the men room for outlining those *any terms* for a handshake and excused herself from the table. Ben stood up for her, and as she slid by him, he whispered in her ear, "I want you to know that as long as I have a face, you have a place to sit on." His good-bye. Melody blushed but realized she was truly off the hook. She glanced at Ben with appreciation and hurried out.

The telephone in the ladies' room was enclosed by a swinging door. Carla wasn't there. *Where did she go,* Melody wondered.

Melody quietly headed toward the back of the dark hallway.

"I'll meet you there. Just name the place," Carla spoke in low, soft, rapid tones. Melody held her breath.

"You don't have to threaten me. I'll cooperate. He means nothing to me. I want the money and the protection," Carla continued.

Melody didn't see Carla reading a note given to her by the other person, nor did she see Theo step back into the darkness.

"I'll let them think I'm wasted," said Carla, and turning quickly, she headed back to the table.

Melody was stunned. If she warns Ben about this conversation, she may cut off her own exit. Dilemma. Save Ben or save herself?

She casually returned to the table, observed Carla holding both men's attention. She saw a Mexican busboy scurry over to a tall, distinguished-looking gentleman and instinctively felt that her tablemates were the topic of the quick exchange. She leaned back, reentering the conversation.

"This place looks awfully familiar. Who owns it?" She looked at Ben.

"You mean you don't know?" Carla interjected.

"Ben, can you believe that we're all here because of Melody and . . ."

"Lara and . . . Bill." Melody finished the sentence, letting her voice trail off softly, leading her back to fragmented memories, the devastating effect her short-lived relationship with Bill had on her entire being. How she became Ben's puppet in order to be out of the normal life flow.

She saw, as if through a fog, Bill Benton and Chuck enter the restaurant, walk toward their table, clearly intending to join them. Lara's restrictions were ineffective during her absence, but Melody didn't know about that anyway.

"How cozy" was her first thought. "I don't belong here" was the second one as she rose, coldly looking away from Bill.

"Ben, I'll never break bread with certain people, and you should know that."

Ben jumped up, followed her to the exit.

"Never mind. I'm taking a taxi to the house. You stay, OK?"

Ben was flabbergasted. "What happened, Mel? What's wrong?"

Melody looked at him as if she suddenly gained the power of being able to predict with precision an impending earthquake and no one believed her.

"That is Bill Benton!"

Not taking an extra second, an extra look at anyone, Melody exited, leaving a bewildered Ben Taylor in the doorway. The effect Bill Benton's presence had on Melody was unsurpassed by any other *don't invite 'm together* people he had ever known.

Theo posted Martin on the *who is who* that he needed to know, and the ring began to appear closed, save for the young woman who had just left. Yes. Martin was impressed. Theo carefully turned the table into his fingerprint land. Carla adored being who she was and where she was. All the men loved Carla. She made sure Melody would not be missed. It was going to be her own exciting night.

Melody went back to Ben's house in Holmby Hills. That was probably her favorite of all of Ben's homes. Her belongings from the loft had been crated and awaiting shipping instructions at an air freight warehouse. She always traveled lightly with one suitcase and a carryall shoulder bag.

As she got out of the cab, Maury was at the door, letting her in.

"Oh, no!" The cab was slowly making the loop of the driveway as she yelled after him.

"Driver, come back!" He backed up to the front door. "Maury, I know you were expecting Ben. He's having a little party. Exactly what you like. The driver will take you there."

Maury smiled. Apparently the houseman let the unexpected guest in, and he got loaded while waiting for Ben. He headed out to the taxi in shirtsleeves. Melody grabbed his jacket, threw it after him, just making it into the cab as the door closed. "Driver, back to The Place, or whatever it is called."

The houseman handed her a telegram. She tore it open. *Melody. I am sending this telegram to all of Ben Taylor's addresses to find you. My last stop is Vienna. Hotel Imperial Wien, through Saturday, October 20. Meet me there if you want to live with me forever. Peter.*

She laughed, screamed, and hugged the houseman.

"Hey, you know somethin', it's October 14."

The houseman nodded in agreement and was anxious to leave the room. Melody headed for the telephone and dialed Ben's travel agent.

Chapter 38

SCHWECHAT AIRPORT, VIENNA. A welcome sight for Melody. She had spent eight hours on the Super G. Constellation to New York. She had a first-class sleeper compartment but could not sleep, ended up sitting around in the cocktail lounge most of the time, reading, drinking Perrier, and talking with other insomniacs. During the layover in New York, she grew sleepy; but as soon as she boarded the Lufthansa flight to Europe, she came wide awake.

Finally, she fell asleep, took a brief nap before the stewardess woke her. It was time to freshen up and face her newly elected world. The plane landed.

She collected her luggage and headed for the taxi stand when she heard her name! "Melodyyy!" pronounced with the gentle, gurgling sounds of a Continental accent. She turned. Jacques Martel and Maj, looking as if they had just stepped out of a fashion magazine, were approaching her.

The surprise was mutual. They rapidly asked about Ben, asked whether she was traveling on business or pleasure. They came in from Rome where Mme. Martel was staying for special treatment, and they had to pick up a few things for her.

Melody was overwhelmed by their fast chatter and the way they closely surrounded her. Both of them had their arms around her, her suitcase joined theirs, and the porter got them to their limousine. They insisted on her driving into town with them and invited her to dinner at the Bristol where they had a suite.

Melody could not object to riding with them. She accepted a gold-trimmed Gauloise from Maj in the car and refused the champagne because she felt too tired for drinking after the long trip.

She leaned back. Jacques drew the drape of the limo, excluding their driver from viewing their hands eagerly reaching for Melody.

"Hold it! Hold everything." Melody tensed her body away from them.

"Maj, you're like a bull in a china shop."

"Too rough, *cherie*? Here, let me show her how." Jacques bent over her as Maj laughingly pulled back.

"Both of you, stop it, please. Stop it. I mean it."

Somehow the seriousness of her tone reached them.

"You mean you haven't missed us like we missed you? That's sad." Jacques was believable.

Lighting fresh smokes, they looked at her with genuine hurt in their eyes. Melody felt strangely guilty. She took their hands as she spoke.

"I did miss you. Both of you. But it's all different. I am off the drugs, I am off the groups, I am getting married. I am clean and in love with one man. What I always wanted. Can you understand that?"

"Love, of course we understand love." Maj sighed. "I'm in love with one man, and he is in love with his one wife." She looked at Jacques.

"Well, could we be friends? Straight friends? After all, I'll be living in Europe."

"Where?"

"Budapest."

"Magnifique. A city of sheer delight." Jacques could taste the pleasures of Budapest. "You are marrying a Hungarian? Is that so?"

"Anyone we know?" Maj giggled. "And even if we don't, now we shall, right?"

Melody gloated on their anticipation before she divulged her secret.

"You know him. Maj, I am definite that you know him better than Jacques."

"Oh, noooo!" Maj shrieked with delight. "You got the Hun? *You* got him! That's outrageous! I love it!" She was happy. "I'm especially glad it's one of us, Melody, we'll come to the wedding."

They arrived at Melody's destination and dropped her off. She stood in awe of the architectural masterpiece the Hotel Imperial represented. She experienced an involuntary hesitation at the front entrance. Partially she was overwhelmed by the beauty and grandeur of the building, and partially she was nervous about dropping in on Peter unannounced.

Maj got out of the limo. "What's the matter, dearie?" Her lanky blondeness sparkled against Melody's dark, velvety look.

"I'm afraid to surprise him like this. I never told him when I was arriving."

"If you're going to find him with anyone, it better be now, so you know. Go on and call us, anytime, qui?"

One more hug and Melody bravely marched through the door held open for her and her bellboy by the doorman. She announced herself at the desk and was immediately taken upstairs.

Peter came to the door, opened it, looked at her expectant, anxious face and said, "Good . . . just one minute." As if in oblivion, he walked away from the door, left her standing there. The bellboy brought the suitcase in. Melody tipped him and checked that he locked the door behind himself. She was startled by Peter's rudeness. She stood motionless in the middle of the living room and heard Peter's voice. He was talking in Hungarian. She could not see that he was on the telephone.

"Anya, igazad volt, mint mindig. Melody megérkezett, Ott leszünk szombaton este. Csókollak."

He hung up and slowly, as if walking in a dream, approached Melody. He reached for her two hands. She let him raise them to his lips. Then he kissed and kissed her hands, and she could feel teardrops from his eyes.

"My mother"—he nodded toward the phone—"she knew you would be here. She, a woman, knew."

God, to be this happy, to be this loved, to be with such a man, were all the things she didn't know how to even dream about. Overcoming the tears, his voice became crackly and weak.

"Ever since Frankfurt, when I didn't hear from you, I wasn't sure if you were coming or not."

They laughed, cried, embraced. He looked at the medallion on her neck chain, the seashell in the gold enclosure, and repeated what he said that long ago weekend in Carmel, "You build solid strength around love so that it may remain in permanence."

Melody didn't want to go to sleep. She wouldn't admit to being tired until he forced her to take a nap. The drive to Budapest will be long, and he didn't want her to miss anything by sleeping on the road. He picked her up and carried her into her bedroom. They held on tight. The amount of energy they felt surging in them as their bodies touched was amazing. Peter sat on the bed. They yearned for each other.

"I want to live with your moral values, Peter. Don't let me, our love, make a small man out of you. Let me try a little self-discipline. Help me."

He reluctantly left the room.

*

Early next morning they started their drive to Budapest, leaving behind sunny Vienna. Melody was excited about his new car, insisted on leaving the top down in spite of the brisk October dawn. It gave him special pleasure to have a real American go crazy over his Mercedes Benz. He was happy, happy, happy about everything.

They reached the border in what appeared to be a short period of time. He handed the guards his passport and her visitor's visa. Everyone knew him. They were processed fast. The border guards congratulated him on his new car and asked about his next record.

Back on the road, she picked up the visa sitting next to him on the seat, studied it, and realized that it was merely a visitor's visa.

"That's nice. You know, Peter, this is really nice." The way she said the word *nice* could have been the word *shit*.

"What?"

"What? What!" Her voice rose in anger. "A visitor!" She waved the paper in front of his nose, and he was unable to grab it out of her hand.

"Stop that waving. Stop waves."

"Maybe that's what I should do. Not stop waves but make some waves. How come is it that I am expected to make a final commitment and show up here and throw away my past, but you're not expected any kind of final commitment, neither is your country? How come? Why didn't you get me a permanent visa? Why? Did you even try?"

"Yes, I did. And I am still trying, and I will get it. You relax. All is well."

"Hah!" She looked away, upset, defiant. She didn't understand why this had happened. She got scared.

"Why?"

"Because of the dope."

He slowed down at the railroad crossing, and before he could offer any more explanations, she threw the door of the moving car open, jumped out, rolled over, got up, ran with fury toward the wide open fields. The tears poured as she cursed and screamed with anger and fear. Would she never be able to get away from six months of dope. Will it be a permanent stigma?

She completely lost contact with reality and was blinded by the steady stream of tears. She ran out of breath, slowed down, and he caught up with her.

"I will get the permanent papers. I know I will."

"You're a fuckin' patsy!"

"A what?" This was new to him.

"A fuckin' patsy!" She walked fast, kicking up soil on her well-tailored pants.

"You're a fuckin' radical," he screamed.

"A what?"

"A fuckin' radical!" He was mad and had no idea what either of them were talking about.

"Ya have no idea what we're talking about, do ya!" She was frustrated.

"Is this how all our fuckin' fights will be? We won't be able to do it right because we won't have the words?"

"We'll have the fuckin' words! We will have fuckin' everything and have fuckin' good fights and fuckin' good fucking. How's that?"

She started laughing. He moved close to her.

"Hungary does not believe in drugs and dope for fun, you know. So they figure anyone who does is dangerous and should be kept out of the country. There is no crime in Hungary. You can walk around any hour of the night. It's a good place. They know you're cured. But I agreed to go along with the rules. In the long run, I will have it my way. I always do."

"Maybe you're not a patsy."

They kissed. The kiss wouldn't end. They fell on their knees and felt the freshly tended farm land get under their clothes as they loved, becoming part of the great Hungarian earth.

*

It was after midnight when they arrived at his home in Budapest. A spacious apartment on the top floor of the three-story building. Once Peter started to gain fame, the Szabó family broke through some walls and connected two apartments which were rightfully theirs, since Peter was allowed to have one of his own. They also built a roof garden.

The front of the building on Klauzál tér was decorated for his birthday, people had ribbons hanging out of their windows, and the stairwell to the third floor was dressed up for the occasion.

Mrs. Szabó opened the door for them with the happy faces of Mr. Szabó and Peter's seventeen-year-old sister Erzsi behind her. The hugging and kissing was genuine. Melody found herself bowing Asian style several times. It was silly. Being a foreigner was confusing. Hot toddies awaited them along with a telegram from Wade Nash asking that he be picked up at the airport first thing Sunday morning.

Melody was no longer concerned about Peter's contacts with big stars. If anything, she was impressed by the fact that someone like Wade Nash would make a point of getting to Budapest for Peter's birthday party. His mother explained that generally everyone who was anyone in show business and sports, working or vacationing in nearby countries, usually came to Peter's birthdays.

Then she showed Melody to her room and sent Peter off into his own. No one argues with a mother.

They had to get up early in order to be back from the airport by noon Sunday when the festivities of the block party were scheduled to start. Melody thought she might never stop smiling as she went off into a deep sleep in the cushy, dawn-filled pillows and comforter.

Chapter 39

THE SMALL AIRPORT OUTSIDE Budapest was quite different from the oversized, busy airfields of large Western cities. This was functional, colorless, unimpressive. Peter the Hun enjoyed the celebrated Million Mile Traveler status, clearly an overstatement under the circumstances, but the label carried a great deal of importance with it. He took Melody to an unobtrusive side door which, in fact, was the private VIP entrance in the land of equality. A corridor led to the receptionist's desk fronting the offices of operating personnel.

Happy faces greeted him. Cheerful hellos came from all directions along with the information that his friend was about to land. Peter took Melody to the observation deck where they witnessed the smooth landing of a Cessna 310 twin engine craft. Peter and Melody hurried to meet the plane as it taxied to its assigned area.

To Melody's astonishment, Lara Burns climbed out of the cockpit. Wade followed from the copilot side. The men shook hands, hugged, kissed on the cheeks. Lara and Melody froze, stared at each other.

No introductions were needed.

An uncomfortable ride followed. The men couldn't imagine what was wrong between the two women. Their casual chatter mostly covered show business friends. Peter dropped them at the Royal Hotel, agreeing that they would check in, shower, change, take a taxi to Peter's apartment before eleven thirty, and be able to participate in the festivities from the beginning.

Peter drove down Lenin Kőrút silently, turned at Wesselènyi utca toward Klauzàl tér. She liked the fact that Peter never moved out of his neighborhood. Instead, his own money beautified the building he was born in. He reconstructed the apartment, adding some luxury features and creating the roof garden for anyone's use. His presence gave the area class it had never known before.

"Do you want me to wear the . . ."

He sharply interrupted, "I want you to wear your white jumper dress, no furs, little jewelry. This fox looks very good on you, but not here and not today."

"It was your gift, Pe."

"There are times when it is wrong. There are times when a lot of my gifts that are right in one place are not right in another place. With me you are part of me. You represent me. I want you to remember that with me you are always a gracious hostess to each and every one of our guests. Each. No matter what you think of them privately."

"OK. OK, already. I hear you, Captain Queeg, sire. And I obey you, my master."

She hurt. She had never heard Peter use that tone to her. He had scolded her before only about her own insecurities and jokingly at that. She sulked, pulled her fox collar close around her face, and slouched low in the seat. *He had a point. But why get so upset?*

They did not look at each other. Peter realized he was too harsh, it was the wrong approach, but he was inexperienced in backtracking and apologizing. Nyár utca, a narrow, almost dark, old-fashioned cobblestoned street lined by three and four-story graying apartment buildings, was where he turned. They barely got into the long block when they heard a whistle, and the band started to play at the other end of the street. It wasn't noon yet.

"Oh, my god," said Melody, pulling her fox security blanket tighter, trying to disappear in attempted simplicity. She looked at her hand with the huge diamond pinky ring and the famous antique opal cocktail ring Ben got her. Gifts of lust. She felt like the bourgeoisie all-Americans were believed to be in these parts of the world. She touched the gold framed seashell hanging off her neck and was a lost little girl. She didn't think she would ever have to feel like that again. Her eyes were increasingly moist.

The convertible top was down.

"Smile." Peter squeezed the word out of his own smiling teeth, looking at the oncoming crowd.

They had to slow to a creep because people were trying to get close to him, to touch him. It seemed that the celebrating friends and neighbors started to gather ahead of time, expecting him and his family to come out of their building at noon. But as they spotted them sooner, spontaneous enthusiasm overtook everyone, and the party began.

There were ribbons, confetti, and noisemakers. The sun came out by that time, warming the clear fall day. Peter graciously waved at the people from the car, calling many by name. She started smiling. The spirit of the moment gradually engulfed her. She waved. Warm from the excitement, she took her coat off.

Klauzál tér, a plaza, a square-shaped park, connected seven streets, and boasted one of the largest indoor markets of the city as well as a children's playground, tables of stone made for playing chess or cards, and a well-stocked newspaper kiosk.

They parked the car in front of building No. 6, his apartment house. Peter helped her up the steps to the wooden podium built for the occasion in the center of the plaza and held her close. Feeling his excitement, feeling his love for these people, she couldn't help but shine on his arm.

She forgot about her capitalistic appearance. Wearing a plum-color stretch jumpsuit, which somebody had specially ordered for her from some famous designer, her long scarf loosely flowing around her hips, she felt and looked beautiful.

In a few minutes, his parents and sister came downstairs and sat alongside them. The crowd cheered as other celebrities arrived, Hungarians as well as foreigners. The music was continuous, switching from some of Peter's hit songs to favorite marches. The marching band started up the street, came toward them, and surrounded the podium as if they were an honor guard. Newsreel cameras rolled, and many amateur photographers took pictures of the event, of Peter, and of his woman.

Peter spoke to a young man by the stage, who took off.

A pretty teenage girl, representing all the Hungarian women who adored him and who felt as if he were their son, made a short speech about that. She handed him flowers and gave him a very, very long kiss.

Then a handsome young man, representing all the Hungarian men to whom he had become a national hero, one who sang of love and believed in love and morality, gave his enthusiastic talk about that. He presented Peter with a red triangular silk scarf, symbol of the pioneer youth organization of the country.

They posed for pictures. Miklós Barát drove down the street in a government-issue Czechoslovakian Skoda and appeared on the podium to deliver his usual semi-political message.

During all this activity, a taxi arrived with the young man whom Peter dispatched earlier hanging off its side, guiding it to the spot Peter specified. He opened the door for Lara and Wade. Lara had changed into blue jeans, a slinky T-shirt, and carried a short fur jacket on her arm. Wade wore a jacket over a turtleneck sweater. The young man guided them through the crowd. Melody felt Peter's scrutinizing look on her and would not give him the satisfaction of acknowledging it. *She will show him*, she thought, and a challenging smirk appeared on her face.

She got up from the bleacher seat, walked down the steps, took Lara by one hand, Wade by the other, and brought them up to Peter on the podium. Melody glanced at Peter with challenging coyness, as if asking "Have I redeemed myself?" A pregnant four-way look. Lara and Wade had no doubt they were really welcomed this time, but it was Peter taking Melody's hand once again that signified real peace. They laughed, hugged, and finally settled down to the sounds of a teenage chorus, in uniform blue skirts or pants, white shirts and red scarves, singing one of Peter's hits.

Lara turned to Melody. "Thanks. You always could put people at ease."

"Or ill at ease, whatever the case may be. But you have to admit it was a shock. It's over now. The past doesn't belong here."

They watched the celebration and watched how Peter was adored, how he was getting gifts of scarves, poems, several red-white-and-green handcrafted things, boasting of the national colors and talent. There were songs written and performed for him, and hand-knitted and crocheted memorabilia.

When Peter's accompanist arrived, Peter took his turn to sing, to return the love that was bestowed upon him. He sang for nearly an hour; then he thanked everyone and asked them to enjoy themselves at the eats-and-drinks stands. Dance music started. Couples plunged readily into the fun and merrymaking. Peter asked Melody to dance. They have not danced together before. Melody had not danced since Bill. Peter's arms around her settled her nerves, and soon they moved as one.

"This was worth living for," she whispered in his ear.

"Ya betcha, or you bet," he said with a grin.

Amidst their laughter, looking at their friendly faces, she realized that she had been delivered into the heart of a kind and generous people. Lara and Wade danced like newfound lovers, savoring the essence of every second.

Miklós came over and Peter introduced him to Melody.

"I have heard a great deal about you, Ms. Melody Shorr."

"He arranged your visa, you know." Peter emphasized the man's power. She was happy to meet him and with Peter's permission didn't mind taking a couple of turns on the dance floor with Miklós. He had never had such a woman on his arms and prolonged it for a few minutes. Then he spoke softly into her face.

"Let's go for a little walk, shall we?"

"Of course." She trusted him.

He guided her toward his car. A burly man stepped out of the crowd and closed in on them.

"I'll take you for a little ride. Show you around. You see, my dear, this visa is only good for a few days. So you may dream on, for Hungary doesn't want any addicts."

She froze in her step. The burly man took her arm. Her voice left her. She couldn't scream as the two men tried to force her into the car. Peter noticed her absence and spotted the action around Miklós's car. He ran toward them and yelled out "Melody!"

Miklós quickly bent down to kiss her hand as if saying good-bye.

"Miklós, going so soon?"

"I have business to attend to. I'll see you at the banquet at the Gellért."

He and the man drove off. Peter saw how shaken Melody was.

"Sweetheart, what happened? What did he say to you?"

Melody trembled. "That . . . that Hungary doesn't . . . doesn't want addicts."

A small group of onlookers tried to figure out what was happening, but their good manners did not let them get close enough to hear anything. They knew it was private, but they wanted to be available.

"I apologize for him. He is a moron."

"It's all right. In a way I understand him . . . somewhat. But and please don't be angry with me, I just think that I have to seriously decide if this is the country I want to live in."

"Correction. We want to live in."

Chapter 40

THE BIRTHDAY BANQUET LASTED into the wee hours of the morning. It behooved Miklós to send his regrets. A Washington diplomat's wife couldn't have been more gracious than Melody. Wade and Lara continued discovering each other while growing pleasantly attached to what they discovered. Wade could not get over his delight of having a nondrinking, non-user in his life. Obviously, what he didn't know didn't hurt him.

Monday was a family day. Erzsi had to go to school, but the adults stayed together. Melody, who had never had a real family, fast became involved with Peter's loving surroundings. She planned to take Hungarian lessons, and the thought of cooking crossed her mind.

Erzsi, a pretty high school senior, was also an athlete but more important was a recognized literary figure in school. She was hooked on literature of every kind, knew and remembered everything she had ever read, started to write her own short stories and recited her own poems in the literary group as a sophomore, two years ago.

Erzsi invited Melody to the Tuesday afternoon literary circle meeting then realized that six words of Hungarian were not going to be sufficient for such an experience. But amidst a great deal of sign language and nodding, they agreed about looking forward to being together for supper.

Peter suggested a sightseeing tour of the city to his guests, the Opera house, the original Turkish baths, and other famous points. Wade and Lara were scheduled to leave after supper because he had to return to work Thursday. Lara also thought more and more about her work, the restaurant, and missed it. Wade's flight plan was cleared, the plane serviced, ready for takeoff anytime. They were paid up at the hotel although not checked out and carried their light luggage in Peter's car trunk.

They had an exquisite lunch at the Országhâz Vendèglő, an old, old historic restaurant. Next to the once royal palace, on top of the Buda hills, it offered a breathtaking view in addition to the fine food. After lunch, they walked around before heading to one of the picturesque bridges over the Danube River, to cross back to Pest. Around the University of Technical and Engineering Sciences, a crowd of students excitedly gathered with signs and flags. Peter decided to stay out of the crowd and intended to take another bridge. However, Wade was curious about the reasons for the gathering.

*

The after-school literary circle discussion addressed itself to the more intellectual students. Erzsi became deeply involved. It was nearly six o'clock when she realized that she couldn't be late for supper. Darkness came early, and the air turned chilly. Bundled up in her coat, she hurried along. She crossed the street where Hungary's one and only two-channel radio building stood, and a short block away she had to tell herself not to stop to look at the photos and program information posted on the walls of the National Drama Theater. She loved that place. Her goal in life was to one day be a writer and director in that very theater. She put that out of her mind for now. Tonight was special. No time to dillydally.

Near the radio building, she heard noises. It was not just any noise. It was her brother leading the singing. He'll be late for supper too.

The crowd of students, joined by hundreds of other people, filled the entire street. Peter stood on a newspaper stand, singing a patriotic song from the revolution of 1848. She fought her way through the crowd to join him. Melody, Lara, and Wade enthusiastically clapped to the beat of the tune. *Gosh*, she thought to herself, *these people must think that Hungary is just one continuous Oktoberfest.* She joined in the singing.

Several of the university students appeared on the balcony of the radio building overlooking the street. They read a ten-point demand notice addressing the Soviet government, the ruling power of Hungary since the end of the Second World War in 1945. The ten points reclaimed Hungary's political, industrial, agricultural, and cultural independence. Amidst the crowd's jubilant approval, the students took over the radio station and began to broadcast the issues on the air.

The procession marched up Rákoczy út toward Dózsa György út and Városliget, the city park that was more than merely picturesque. It was rich in history, well maintained. It was a place to feel free, become part of nature.

Josef Stalin's gigantic bronze statue dominated Dózsa György út, named after a long-ago revolutionary. The statue was a magnificent piece of pure modern bronze art. An homage, it served as the centerpiece of all parades since the Soviet liberation of Hungary.

One and all, they marched hand in hand, singing. More and more people joined, swelling the crowd to an endless river of bodies.

Peter squeezed his sister's hand.

"Go home. This is no place for a young girl."

Somehow she thought she could defy him this once, but she had never done that before. She had better obey him, as always.

She pulled out of the line, watched the rows and rows of people march on, until suddenly there was silence and darkness around her. She was nearly at home when she thought she heard the faint sounds of what seemed like gunshots.

There was no way she could be sure. A very little girl during the war, it was more than eleven years ago since she first and last heard gunshots. She began to tremble, and in spite of her weakening knees, she ran the rest of the way. Her parents sat in the living room, listened to the radio, which was overtaken by confusion.

Her father gravely announced, "This is a revolution. Mark Tuesday, October 23, 1956, on the Hungarian calendar as an uprising of revolutionary stature."

Erzsi told them what she saw. They heard Peter's singing and did not need an explanation as to his whereabouts. They grew worried with the definite sounds of armed opposition. Not able to eat, or rest, they just sat around, listened to the shots, waited for Peter and his friends to get home.

An endless night. Nothing like this had happened in Hungary in over one hundred years, since 1848. Hungary was a peaceful, productive, growing country.

Mr. Szabó, a retired historian, pointed out that something like this was inevitable. The college students, who were babes in arms during the war, were, in fact, a new generation, creating their own politics and able to follow their own ideals.

At about two o'clock in the morning, there was banging on the door. Secret servicemen looking for Peter. They were told that he was out on the town with his friends.

The AVO men promised that they would be back later to talk with him.

Erzsi tried to telephone the Royal Hotel immediately, but the lines were dead. What could be done? She would have to go over to the hotel. Her father objected at first then realized that he should not be pulling rank against the feeling of duty and reason. He, himself, couldn't go. He was too old and too slow. Erzsi had a chance of making it.

The streets were dark, lit by a few overhead streetlights attached to wires stretched between opposite buildings. She crept along unnoticed and undeterred.

The Royal, a fine old hotel, where only the famous and rich could afford to stay, filled up on weekends ever since she could remember. Budapest was a well-known weekend getaway. Her mother said that people returned for the Hungarian wine, women, and violins. There was nothing like it anywhere in the world. Her mother never mentioned the theater, sports, good climate; but Erzsi just about figured out that all of those elements had added to the others, making the city a haven for visitors.

The hotel was busy. Newspaper people were trying to reach the only working telephone. She didn't know whether any of the foreign wire service reporters were actually staying there, but at that point, the lobby was buzzing with Babel-like confusion.

The young desk clerk was invincible and would not give her Wade's room number. No hotel of any reputation would do such a thing.

A man showed up carrying a doctor's bag, asking for Wade's room. He instantly got the number. Erzsi followed without fail.

The doctor was practically pushed through the door by Erzsi. Inside, she saw an injured Wade on the bed. The doctor proceeded to administer medication to try to make him comfortable with a gunshot wound in his ribcage.

"What happened?" said Erzsi.

"The shooting started. It was aimed into the crowd randomly," said Peter.

"Wade just happened to be in the way," said Lara, tears in her eyes.

"Will he be all right?" said Erzsi.

"He needs to go to the hospital. Would you like me to arrange it?" The doctor did not meddle. "No," said Peter. The doctor left.

Erzsi quickly related the secret service request to Peter. That was bad news.

Lara and Melody were helpless. "My god," Melody whispered. "What are we doing here? We're smack in the middle of a revolution. A new junta is coming."

"They told me to stay away from these exotic, hot-blooded countries." A wry Lara.

"Not funny." Melody was pale, lifeless. Erzsi hung on to her brother, who held Wade's hand.

"You have to go," said Peter to Erzsi. "Can't stay here."

She kissed him *good-bye.*

"Let's order some coffee." Melody, almost eerie. Erzsi headed for the phone, but Melody stopped her. "We'll do it."

"Espresso in this town. Gallons and gallons of it," said Lara.

Lara got the dictionary. Erzsi watched in amazement. Melody walked to the phone as if fulfilling an important assignment. Together they found the numbers for the room. Melody dialed.

"Hello, room 528." Lara helped out. "Öt, kettö, nyolc." Melody repeated the numbers Lara got from the dictionary and then added, "Espresso. Kérem. Köszönöm."

She hung up. They looked at each other. Both were drained. Melody reached out for Lara, held her as a mother would hold a crying child. Melody cared, and this time Lara knew it.

Erzsi smiled and nodded. The coffee arrived in minutes.

Wade was woozy with morphine. The room, quiet. The crackling gunshot sounds could infrequently be heard over the street noises.

Peter spoke in English, holding his sister by his side.

"We have to get out. The secret service is looking for me. That's bad news in any country."

"Do you mean *out* by *out* of the country?" Melody asked.

"Yes."

"That'd make you a fugitive. A political refugee."

"Can you live the rest of your life with a fugitive? A political refugee?"

Melody squeezed Lara's hand tighter as she answered.

"I can live the rest of my life with you."

"Then it's decided. The plane was ready for you hours ago. The question is how to get there faster than they. We can't take my car. It's a dead giveaway. And Wade?"

Wade's voice was faint. "I can make it."

They dressed him hurriedly. Erzsi took off her gold necklace and put it around Peter's neck. She took off her shawl and put it around Melody's shoulders. Squeezed Lara's two hands as good-bye.

"You'll send word?" She kissed Peter. One more hug and she was gone.

"We'll have to take the stairs." Peter organized their actions. They grabbed Wade and painfully slowly proceeded to the stairs.

"That won't do." Peter picked up Wade's 6'4" body, put him over his shoulder, and led the way to the back entrance of the hotel.

"Wait here." He put Wade down on the bottom steps and disappeared in the night. The minutes passed like hours before he was back with a taxi. In the car, Lara started to tremble violently. Melody took hold of her.

"What's wrong?"

"I . . . you know . . . I . . . Wade's plane is a twin engine . . . I never checked out on it. He . . . he let me land it as a lark . . . that's what." She closed her eyes tight and bit her lips.

Melody and Peter looked at each other. Peter, the man, tried to ease the tension.

"I certainly could have done better without this news and go on believing that you were as good as you looked when you got out of that plane."

"Me too." Lara, with a frightened stare.

There was nothing else to say during the rest of the ride. The pilot's license seemed a small problem. Peter's primary hope was that the secret service wasn't thinking quickly enough to figure out what his next move might be. He had hoped that the Hungarians, true to form, would be as gullible regarding him as they generally were regarding most things. He counted on the slow thinking of his peaceful people, regardless of the uniform they were in.

Melody tried to imagine the crackling sounds, fading in the distance of the city, to be noisemakers and fireworks instead of gunshots.

Peter paid the driver generously and told him to forget he made the trip.

Peter carried Wade in the dark all the way to the plane. They laboriously put him inside. Peter pushed Lara into the pilot's seat, strapped Melody into the copilot's seat. As he jumped in, the searchlights came on; and when they found the plane parked in its original spot, the lights remained trained on it.

"Duck down," Peter ordered. Melody obeyed, but Lara did not seem to hear him!

"Lara, we must go and we must go real fast. They don't know we're in it." Peter squeezed her arm, shook her hand, trying to bring her out of her trancelike state. She didn't move.

"And Wade. Look at Wade. His life is in your hands. Please. Think! Remember."

"It doesn't matter when you got your license, Lar. What matters is that you got it. I don't got it. Peter ain't got it. You got it, so get your ass in gear!" Melody wanted to scream, wanted to give Lara courage, but instead she was losing her voice. Hoarse, croaky sounds followed her rational statements. Losing self-control. Panic was next.

"I neeeed a fix." Harsh whisper.

"Not on your life!" Lara screamed. "Not on your goddam fuckin' life!" Lara had the look of a crazed woman, with eyes burning wildly, her teeth gritting; and she stared at the machine.

"Taking off is landing in reverse!" Melody's failing logic reached Lara.

"I shoulda' thought of that! They shoulda' given you the pilot's license two weeks ago!" A maniacal laugh accompanied her response. "But the fools gave it to me, man! Me! Funnyyyy!"

Strapped in behind the yoke, Lara's ears were filled with "Negative clearance! Negative!" coming from the control tower repeatedly in several languages, including English. Her newfound love, morphined out of his mind, slumped low in the seat behind her. What's the word? She was trying to remember the simple word guiding the amateur pilot through checkout. *Cigar!* "Controls! Instruments! Gas! Attitude! Runup! Fuck 'm!" She laughed, screamed, cackled in hysterics with each word. The other man, the political refugee, knew of the electrically charged barbed wire fence enclosing the airport, but why bring it up now.

She saw uniformed soldiers running in the floodlight aimed at the Cessna, pointing their machine guns at them, and went for the ignition. Melody's fear-filled eyes chilled through Lara, and she screamed at the top of her lungs. "Fuuuck!"

The plane jumped out; and with the shortest, fastest taxiing in history, they were airborne. The shooting was straight. The flying wasn't.

They swept into the thick, black velvet night, traveling at maximum speed, hopefully westward.

Somebody up there decided to help the fantastic four. The sun emerged. They had a direction.

Chapter 41

TUESDAY MORNING, OCTOBER 23, played a little differently for Bill. On arrival at his office, he found Malcolm behind his desk, going through his papers and notes.

"What are you doing in my desk?"

"Taking a look at what's really going on around here. It looks to me that you have not been attending to our business satisfactorily, Bill."

"C'mon, not you!"

"The name of the game is money."

"Whatever money you're not making here, you're making on the other end. I took care of that."

"That was not the deal. I want money on every end. You've been faltering too much." Malcolm looked straight at Bill. "It's time to go packing."

"But look at all I got going for you! Look at you! A rich tycoon! I turned you on to wealth and glamour. You never had it so good!"

"I thank you for that. And to show my appreciation, I am prepared to pay you through the balance of the year, computed on the basis of your performance here at the Associates during the past six months. That's fair, I should think."

Bill sank in the chair across from his desk. He didn't know what to say. Chuck had been traveling a lot lately. Bill found himself nothing more than a bag man. Instructions came to him in all forms and shapes, and he would deliver and pick up and deliver. He would go to the office daily, give his regular pep talks to the new staff members, encourage the old ones, make a few calls to keep his private cash flowing, although his attention span had decreased and so did his private cash. He wouldn't admit to being hooked on cocaine, but he was. That cut into his budget considerably. Priscilla was ordered by the court to leave town and move in with her grandparents. Bill missed her the most. Other girls were a faceless turnover, and Chuck remained the only male in his sex life.

He came out of his daydreaming and suddenly realized that Malcolm was still in the office, still behind his own desk. He looked up. Malcolm stared at him.

Bill slowly rose, went around the desk, pulled out the drawers as Malcolm remained motionless, found his personal things, put whatever did not fit in his briefcase in a manila envelope, and walked out. His secretary had tears in her eyes. His young aide, Barry Sherman, jumped up and headed for his office. Somehow Bill knew that Barry was moving in behind his desk. Sweet Barry. He trained him, and he was phenomenal. Overkill. Malcolm's new son.

He drove. The only solace. He drove while swallowing deep tokes of marijuana. Before long, he was at the beach, the same stretch of beach where Melody took him when they were on the verge of getting married. All that wonderful fairytale took place exactly one year ago. Everything had turned to shit ever since. She was poison.

He wondered why Melody knew Ben. He wondered why Ben became less trusting toward him after the scene with Melody when he arrived at The Place that night. What did Melody say? He never imagined that Malcolm had been doing the talking. He knew as a given that Carla was hooking for Ben but had no idea there might be an angle. The thought of Carla having an angle of her own never occurred to him. He wondered why Melody was friends with a hooker? But Melody was weird, high and mighty. Her tastes unpredictable. Look at the connections she made. Bill was unable to fit the puzzle together.

Frustrated, he broke out laughing. He opened his eyes and through the windshield saw a pretty girl running light-footedly on the beach. He unzipped his pants, reached for his Big Rex, and did what he had to do.

Theo Sanchez popped into his fantasy. Skin shining with a constant gloss, his white teeth always showing through a friendly smile. Ever since they first met, Bill trusted the guy. Theo respected him, ran errands for him, never asking questions, never bargaining about the payments.

Now there's an idea. A poor slob of a Mexican like that must have some friends who could help him solve his problems with Malcolm, Ben, and maybe even Chuck, permanently. A cheap contract. That way he could run the entire show, no one telling him that he was faltering at anything. Great idea!

He was pleased with himself. The orgasm appeared to give his brain a new surge of power. He was satisfied with his own creativity under duress. He headed back to town. He would make a good deal with Theo. That was his man.

*

Even California had ways of dressing into fall colors, and the restaurant began to reflect the earth tones of the season. Lara not being around, he felt safe going in. The Place offered a coziness with the flaming fireplace, oversized rust-colored daisies on each table as well as on the bar, ready for the happy hour.

Everyone looked familiar to him, although he never met Don Curtis, who was sitting with Martin, talking over cappuccinos. The players in his ballpark grew fuzzy. He had no definitions, no clear recollections. A woman sitting at the bar reminded him of Bonnie long-legs who had since become a well-paid hooker at Monty's. Bill headed directly for the kitchen.

Theo was in the vegetable basement. Its upkeep and inventory had become his main responsibility in addition to bussing tables. Nobody else had reason to go down there although he kept his equipment well concealed at all times, leaving no room for being discovered. He utilized the ducts he had found on his arrival to build his own electronic communications center.

Bill had never had any reason to go to the basement before. He found Theo behind a set of crates, sitting low, only his head showing. He looked up when Bill entered, didn't say anything, letting Bill go with it.

"Theo, I've gotta talk. Stop working. We gotta talk."

Theo had a sadness in his eyes as he spoke to Bill, "They've got you, haven't they?"

Bill's earlier sex fantasies about Theo vanished. He was stunned. Flabbergasted. He wasn't sure that Theo knew what he was talking about, yet somehow, he was. He backed away from Theo, who made no physical move. He didn't have to threaten Bill. Bill did it all to himself.

Bill exhaustedly dropped on the bottom step to Theo's undercover workshop. Theo reached for his earphone, which was all Bill could see. None of the code equipment and portable duplicating equipment were visible from his vantage point. Theo continued eavesdropping.

"What are you doing?" The whole thing looked inexplicable to Bill.

Theo didn't answer. He was writing. Bill got up, walked around the crates, and observed Theo and his gadgets in action.

"What are you doing?"

"Monitoring your house."

"You mean Sheila's?"

"It's Chuck Pui Hung's. You gave it to him."

Bill paced slowly in an involuntary reaction, attempting to put the pieces together, attempting to get a clear picture of something through his blurry mind.

"And you are . . ."

"Special investigator Theo Sanchez, Metro police."

"You had me pegged."

"For a long time," Theo added.

"You know somethin'? I was gonna offer you the biggest deal of your life. How does that grab you?" He slumped back on the bottom step.

"You know, I always thought when this'd come to an end I'd be very rich, very powerful and could walk away without a trace. Instead, I'm very broke, very tired, and feel no rage. Is that normal? I feel no rage." He took out a fresh roach and lit it.

Chapter 42

LARA'S EXCITEMENT KNEW NO limits when she approved Don's layouts for her grand opening campaign, which included several magazines, weeklies, and daily newspapers, doing interviews, running the full-page ads, increasing the letters of the name of the restaurant in each subsequent issue. She had developed a small daisy as a trademark, inside the arch of the letter *C* in the word *PLACE*. She identified with the small simple flower, as she learned to understand how simple life really was.

. . . Place
. . . s Place
. . . 's Place
. . a's Place
. ra's Place
. ara's Place
Welcome to Lara's Place

The sign with the daisy that was going up on the marquee the very day after Christmas when people were ready for going out again.

In a way, she began to believe that you get back what you put out. She realized she could no longer be had. Nor fooled. She was not afraid to think, now that she knew that she could think, and she was not afraid to tell anyone her thoughts. Yes, she was pretty happy. She had learned to protect herself from unnecessary pain. She still experienced pain, but it was different.

Leaving Wade in a Swiss hospital was pain. But a good pain. He was fine in a few days, he could resume filming, and he would be back in Los Angeles for Christmas. He will be back in Los Angeles for Christmas because of her, because of his need for her, because of his respect for her commitment to her business, but mostly because she had the courage to ask him to spend the holidays with her. Not in his expensive home. Not in his milieu, but in hers. To find out together if they are for each other. They had no doubts about wanting to settle down to the wonderful world of living happily ever after.

Lara also found the rediscovery of Melody a dear addition to her life. They had both been on both sides of love and life. She didn't know until the days in Switzerland around Wade's hospital room that Melody was considered an addict by Hungary, and she was insulted for her.

"Six months of messing around does not an addict make," she said.

Melody laughed. "I never thought you'd be the sage of the house."

Wade slept restfully while Lara and Melody sat in a corner of his hospital room, talking quietly.

"You started it, Melody," said Lara. "You started me reading. Apparently, that was the push I needed. I read the trade papers, restaurant and food magazines but I am widening my horizon."

"How wide?" asked Melody.

"Very. You won't believe this but Khalil Gibran caught my attention. He speaks to me."

Lara's face reflected her joy of reading.

"I just read *Desiderata* by Max Ehrmann. Gives me goose bumps."

"I can hardly wait until you discover Plato's *Republic*," said Melody with a little chuckle.

"Do I want that?" asked Lara?

"Probably not, but I will read it with you," said Wade.

Lara rushed over to his bed. Their moment, eyes locked, fingers locked, lingered on. Melody slipped out of the room.

*

The day before Christmas, she was harshly awakened by the doorbell. Martin with his gift.

He stood in the doorway, holding a huge box, gift wrapped with everything that a Christmas gift wrapper could dream up. Lara thought the gift wrapping may be as expensive as what's inside . . . if anything . . . haha.

It was early morning, and he came by before going to his office for a few hours. It didn't matter. They were friends. Lara made coffee and sweetened it with Ovaltine.

"Here, this should give you a cappuccino feeling."

"Looking at you is everything I need."

Lara shuddered. Was this a new come-on? She felt undressed in her slinky robe over her naked body. Or was this her friend? The friend she thought he had become. Could she ever be sure? Will somebody come down on her for her body all her life? She looked bewildered. Martin went on, slowly stirring the cappuccino.

"I raised three children to adulthood. They have messed up more than you ever had, even at what you think was your worst."

Lara still wasn't sure of what else was coming. It's a hard price to pay for a large Christmas gift.

"You went out and down in the streets and tasted the dirt and knew you didn't like it, and as soon as you knew you had a choice, you made it.

"They didn't go out and down in the streets. They brought dirt into their lives, tasted it, and liked it because they could get away with it. They brought dirt into their lives, into my home, into their friends' lives, and they all liked it so much that they are still living it. But you, Lara Burns, you thought you were a hooker and a doper and a sickie, nonetheless you were never dishonest to yourself. And that's what it's all about."

Tears rolled down her face. She was motionless. This was good. Better than anyone could've done by her. This was the confirmation of her true rise out of the gutter and into life . . . life as she wanted it.

He got up, kissed her on the cheek. "Open it."

Her hands were shaking as she began to undo the elaborate wrapping, trying not to damage the wonderful trinkets. Martin motioned her on impatiently.

Inside the box she found a four-foot handcrafted glass daisy, bent exactly the way she designed hers for the top curve of the *C*.

"There are some special hooks in the box. Do you want me to hang it up for you?"

They looked at each other with moist eyes.

"Wade will be here this afternoon. He'll hang it."

"See you at the party." He walked out of the door.

Lara watched him leave and hated herself for being such an emotional mush.

At the restaurant, she had called her staff together, gave them each a bonus, showed Bobby a new printed menu with his specialty dishes bearing his name, Larry's specialty drinks bearing his name in print. She had announced that Walter was no longer the maître d' but the manager, and Walter now had the authority to interview for a new maître d'. Before sending them back to work, she held up the full-page ad in several publications. One more day, one more letter!

Chapter 43

CROWDS, KLIEG LIGHTS, MUSIC marked the grand opening celebration of *Lara's Place*.

Everyone who had enjoyed the restaurant, Harry's as well as Lara's, came to watch the unveiling of the new sign with the same excitement as if it were a work of art.

Wade stood by Lara's side. Martin brought his wife, daughter, and son-in-law, the presentable portion of his family. Malcolm also arrived with his wife and joined Ben and Chuck at their table. They talked hurriedly, exchanged looks with a couple of casually dressed Asians. Capacity crowd. Capacity noise.

Carla was dropped off by a car away from the main entrance. A man's voice called after her.

"See you inside. Keep him on your left and keep your eyes on Theo."

She entered, looking show-stopping gorgeous. People, like the Red Sea, parted for her. She hurried over to Ben and Chuck.

"So sorry I'm late, Ben, gentlemen."

Ben's look softened. "You're here now," he said.

"I couldn't decide what to wear. Can you forgive me? Do I look OK?"

She leaned close to Ben. He saw what she wanted him to see, glazed eyes rolling demurely at him, and he believed that she was spaced out. She sat down between them, with Ben on her left.

Carla's eyes roamed around. Someone brought her a Perrier with lemon. She noticed Ben's scrutiny, but his concentration was not on her, mostly on the entire room.

Lara was graciously greeting everyone. Wade posed for photos but refused any interviews, announcing that this was Lara's night. Wade finally sat down with the lesser-known Peter the Hun and his lady, Melody. The photographers had a field day; and the press, true to form, was predicting all kinds of improbable occurrences.

Kay felt humbled by the standing ovation she received as she sat down at the piano. Lara's love and conviction in her talent made this her home, exposed her work to the world, and she had her first record deal in the works. Lara's love spread over all those who were good to her.

Chuck caught a glimpse of a pair of familiar eyes. It was a fast glimpse. It stirred him.

Lara, on her way to greet Martin and his family, was intercepted by a well-dressed, tall, skinny female. The woman's eyes cast down, she headed in a definite direction.

Carla checked on the position of the undercover team. Theo watched Chuck.

The skinny woman was nearing Melody's table. Melody looked at the heavily made-up face and cringed back into Peter, recognizing the woman's eyes to be none other than Bill's. Out on bail. Awaiting arraignment.

Chuck recognized the movements of the woman to be Bill and signaled his Asian henchmen, who responded by quickly making their move through the crowded room toward Bill. Theo headed that way too. The undercover cops positioned themselves closer to Carla's table.

"You were my ruin, Melody." Bill spoke into Melody's face with a crazed hoarseness in his voice and raised a small automatic hand gun. Chuck signaled his men. Bill pulled the trigger. A shot knocked his gun out of his hand, another one hit his heart. He was falling dead on Melody as Peter grabbed and pulled her out of the way.

The crowd of diners froze. The silence was thick for a split second; then everyone began to talk at once. Chuck helplessly looked on as his two men were arrested while attempting to flee through the back door.

Carla looked from Chuck to Ben. Ben caught the glance of clear eyes, unlike the stoned look of her entrance. His self-defense antenna raised. He instinctively reached for Carla, pulling her into his arms and in the way of the bullet that she had planned for him.

Melody screamed. Everyone screamed. The emergency vehicles screamed as they converged on the restaurant.

Lara, Wade, Peter, and Melody watched Theo's squad take charge.

*

Two thirty in the morning. Lara's Place was dark and empty.

"A nightcap. That's what we need. An adrenalin-curdling nightcap." Lara got busy preparing French connections for her friends.

"Anticlimactic as it seems"—Peter appreciatively sipped on the aromatic liqueurs—"we got a notice of official pardon from Hungary and invitation to return as husband and wife."

Lara and Wade's glasses stopped in midair. Melody grinned. She held Peter's hand and leaned close to him.

"This is home for us. The land of freedom," she proudly announced their decision.

CPSIA information can be obtained at www.ICGtesting.com
Printed in the USA
BVOW03s1902071113

335735BV00002B/113/P